D0629359

Hypnosis
Is For
Hacks

By Tamara Berry

Hypnosis Is For Hacks

Curses Are For Cads

Potions Are For Pushovers

Séances Are For Suckers

Hypnosis
Is For
Hacks

TAMARA BERRY

KENSINGTON
PUBLISHING CORP.

www.kensingtonbooks.com

KENSINGTON BOOKS are published by

Kensington Publishing Corp.
119 West 40th Street
New York, NY 10018

All Kensington titles, imprints and distributed lines are available at special quantity discounts for bulk purchases for sales promotion, premiums, fund-raising, educational or institutional use. Special book excerpts or customized printings can also be created to fit specific needs. For details, write or phone the office of the Kensington Special Sales Manager: Kensington Publishing Corp., 119 West 40th Street, New York, NY, 10018. Attn. Special Sales Department. Phone: 1-800-221-2647.

The K logo is a trademark of Kensington Publishing Corp.

Library of Congress Card Catalogue Number: 2021938936

ISBN-13: 978-1-4967-2934-7
ISBN-10: 1-4967-2934-X
First Kensington Hardcover Edition: November 2021

ISBN-13: 978-1-4967-2931-6 (ebook)
ISBN-10: 1-4967-2931-5 (ebook)

10 9 8 7 6 5 4 3 2 1

Printed in the United States of America

Chapter 1

❧

"This tea tastes like the inside of an earthworm."

I pop my head around the corner of my kitchen, taking in the sight of my brother sitting at the table and sipping tea like a proper Englishman. Liam has only been visiting me for two days, but he's already settling into the bucolic lifestyle afforded by my Sussex cottage. He dips toast soldiers in his tea, refuses to go outside without a tweed hat on top of his dark hair, and peppers his speech with things like *boot* and *loo* and *bobby*, which are the only British words he knows.

"Where did you get it?" I ask.

He waves a hand in the general vicinity of the pantry. "I don't know. In one of those canisters." He takes another sip and grimaces. "How you people can drink this stuff morning, noon, and night is beyond me. Especially in this heat."

Although I will defend the local custom to drink tea at all times of the day to my dying breath, he's not wrong about how hot it is. My little patch of England is currently experiencing a heat wave. For weeks, the temperatures have been soaring well above the annual average. It's great for my herbal garden out back, but not so great for my comfort level. Ancient thatch cottages aren't designed for summers like these. Even the smallest air conditioner overloads the electrical system.

"Hot tea makes you sweat more, which in turn evaporates and cools you off. It's science." I take the floral teacup from his hand. I don't need to bring it all the way to my nostrils to smell what it is. "Uh, Liam? Did you grab this from one of the normal canisters or one of my special ones?"

He blanches, his already pale skin growing paler. As two parts of a set of triplets, he and I share the same pasty complexion. "Define *special*."

I laugh and set the cup down. "You'd better finish it. This is the good stuff. I sell it for ten quid a pop."

This news doesn't appear to comfort him. He pushes back in his chair and narrows his eyes. Like the ghostly pallor and dark hair, his eyes are also the same as mine. In the right light, they look almost black, the pupil and iris blending into one.

"What did I just drink?"

"Nothing toxic, so you can quit looking at me like that. It's mostly senna and marshmallow root."

"Ellie." He says my name as a warning. "What's going to happen to me?"

"You mean, other than turning into a frog by the light of the quarter moon?" I shrug. "A slight disruption of the bowels. I wouldn't go too far from home tonight."

"Ellie!"

I hold up my hands to ward my brother off as he leaps to his feet and pounces toward me. Liam might not know anything about herbal remedies, but he's an elementary school gym teacher. He's in phenomenal shape.

"I warned you about the pantry!" I cry as I dash behind a chair. "I have limited storage space. That's why I have everything carefully organized. I wouldn't want to accidentally serve my brother a laxative at teatime."

Liam lets his emotions loose in a torrent of threats from our childhood. Unfortunately for him, traumas like locking me in the bathroom overnight or sitting on me until I'm sorry don't have power over me anymore. A long soak in a cold tub sounds lovely, and I know for a fact that Liam would grow bored of pinning me to the ground long before I did. I've always had more patience than he does.

"If you want, I can give you some fennel tea to try and counteract the effects," I offer, still laughing. "But I think you're better off riding this one out."

"You have serious problems, you know that?" Liam gives up trying to wreak his vengeance and falls to the kitchen chair with a plop. He pushes the teacup as far from his person as it can get. "Ordinary people don't stock their cupboards with weird, mystical concoctions."

"My weird, mystical concoctions bought your plane ticket out here." Before I can say more, the younger of my two cats, a black animal with white-tipped ears named Freddie, slinks into the kitchen and plants herself at my feet. I pick her up and point her at my brother. "See? Even Winnie knows what a momentous occasion this is. We haven't all been gathered in the same place for years."

Liam's look of doubt speaks for him. He might be willing to accept that the herbal elixirs, tonics, and remedies I sell to the local populace make for a thriving and well-paying career, but that's where his belief in my witchlike abilities ends. *I* know without a doubt that my cat acts as a conduit between this world and the next, tying me to our sister Winnie in ways that defy reason and logic. Liam, however, has a hard time with it.

I try not to blame him too much. When Winnie died, almost two years ago, I also thought that would be the end of my connection with her. Thanks to my cats and what can only be described as my own sixth sense, however, she's still very much a presence in my life.

What am I, chopped sardines? asks another voice.

That's the other part of this whole bargain. Apparently, it's not just Winnie's spirit I can hear from beyond the grave. Ever since last fall, I've also been able to communicate with a woman named Birdie White. She was once a fake medium, like me, and has turned out to be a real pain in my neck.

"Is Winnie talking to you now?" Liam asks with a hint of suspicion.

I smile and shake my head. I haven't yet mustered up the courage to admit to him that I hear multiple voices now instead of just Winnie's. Liam is a good brother, but he's only willing to be pushed so far.

"No, but I can feel her presence. She's probably giving you a few days to settle in before she starts predicting your future. Is there anything specific you want to know? A hot guy you've got your eye on?"

At this, Liam visibly perks. "She can do love spells?"

"Not to my knowledge, no. But there's no saying what can happen if we put our minds to it."

He slumps in his chair like a deflating balloon. "You're cruel, you know that? Don't promise the power of romance unless you can deliver."

"Oh, I can deliver. If you'd grabbed the canister with the pink sticker on it, you'd have had the entire village lining up outside your window to serenade you instead of tummy troubles." I sling an arm around his neck and drop a kiss on his cheek to show him I intend no harm. I mean, there's a good chance he's going to seriously regret that tea in a few hours, but I did warn him about the cupboard. "Don't worry. I know just the thing to cool you off in the meantime."

"Are you having air-conditioning installed?"

"Better," I promise. "I'm taking you to a drafty castle. Between the ghosts and the ancient stonework and the welcome we're likely to receive, that place is colder than a tomb."

* * *

"It's hotter than Hades's lair in here!"

I'm already sticky with perspiration when I step into Castle Hartford. The walk over was a hot, humid affair, made all the hotter and more humid because we had to turn back at the halfway point when Liam decided he needed a sun hat. My black dress, though gauzy and made of linen, is soaked through with my sweat and the heat of the afternoon. Even my hair, which is pinned up in intricate coils off my neck, seems to have directly absorbed the sun's rays.

"What devilry is this?" I demand as I take another step into the castle. If possible, the heat increases the farther I draw into those stony walls. "Vivian, did you install a nuclear reactor or something?"

Vivian Hartford appears at the top of the grand staircase that leads up from the black-and-white-checked marble foyer. She's wearing nothing but a yellow skirted swimsuit and a pair of rain galoshes. One might think that a woman her age would look ridiculous in such a getup, but she makes it work. Her white-threaded hair is even pulled into two youthful braids to add a final touch.

"I'm disowning that man the moment he returns," she announces. The reason for her clothes—and for her mood—is explained by the tinkle of ice in the tumbler she holds aloft. In summer, that woman lives off gin, but it doesn't always give her sound judgment. "I'm writing him out of my will and casting him to the wolves."

I don't blame her for this plan. Nicholas Hartford III, Vivian's son and my longstanding beau, is away, as he so often is, traversing the world to keep his fortune intact. I'd hoped to finally introduce him to my brother during this visit, but, alas. Millions of dollars aren't just going to make themselves.

Believe me—I've tried. Transmutation isn't the spell it's cracked up to be.

"Vivian, I don't believe you've met my brother, Liam," I say. "Liam, this is—"

"Do you know how to make a gimlet?" she interrupts. She begins a slow descent down the staircase, one leg crossing over the other like an aging Hollywood actress making her final appearance. Before she reaches the bottom, she's already holding out her arm, though whether she wants Liam's support or for him to take her glass, I can't say.

"Gin, lime juice, simple syrup," Liam recites. In a gallant gesture that does him credit, he accepts both Vivian's arm and the empty drink. "Who are we disowning, and what can I do to help? These conditions are inhumane."

None of us disagree.

"My son has decided to fix the heating in the castle," Vivian says. "There's a new furnace below stairs, and every chimney in the place is being cleaned and tested. I've lost eight pounds in sweat since yesterday."

I'm the first to react. "Oh, that will be so lovely in winter!" I cry. Vivian might not appreciate Nicholas's attention to things like household repairs, but the man has been trying to update the castle's infrastructure for years. The only real surprise is that he's finally succeeded. Vivian is not an easy woman to move. None of the Hartfords are. "Think of how cozy it'll be during the holidays."

"Don't speak to me of the holidays," she retorts. "If anyone in the village gets wind of this, they'll be after me to start hosting our annual Christmas ball again. I was hoping that tradition would die with my mother. The cart's right there, love, and I prefer it shaken."

The second half of this commentary is for my brother, who gets right to work mixing Vivian a cocktail.

"I'll admit that it's uncomfortable *now*, but surely you can open some windows or something?" I say. "Nicholas can't have intended for you to live like this while he's gone."

Vivian blinks at me. "That son of mine is the most unfeeling, heartless, *ruthless*—" She breaks off to accept her glass from Liam. She takes a tentative sip and sighs her pleasure. "I do love a man who knows his way around a shaker. Now, where was I?"

"Your ruthless son," Liam supplies.

She flashes her smile at him again. "Ah, yes. So I was." The smile drops as she points an accusatory finger at me. "He had the audacity—the *nerve*—to send me away while all this work is being done. Like I'm a piece of rubbish three days gone."

I know better than to believe a word out of her mouth. Nicholas might be annoyingly dedicated to his work, but he's unfailing when it comes to caring for the people in his life. If he made a plan to send his mother away while the castle is undergoing repairs, I can only imagine it's somewhere decadent, appealing, and expensive.

"Vivian, are you telling me that he booked you a vacation? And you're refusing to go?"

She knows this for the attack it is. Her gaze shifts to a spot a few inches above my head.

"I'm not saying any such thing," she says. Then, because however curmudgeonly Vivian is, she's always honest, she adds, "Brighton isn't a vacation. It's where tourists go to multiply."

Liam squeaks. I can't tell if it's a squeak of excitement or dismay, but it doesn't matter. Any response other than one of complete sympathy holds no weight with Vivian.

"What's an old woman like me supposed to do in a place like that? Play carnival games? Visit the Pavilion?" She scoffs. "I'm not sure which is more likely to give me a heart attack."

"Vivian, when were you supposed to check in?"

She ignores me. "I have a perfectly good home right here."

"And how long is your stay booked for?"

She holds her cold glass against the back of her neck and

sighs. "At least, it *used* to be good until Nicholas got his claws into it."

"I would love to go to the seaside right now," my brother says. Without waiting for a response, he begins mixing a drink for himself. "Just think of all those ocean breezes, the tropical drinks, the cabana boys. . . ."

"It's coastal England, Liam, not the Bahamas. Besides, I thought you came to see the village where I live."

Liam rolls his eyes at me. "I *did* see it. The pub and the church and the un-air-conditioned thatch cottage you call home. What's next? The butcher? The baker? The candlestick maker?"

Vivian doesn't bother to hide her snort of laughter.

"It's not that bad," I protest. Small, yes, but that's its charm. Living here is like stepping back through time. "You're standing in a real-life castle, for crying out loud. I haven't even shown you the secret murder passage yet."

My brother manages to contain his excitement. He pours his drink into a glass and takes a long sip, his attention fixed on Vivian's face. "I think we should all go," he says. "Especially if the hotel is already booked. How long will it take to get there?"

I assume he's talking to me, so I don't hesitate over my answer. "It's not far, but the trains can fill up this time of year, so—"

"The car service Nicholas hired will have us there in an hour." Vivian nods once. "Eleanor will pack my things."

"I will?"

"There's a trunk somewhere in one of the guest rooms with everything I'll need. Sun dresses and hats and the like. Bring at least three of my good gowns. And my rubies."

"Your *rubies*? Vivian, I'm all for you getting away from this castle, but I hardly think you're going to want—"

"You're right. Rubies are more of a winter jewel. My diamonds, then, and perhaps the sapphires."

I look to my brother for help, but I should have known not to bother. Now that the offer of a vacation at a beachside resort has taken hold, nothing I say or do—short of another herbal remedy—will stop him.

"Did you bring a tuxedo with you to England?" Vivian asks Liam. She makes a tsking sound with her tongue. "No matter. We'll buy you one when we get there. I expect Eleanor will need an overhaul of her wardrobe, too. I've seen what she passes for elegance. We'll put it on Nicholas's account."

"Now wait just a minute." This is where I put my foot down. "I'll go on this trip with you, Vivian, and I'll even do your packing and hunt down your diamonds, but you will not buy me or my brother anything with Nicholas's money, got it?"

"But, Ellie," my brother begins, a plea underscoring his voice, "I've never owned a tuxedo before."

I whirl on him. "And you aren't going to start now. I'll rent you one if I have to, but it's not Nicholas's job to foot the bill for your extravagancies." I cross my arms and glare at the pair of them. Vivian might be a matriarch marching through her eighth decade in a yellow bathing suit, and Liam a grown adult with a decent-paying job and good long-term career stability, but I might as well be facing a pair of toddlers. "We'll stay in our own hotel room at our own expense, and we'll split all the meals, got it? Even ones that require tuxedos and diamonds."

Both of them nod meekly. Another woman might take this as capitulation, but they follow it up with a side-eyed look of delight that neither one of them bothers to hide. I've solved enough mysteries in my lifetime to recognize what I'm seeing.

"You did that on purpose!" I accuse, but without any real heat. I know when I'm facing the inevitability of fate. "You only said all that to trick me into agreeing to go."

Vivian gives a lofty toss of her head and takes my brother by the arm. I have no idea where she plans on taking him, but I assume it will involve more gin, zero packing, and plenty of plans to spend Nicholas's millions.

"Don't forget to call and have them stop the mail delivery, dear," Vivian says as she and my brother trail away in the direction of the first-floor salon. "For two weeks at the very least. If I'm letting you drag me all that way, I intend to make it count."

Chapter 2

"Are you absolutely sure we don't want to take that other suite?" Liam stands at the threshold to our hotel room, a suitcase in each hand. "Vivian did say she'd prefer to have us next door."

"You're more than welcome to take her up on the offer." I brush past him and survey our surroundings. After a quick glance, I decide on the bed closest to the window. "But I'm warning you right now that it won't be worth it. She'll have you running her errands and making her drinks at every hour of the day and night. She's exhausting."

I set my own bag on the bed. It contains the haphazard mix of clothes and toiletries I managed to pack up in the five minutes that Vivian insisted was all I needed. "Everything you own looks the same anyway," she'd said. "Black and depressing."

She's not wrong. Most of my clothes do fall on the darker end of the rainbow, since I like to project an aura of gloom and doom whenever I'm on the job. But a girl can't *always* be working. This far away from the village and from the persona that makes up my livelihood, I'm determined to enjoy myself. I even packed a sundress to prove it.

"I like her," Liam says.

"Me too," I admit. "But in order to maintain that sentiment, I need my own space."

The space, in this instance, is the smallest room the hotel has to offer. The Brighton Luxe is everything the name promises—regal and imposing and far more glamorous a resort than I'd have chosen on my own. Vivian is installed in one of the suites upstairs, a huge, elegant apartment that could easily fit four or five of these rooms inside it. It also contains a safe, where I insisted she keep her jewelry. I'd had no idea, when she mentioned the family jewels, that there would be quite so many carats dazzling up at me, but the Hartfords don't do anything by halves. Their castle is a rotting heap of decay and gloom, but their family fortunes are so impressive that they could buy and sell several of these hotels should they have an urge to enter the hospitality trade. It's all or nothing with them.

As if thinking along the same lines, Liam tosses his bags on the crocheted white coverlet and casts a sidelong look at me. "You're not really doing this whole dating-a-millionaire-thing right, are you?"

I don't have to ask him to clarify. One of the good things about being a triplet—and being a medium—is that I can see to the heart of almost every question. "If by 'not doing it right' you mean I insist on paying my own way and asserting my independence as a woman of means and intelligence, then, no. I'm not."

When he doesn't say anything right away, I drop my façade. It's not a condition that suits me, but serious times call for serious measures.

"Liam, you wouldn't really want the man I'm dating to pay for your luxury vacation."

He shifts uncomfortably. "Well, no."

"And you wouldn't be happy if I was letting him buy me expensive gifts and pay my bills."

"I mean, the *occasional* expensive gift wouldn't kill you."

I laugh and wrap my arms around my brother's neck. He smells like the cotton-scented cologne he's always favored, and I bask in it for a moment before smacking a kiss on his cheek. "I'm happy, Liam. I have a home and a steady income and a man who seems to love me exactly the way I am. I like his family enough to willingly spend time with them, and I'm in a beautiful beachside resort with my favorite brother in the world. What more could I want?"

The answer to that is a loud knock at the door. It's my common sense rather than my sixth one that tells me who's on the other side.

"And now that my babies are here, the real party can begin."

Liam shakes his head. "You are so weird, Ellie. I don't know any rational adult woman who brings her cats to the beach with her."

Yes, well. That's because he wasn't present the last time I tried to travel without them. Nicholas had to drag them several hundred miles to help me solve a double murder. I'm not taking any chances this go-around. The driver of the town car that brought us here promised to carry them to our room as soon as he managed to sneak them past the front desk. This isn't exactly a pet-friendly hotel.

"Come in!" I call. Whether because the driver can't hear me or—more realistically—because he's holding the basket containing my fur babies, he makes no move to open the door. When the knock sounds again, Liam goes to open it.

"Have they scratched your eyes out already?" he asks as he pulls the handle. He pokes his head into the hallway. "Hello? Where did you go?"

"He left? Drat. I wanted to make sure I gave him a good tip." I join my brother at the door, repeating his motions when I realize that not only is there no driver standing there, but there isn't the basket containing my cats either. We see nothing but empty hallway extending in either direction. "Where are Beast and Freddie?"

"With any luck, they've found a rat's nest in the basement and have decided to stay there," Liam says as he shuts the door. "I guess we imagined it."

I don't believe that for a second. *One* person can imagine a knock on the door, especially in a place where pipes and ancient woodwork are constantly in motion, but the likelihood of two people hearing the same sound at the same time is low. However, I'm far too rational to feel alarmed. For all we know, there are kids staying across the hall eager to get into mischief. This *is* the cheap floor.

"What should we do first?" Liam asks as he throws himself onto his bed. "The beach? The bars? The boardwalk?"

"*I'm* unpacking and then taking a nap," I say. It's not the most exciting way to enjoy our first afternoon on holiday, but I've spent the past few nights on the couch. My cottage is too small for a guest bedroom, and Liam gets cranky if he doesn't have four posters and a full-size mattress to sleep on. "If you want to go exploring, I won't stop you, but—"

The knock sounds again. This time, there's no mistaking its existence or the fact that it's not caused by a pipe in the wall. That's good, old-fashioned knuckles on wood if I've ever heard them.

"*That's* probably my cats," I say. "Which is another reason why I don't want to go out right away. The poor things will need a few hours to calm down and get used to the room. They don't like to travel."

Liam heaves a sigh of disapproval, but he's too lazy to get up from his prone position on the bed. I pause a moment to toss the television remote at him before opening the door, which is what I blame for the sight that greets me on the other side.

And by *sight*, I mean nothing. There's no driver, no basket of cats, no sign of anyone bringing fresh towels to the wrong room. In fact, the stillness of the hallway is so profound, it's almost supernatural. The plush gray carpeting appears untouched by feet or time, the scrollwork on the walls as stalwart as if it's stood there for centuries.

Which, technically, it has. This is a very old hotel.

I narrow my eyes and step out into the hallway only to be yanked back by a strong, gym-teacher hand.

"Are you trying to get me killed?" Liam drags me into the room and slams the door. "I've seen horror movies. I know how this ends. A hint—it's not great news for the good-looking gay guy on vacation for the first time in years."

I snort, but only because my brother wouldn't mind dying a gruesome and obscene death as long as the newspapers promised to include that bit about being good-looking. "Relax," I say. "It's probably someone playing a prank on us. Vivian, most likely. She'd get a kick out of slipping a bellboy a ten-pound note and telling him to do his worst."

Liam puts his eye against the peephole and waits a full twenty seconds. "There's no one out there. Bellboy or otherwise."

"I suppose it could be Winnie," I say, but only because I know it will get a rise out of my brother. "She doesn't normally manifest physically, but—"

"Why would you say that?" He whirls to face me, predictable to his core. "Winnie wouldn't try to scare us."

I laugh. "No, but you should totally see your face right now. You're as white as the bedsheets."

"So are you, if we're being honest," he retorts. Determined, as he always is, to get the last word, he nods and adds, "That decides it—we're hitting the beach first. Your lack of vitamin D is starting to scare me."

He makes good on this threat by gathering up all the supplies we'll need for the beach: towels, swimsuits, and enough suntan lotion to block any and all vitamin D from entering our systems for years. "We'll have to go out the window if we want to avoid the murder hallway out there, but it'll be worth it," he says. "I saw people rollerblading. Do you think we could go rollerblading?"

The thought of going anywhere on wheels is one I don't much care for under normal conditions. In weather that's capable of frying an egg, the thought of going anywhere on wheels is downright ludicrous. I'm in the middle of trying to convince Liam of this when the third knock comes.

This time, I'm ready for it. I pounce at the door and pull it open before the person on the other side has time to disappear. Liam tries to stop me, and even dives across the room to grab at my ankles, but he misses.

To my dismay, our driver is standing on the other side. Although he's a nice enough guy, and he even turned the radio to whatever station we wanted on the way, he's not as exciting as a bellboy caught in the act or the ghostly apparition of our sister come to pay a visit.

"Oh. Hi. It's you." I try not to sound as disappointed as I feel. "Did you see anyone else coming up or down this hallway?"

"Just me and the cats," he says, lifting the basket in his hand. It shakes and mewls a protest. "But you'd better hide them well. The doorman is already suspicious. I only made it past him because I said I was bringing the live lobsters for your dinner."

I accept the basket, which is much heavier than it looks. "That was quick thinking," I agree. "But where does he think I'm going to cook them? The rooms don't come with kitchens."

"That was what worried him. I told him you prefer them raw."

This doesn't bother me nearly as much as it does Liam. Eating live shellfish wouldn't be the worst thing I've been accused of in this lifetime.

"You're a marvel of man, and I can't thank you enough." I manage to extract a folded bill from my bosom and pass it to him. From the surprise on his face, I surmise that he's either unaccustomed to tipping or to receiving money from a woman's brassiere.

"No pockets," I apologize with a gesture over my person. "But it's clean, I promise."

Liam steps back and watches as I lift the lid off the basket and release my pets into their temporary home. In true Beast fashion, my oldest cat casts one disdainful look around her and decides that both the room and I are unworthy of her attention. Freddie mewls pitifully, so I press her to my chest until she grows accustomed to her new surroundings.

"You're really going to stay here with your cats and take a nap?" Liam asks doubtfully. "Am I supposed to stay and protect you?"

"From what? If there really is a ghost in the hallway, Beast will take care of him. And if it's a prankster, well . . ." I glance down at the cat in question, who is serenely licking her paw. I take more comfort from that sight than my brother will ever know. After the things Beast and I have been through together, a few empty knocks at the door don't scare me.

"It might not look like it, but she and I have our own way of getting to the bottom of things," I promise. "We've never failed yet."

When I awaken, it's to find that the entire world has gone black. The room, the window, the skies—all of them are plunged into a darkness so profound that it makes me feel as though I've been asleep for days instead of hours.

The heavy press of two feline bodies at my feet indicates that things might not be as dire as they seem, but that doesn't stop me from calling out. "Liam? Winnie? Birdie? Is anyone there?"

No one is—or, if they are, they aren't willing to own up to it. Glancing at the bedside clock, I note that it's only six o'clock in the evening. I've been asleep for a little over two hours, which should place me in an ideal position to take in the balmy summer evening. I cast the blankets aside and move to the window. There's nothing balmy or summerlike about the conditions outside. The heavy sag of black clouds overhead seems to be roiling up from the direction of the sea, covering everything like a blanket. The lights of the shops and restaurants are fully lit in an attempt to counteract the gloom, but huge gusts of wind are preventing anyone from wandering around in the open. The feeling that I've pulled a Rip Van Winkle and slept my way through to another season is strong, but one glance at my cell phone confirms that the date and location are the same as they ever were.

I pause just long enough to grab my purse and wrap my favorite white shawl—the only warm item of clothing I brought with me—around my shoulders before venturing out in search of my brother. I expect the hallway to be a little more bustling now that we're nearing the dinner hour, but it remains a long stretch of empty, elegant nothingness.

Well, mostly empty.

"What the . . . ?" I bend down and pick up a small porcelain doll that's sitting outside our door. She's tiny, no bigger than the palm of my hand, and appears to be of ancient origin. I say this not just because the porcelain is yellowed and cracked, but because I've never seen such a terrifying plaything. Modern dolls have big, kewpie eyes and adorably painted bow lips. This monstrosity looks as though she clawed her way out of the depths of a grave, her white dress covered in dirt and her once-blond hair down to a few straggling strands.

"At least our prankster is creative," I muse, dangling the doll between my forefinger and thumb. Her mouth gapes up a silent protest to this treatment. "If Liam wasn't freaked out before, he's definitely going to be now. He has serious pediophobia."

Since I can hardly leave the doll here for my brother or some poor innocent bystander to find, I tuck her into my purse. It's more of a clutch than an actual handbag, and it barely clasps over her head, but at least the doll is out of sight. I have no idea what our prankster's end goal is, but there's no denying that the creep factor is high. Mysterious knocks and vacant-eyed dolls are the stuff of nightmares.

Not *my* nightmares, obviously, but my experience with the dark side is greater than most.

There are no more mysterious gifts waiting for me as I make way to the lobby. The elevator runs smoothly and efficiently, there are plenty of families milling about, and even the storm building up outside is less ominous now that I see people shaking umbrellas as they enter the revolving front doors.

"Came out of nowhere . . ."

"Well, really, Caroline, I don't control the weather. . . ."

"Maybe now we can go to London like I wanted. . . ."

Freak storm, I think with a nod. One that seems to have taken us all by surprise.

Freak something, Winnie agrees. *I'm not sure I like the way this feels.*

I'm not sure I like the way it feels, either, but there's little I can do about it right now. I'd like to ask my sister a few questions—up to and including whether or not she noticed our little prankster in the hallway—but I catch sight of yet another relic across the lobby before I can reach out to her.

"Yoo hoo!" Vivian waves an arm in entreaty, heedless of the waiter's tray she almost upends in the process. She's seated at one of several tables in a cordoned-off dining area, what looks to be a ten-course meal laid within her reach. "Eleanor, love, I'm over here. You'll never guess who I ran into while you were asleep."

I halt in midstep. Sure enough, there appears to be someone seated across the table from Vivian. I blink, unsure at first if this is yet another prank, an attempt to send me screaming from this resort before I've had time to settle in, but that couldn't possibly be, if only because of the timing.

No one knew in advance that I would be here. *I* didn't even know until this afternoon.

Vivian's right about one thing, though. If I'd been given a thousand years and a thousand chances, I'd never have been able to guess who she ran into. Mostly because he's dead. Or, rather, he's *supposed* to be dead.

I should know. I'm the one who killed him.

Chapter 3

〜

I move across the lobby as though walking underwater, my brain a whirl of thoughts that don't seem to fit. They're disjointed, jagged, *wrong*.

I don't believe this, I think.

"I don't believe this." The man sitting opposite Vivian speaks the words aloud. He also rises to his feet in a single, fluid movement. Although Armand's height is a bare few inches above my own and his build like that of a reed trembling in the wind, he's striking to behold, even after all these years—and all that death. His eyes contain a piercing quality that never wavers, not even when he blinks. His voice is deep and rich—I might almost say mesmerizing—but that's only because I know that's what it is.

Mesmerizing. Hypnotic. A ruse.

"It's really you," he says, trying that voice out on me now. "When I saw the hotel register, I thought I must be imagining things, but . . ."

He trails off—intending, I'm sure, for me to finish his sentence. As a professional hypnotist and mentalist who can, alas, give me a run for my money when it comes to manipulating people, Armand knows how to get results.

So I stand and stare, my eyes slightly narrowed as I take full stock of him.

Armand Lamont, my one-time partner in crime, looks remarkably well for a dead man. His black satin waistcoat and purple velvet jacket are exactly as I remember them, well-tailored and cut to impress. His eyeliner is the same as it used to be, too, smoky and seductive and applied with a heavy hand. In fact, if it weren't for a few extra lines around his mouth and a certain . . . exhaustion in the slump of his shoulders, I'd think I was looking at a ghost.

"This hotel doesn't have registers," I say, careful to keep myself neutral. Mentalists are the worst of all con men, and I include fake mediums on that list. They're so good at reading people that even blinking too much can give everything away. "It has password-protected computers and strict guest privacy guidelines."

"Strange," he murmurs, not missing a beat. He doesn't blink, either. "Perhaps it was a vision. I have them now, you know."

"Mr. Lamont had a near-death experience," Vivian informs me with a delighted shudder. She's wearing a silver beaded top that clacks as the sensation runs up and down her spine. "He was struck by lightning. Imagine that. A bolt shot straight from the sky and struck him in the heart."

I don't have to imagine it. I saw it. I manufactured it.

Technically, all I did was lay him out in the middle of a storm dressed in a singed white shirt and charred saddle shoes to give the appearance of having been struck, but the idea holds true. It wasn't my best work, but it *was* the fastest way to get rid of him. The two of us had been working at a haunted mansion in Kentucky at the time. All had been going well enough—ghosts thumping and bumping, a wealthy hotelier paying us an obscene amount of money to remove them in time for his daughter's wedding—until Armand invented a fake charity and started recruiting donations from wedding guests on the side.

A normal person—a *decent* one—would have been happy enough with what was already being offered. Our job was to ensure a smooth and beautiful event for the bride-to-be, and by waving sticks of sage and paying some neighborhood kids to stop flying their drones at all hours of the night, we were well on our way to delivering just that.

But that wasn't enough. Not for Armand Lamont. He'd wanted to keep pushing, keep grasping, keep lining his own pockets. I'd already started to have doubts about him by that time, but that was where my patience ended. A woman was getting *married*, for Pluto's sake. All she wanted was for the day to go smoothly, for everyone to enjoy themselves as she pledged her life to another human being.

Some things are sacred, even to a woman like me.

A tincture of valerian root, St. John's wort, and magnolia bark lulled Armand to sleep just long enough for me to set the aforementioned lightning scene. Afraid of a lawsuit or—worse—a scandal, the Kentucky hotelier had been more than happy to help me cover things up as quickly as possible. By the time Armand had woken up, he was safely in the back of my hearse and halfway to New York.

If you'll excuse the pun, he never knew what hit him.

"It wasn't a near-death experience," Armand says now, his voice quiet but compelling. "I was literally dead. I've been to places no mortal man was meant to go, seen things hidden from those who cannot possibly understand. Go ahead. Ask me anything."

Ask him about the welcome buffet, Winnie suggests.

I don't manage to muffle my laughter in time. Armand turns to me with a quelling stare, but like the voice, it has no power over me. Where this man is concerned, I already learned the most important lessons. Trust no one. Once a con man, always a con man.

If you're going to murder someone, make it stick.

"Winnie would like to know if you enjoyed the welcome buffet," I say.

"Welcome buffet? I hate to disappoint you, Eleanor, but death isn't a catered event."

"That's not what my sister says."

This rejoinder doesn't, as I hope, throw Armand off balance. Instead, his penetrating gaze catches mine. "Ah, yes," he murmurs. "The sister. I was sorry to hear of her passing. I know how much you cared for her."

His words don't bring me comfort. Not only do I doubt his sincerity, but Winnie's death isn't common knowledge. We didn't hold a funeral, and there was no big announcement of her burial. In order for Armand to know that she's gone, he'd have had to deliberately seek out the information.

The fact that he knows about Winnie, that he's at this hotel, that he's not the least bit surprised to find me sharing it . . . Armand's here for a reason. He's here for a reason, and whatever it is, it's not good.

"Don't be sorry," I say. "I'm not. She's a lot more communicative now that she's dead."

He arches a brow. "Is that a fact?"

"So are you, it seems," I say. "If you didn't eat the buffet, what *did* you do on the other side? Winnie is curious."

I've put him in a difficult position with this question, and he knows it. It's a trick we learned and leveraged all the time back when we worked together. If one person claims an authority they don't have, the only way to beat them is to pretend you have something better. For example, if someone sees a ghost, you have to see it *and* hear it. If someone awakens in the night with feelings of dread, you have to start sleepwalking down empty hallways.

And if someone claims to have come back from the great beyond, you have to pull out your dead sister and start quoting her verbatim.

Vivian picks up on the undercurrent of tension and claps her hands as though she's never been more entertained. "I hope you don't mind, Eleanor, but I asked Mr. Lamont to join us for dinner. I didn't know you had such interesting friends."

It's on the tip of my tongue to tell her that Armand is decidedly *not* my friend, but I have no desire to go into the intricate details of our past. For one, I doubt she'd believe the half of it. For another, Liam arrives at the table just then, breathless and pale and with beads of sweat breaking out on his brow.

"Sorry I'm late." He looks at me with such loathing that I can easily pinpoint the cause of his distress. The poor guy must be really starting to feel the effects of that tea. "I'm a little under the weather. I can't imagine why."

"It's probably something you ate," I say, failing to take the bait. And, since I refuse to leave the introductions to Armand—or, worse, Vivian—I add, "Liam, this is Armand Lamont. We used to know each other back in the States. Armand, this is my brother, Liam."

"The brother?" Armand says, once again in a way that indicates this whole thing has been planned. "What a wonderful surprise. I've heard so much about you."

This is a patent lie. Although I mentioned the existence of a brother to Armand during the six months we worked together, I never went into explicit details. It was too risky. Liam is a teacher, a taxpayer, a decent human being.

Armand and I are . . . not.

"He's exaggerating," I say, partly because I'm irritated with Armand and partly because it's the fastest way to derail the conversation. I also help myself to some kind of seafood swimming in butter. These ten courses aren't going to eat themselves, and if the green tinge to Liam's face is any indication, he's not going to be much help. "You rarely came up in conversation."

Liam shows a tendency to pout. "That's not very nice. I talk about you to my friends all the time."

"Complaining about your weird sister who practices witchcraft overseas doesn't count."

"I don't complain. I unload." He pauses, a rueful smile touching his lips. "If it helps, they don't believe most of what I say. They think I made you up."

I'm not surprised by this. Although I'm much more stable now that I've settled down in one place, my life is far from predictable. One look around this table is all that's needed as proof. I can't even go on vacation without running into long-deceased co-workers dressed like David Blaine at a Renaissance fair and finding creepy dolls on my doorstep.

I stop with my fork halfway to my mouth. The bulging clutch purse sits heavily in my lap, a strand of the doll's scraggly hair escaping out the top. *Of course.* I can't believe I didn't realize it the moment I saw Armand. That was no mere prankster who knocked at our door, no unchaperoned child who left us a Victorian antiquity with the devil in her stare.

Armand is messing with me—with *us*. And I, like a fool, almost let him get away with it.

Since the best way to deal with a man like Armand is to ruin his game before he has a chance to play it, I pull the doll out of my purse and place her in the center of the table, resting her back against a basket of rolls.

"Gah, Ellie! What's wrong with you?" Of everyone at the table, my poor, queasy brother reacts the strongest to the sight of her. "What is that thing?"

"I found her," I say, careful to omit the exact location of my discovery. "She's cute, don't you think? In a vintage sort of way? She matches the hotel."

"Matches the hotel?" Liam echoes.

Although my brother gags in revulsion, Vivian reaches out and runs a finger over the doll's cheek. "Oh, how darling," she says. "I had one just like this when I was a girl. Her name was Brunhilde."

"Brunhilde," I agree, liking the way it sounds on my tongue. It might be my imagination, but the doll seems to appreciate it, too, her cracked, crooked lips curving into what almost looks like a smile. "I think that's what we should call her."

"What on earth for?" Liam demands. "If you ask me, she belongs in the garbage. In fact . . ."

He doesn't waste any time. As soon as a waiter passes by on his way to another table, my brother flings the doll at him. "Get rid of this, please," he says. "In the oven, if you can. Otherwise, a trash compacter will do. Make sure she's on the bottom."

Such is the power of my brother's smile that the waiter chuckles and complies rather than giving this request the refusal it deserves.

"That seems a touch drastic," I say, but not without first glancing at Armand to see how he's taking all this. He's careful not to give anything away—like me, he's been doing this long enough to hide his emotions—but he watches the waiter bear the doll away much more closely than mild interest would dictate. "She was old. For all you know, she was really valuable."

"I'll pay you back."

"What if she belongs to a little girl staying at the hotel?"

"Then we just saved her years of therapy. I only saw that thing for thirty seconds, and I'm going to have nightmares for a week." Liam seems as though he has more to say on the subject, but a spasm rocks his digestive tract. He bolts out of his seat, but not before first casting me a look of loathing. "I'm never going to forgive you for this, Ellie."

"Travel doesn't agree with him," I apologize as I return to my meal. Since I have no intention of giving Armand a platform to perform on, I turn my attention to Vivian instead. "How are you settling in, by the way? Is there anything you need?"

She doesn't appear to appreciate my concern. "If you're going to hover over me like a fly, then I'd rather go home to die of heat exhaustion. Nicholas has already bribed every bellhop in this place to wait on me hand and foot. They haven't left me alone for five minutes."

"What a monster," I agree. So far, all I've gotten from Nicholas is a quick text and—horror of all horrors—a heart-shaped emoji, but I suspect it was mostly ironic. "Next time, we should check you in under an assumed name. No one will find you then."

"Nicholas," Armand muses, his gaze level and his tone flat. He's not doing much in the way of eating. Instead, he twirls the stem of his wineglass in a way that's meant to draw the eye and fix the attention. It's no dangling pocket watch, but it's as close as you can get at the dinner table. "That would be your boyfriend, yes?"

"You seem remarkably well-informed about my life," I say by way of reply. I also begin drumming my fingers on the table in a random pattern—the better to fight hypnosis with. "I wonder why that is?"

"Oh, I was just passing the time with dear old Vivian here," he replies. "Sharing war stories, as it were."

Mining her for information, he means.

"Yes, I am seeing Vivian's son," I admit, since it's obviously useless to lie. Vivian doesn't know everything about my life, but she knows enough to give a mentalist most of what he needs to perform his trade. "It'll be—what—two years in November?"

Vivian snorts. "The longest two years of my life."

"How interesting." Armand leans back in his chair, still twirling his wineglass in a way that seems to draw Vivian in. I drum my fingers harder. "For you, two years is practically a lifetime."

I shrug. "It helps that he travels a lot for business. There hasn't been time for him to get tired of me yet."

"And you gave it all up for him?" Armand asks. I know for a fact that he's referring to the life I used to lead—the fake mediumship and the income it brought, the nomad's lifestyle and long-term support of my sister—but he's careful not to spoil my image with Vivian. For whatever that's worth. "Packed up your entire life and moved to . . . Sussex?"

"Yep."

"Sussex."

"The one and only."

"Sussex."

I'm not sure what he's trying to get at, but I don't appreciate his tone. Okay, so a few years ago, such changes to my life and situation for the sake of romance might have been unthinkable, but I'm a different person now. I have roots. Friends. A home. A career, even.

A career that, should Armand choose, could disappear tomorrow. All it would take is for him to waltz into my sleepy little village and tell a few stories about the things we used to do together—the tricks we relied on to strip people of their fears and savings accounts—and my life would be over.

And Armand, leaning back in his chair, knows it.

I stop my drumming as quickly as I started it, drawn not to Armand's wineglass, but to his face. It looks serene and confident and *knowing*. That stunt with the doll is just the tip of the iceberg when it comes to that man's plans for me. Unless I'm very much mistaken—and I rarely am—I'm about to be blackmailed. Big time.

"Speaking of, what brings you to our little corner of the world?" I do my best not to sound as rattled as I feel. "Of all the gin joints in all the towns in all the world . . ."

Armand has an answer ready. "Just visiting an old friend who lives in the area. Ever since my brush with death, my fortunes aren't what they used to be. I found I had an opening in my schedule, so I decided to put it to good use."

Yep. I'm definitely being blackmailed.

"And then I met dear Vivian here, and she invited me to join your party." He places his hand reverently over hers, but she's never been one for affection and tries to shake him off. When that doesn't work, she starts eyeing the crab picks. *That* gets Armand to back off in a flash.

"I'd love to hear more about what you've been up to all these years," he says. "It's been too long."

Not nearly long enough, I'm tempted to reply. I don't do it. For one, I'm not about to wage a public battle with Armand before I know what he wants. For another, my brother appears at the edge of the table, looking like a man who wants nothing so much as a quick and painless death.

"Let's get you outside and into some fresh air." I push back my chair and rise from the table, taking his arm before he can argue. "You'll feel better as soon as you inhale the bracing scent of the sea."

The bracing scent of the sea isn't going to do anything except make Liam hate the ocean in addition to me, but I pull him away from the table anyway. The last thing I need is for him to start swapping life stories with Armand before I have a chance to warn him.

Vivian waves us off with no more care than she'd send away the maître d', but Armand is clearly annoyed—not that you'd be able to tell from his expression. He stands and politely waits for us to depart, but I can read the tense lines of his stance. He's not pleased to let me out of his sights so soon.

Which, *good*. If I'm going to be blackmailed by a former business partner whose life and career I ruined, then I'm going to be blackmailed by a former business partner whose life and career I ruined on my own terms, thank you very much. I may be living in Sussex now, but I'm not dead.

Unlike Armand Lamont.

Chapter 4

◅≈►

Thanks to the darkness and the fact that it starts to rain by the time we make it outside, Liam and I have the beach to ourselves. It's a strange, otherworldly, *dangerous* sensation. Brightly colored beach umbrellas whiz by, carried by the wind and the vengeance of the gods, narrowly missing us on more than one occasion. There's nothing on the water—not a boat or a child or even a floating plaything accidentally left behind—and even the huge pier, where the vibrant lights of an amusement park normally blaze up the night sky, is empty save for a few straggling employees.

"Gah!" Liam ducks and narrowly avoids being hit over the head with a beach chair that's taken to the skies like a kite. "Whose idea was this? Can we please go inside so I can die of your poison in peace instead of being impaled by a sand shovel?"

"Quit whining." I continue dragging him along the water's edge. We're far enough away from the hotel now that I don't fear being overheard, but it never hurts to be safe. For all I know, Armand has half the hotel staff under his spell. Or his pay. "I need to talk to you."

"We could just as easily talk at a chemist's shop," he points out. "I think there's something really wrong with me."

"You're fine," I promise. Honestly, Liam has always been dramatic when it comes to illness. All it takes is a tickle in the back of his throat, and he's pretty sure he has cancer with a side of scarlet fever for good measure. "Besides, this is important. I think I'm in trouble."

Nothing could have been more calculated to get his attention than those three words: *I'm in trouble.* Liam is older than me by mere minutes, but he's always counted those minutes as if they were decades. He stops hunching almost immediately, his head snapping up and his gaze sharp. The wind whips through his dark curls in a way that would make a poet swoon, and he nods once. "Tell me."

It's not as easy a task at it seems. In order to confess what I think Armand is doing now, I need to tell him what Armand and I did in the past. Liam knows that my career wasn't always fun ghosts and happy hauntings, but I did my best to shield him from the worst of it. There was no use in both of us feeling wracked by guilt over a choice that had never really been a choice in the first place.

"Armand Lamont isn't a good man," I say, cutting right to the heart of the matter.

Liam laughs and shoves his hands deep in his shorts pockets, his shoulders hunched against the onslaught of rain. "Well, obviously. You didn't need to bring me all the way out here to tell me that."

"Wait. What?"

"I'm not stupid, Ellie. I could feel your irritation with him from across the lobby. What is he? An ex-boyfriend? A slighted lover? A magician you sawed in half and forgot to put back together again?"

That last question makes me feel much better. So does the fact that my brother seems to require no explanation. I get so excited when Winnie pops up to say hello, providing insight and commentary on my life choices, that I forget sometimes that I have a living, breathing sibling who is capable of the same. No one knows me like Liam does.

"Marketing yourself for the ghost-hunting profession isn't as easy as you'd think," I explain, doing my best to simplify the situation. "It's not like you can just make a website or register with the Better Business Bureau. I struggled, early on, to find clients."

He nods his understanding. He'd been there when I started taking on Winnie's health care costs by myself. Well-paying clients had been the only thing keeping her alive.

"Armand had been in the game for a while and sort of took me under his wing," I continue. "It was great working with him at first. You've met him. He's charming and he looks the part—and most important, he's exceptional at getting people to do things."

"Do things?" Liam echoes.

Big things. *Bad* things.

"He uses hypnosis, suggestion, outright manipulation—I've seen him convince people to act contrary to their very nature. He once got himself put in an old woman's will literal minutes before she died, and so believably that no one in the family questioned it." I shake my head, still awed after all these years. Even the lawyer who'd notarized the documents hadn't found anything wrong with the sudden change of heart. "We didn't exactly part on the best of terms. He crossed a line. Lots of them, actually."

"Ellie . . ."

"I know." I wince. "I'm not proud of some of the things I've done, but I'm *trying* to be better. You know I am."

He doesn't know it—or, if he does, he's not willing to admit as much while standing, queasy and uneasy, in the rain.

"It's not an accident that he's here right now or that he just happened to run into Vivian," I say. "This is all part of some bigger plan."

"What kind of plan?"

If I knew the answer to that, I wouldn't be standing on a dark beach with strands of hair whipping across my face and a serious case of goose bumps breaking out over my skin. I wrap my shawl tighter around me. Liam notices and draws close, his arm slinging over my shoulder in a way that I remember fondly from our youth. It's been so long since we were in the same continent as one another, let alone the same city, that I let go and allow myself to indulge in the embrace. I lean on his shoulder and sigh, the pair of us staring out at the cascading waves of the ocean.

"Maybe he was the one knocking on our hotel door earlier today," Liam suggests. "To try and freak us out."

I'm surprised at how quickly he comes to the same conclusion as me. "I was thinking that exact thing."

"What other tricks does he know?"

The answer to that question is a long list of cons, frauds, hoaxes, and scams that would make the uninitiated run screaming for their lives. My brother, who is about as uninitiated as they come, won't swallow them easily. I'm just about to gently ease him into the world of fraudulent mediumship when a movement out on the water catches my eye. I jump, my whole body growing stiff, as I lean forward to peer closer.

"Liam, look!" I point at the bobbing vision in the distance. As improbable as it seems given the current climate, there appears to be a white dinghy undulating on the waves. I was caught on a too-small, too-dangerous fishing vessel under similar conditions last year, so I'm particularly attuned to the possibility of distress. When the waves are that big and unpredictable, there's no telling how badly a boat like that will get tossed around. "Someone must have gotten caught out on the water. We have to help them."

"How?" Liam asks with a quick glance around us. There doesn't appear to be a single soul in sight. "Do you want me to run back to the hotel?"

"Yes. No. I don't know." My heart, which had started hammering at the sight of that boat, drums a more persistent warning. "I think someone on the boat is waving at us."

Sure enough, the waves ebb enough to give us a clear view of the dinghy and its contents. A man stands in the center, his arms gesticulating widely. He's wearing some kind of bright yellow rain slicker but doesn't appear to have a floatation vest on, so I can only imagine how worried he must be.

"I'm sure he's fine," Liam says, though with a slight tinge of doubt in his voice. "He's not alone. There are those two men with him."

At first, I suspect Liam of toying with me. I can't see anyone else on the boat, though it's dark enough that I can't see much of *anything*. As I blink and wipe the rain from my eyes, however, the two figures come into focus.

Figures is the only word I can think of to describe them. They aren't exactly men, but they aren't not-men, either. It's almost as though they're shadows—vague, wavy impressions of humanity that don't adhere to the rules of existence. They flit in and out of my line of sight, giving the impression of living somewhere between this realm and the next.

"You can see them?" I ask, blinking rapidly. "You can absolutely tell that they exist?"

Liam looks away from the boat long enough to give me a strange stare. "Of course I can see them."

I'm more relieved than I care to admit. So far, my ability to connect with the great beyond is restricted to sound and the occasional otherworldly vision, but I've learned not to accept anything at face value. I wouldn't put it past Winnie or Birdie to start sending ghost figures on top of everything else. Birdie, in particular, would find that hilarious.

"Well, it doesn't matter if there's one or three of them," I say. "You'd better go for help. I don't see how they're going to survive those waves much longer."

"You're probably right," Liam admits, but he clutches my arm with so much strength that I'm forced to cry out. "Only—Ellie. They're pushing him overboard. They're throwing him into the water."

I've seen enough tragedy in my life that I can keep a fairly cool head in situations like these. Murder, in particular, seems to have a way of following wherever I go—and it doesn't take me or Liam long to realize that's what we're looking at. The man in the slicker appears to put up a fight, his hands up and thrashing at the two dark figures, his body whipping back and forth as he tries to shake them off.

But it's no use. The figures each take one of his arms and heave him in the direction of the water.

Liam and I call out as one, both of us running much farther into the ocean than we should, given the impossibility of reaching him in time. The boat is too far out and the waves much too thrashing, but this isn't my first time dealing with either of those issues. I'm about to make the plunge when Liam puts a hand on my shoulder and yanks me backward.

"Ellie, *look*," he says with his mouth pressed against my ear. He lifts his hand and points. I pause long enough to follow the line of his finger. The cool, restless water swirls around our ankles as the clouds open to allow a ray of light—moonlight or sunlight, I can't tell which—to stream through. The moment that light makes contact with the boat, the two dark figures disappear.

As in, *literally* disappear. I blink and rub my eyes, straining to catch a glimpse of movement on board, but there's nothing. No sign of life—or afterlife, as the case may be. There's just an empty, rocking boat that bobs up and down on the waves.

"Get help," I say, and give my brother a push. "I'm going in."

"You can't!" he cries, but he's too late. I already have.

I realize the futility of what I'm doing about two minutes later. Not because I'm weak or not making good headway, or even because I'm feeling the chill of an ocean current that's never passed through the tropics, but because a rescue boat zips by with such ease and speed that I realize I'm only going to add to the trouble. In fact, a second rescue boat slows down, realizes what I'm up to, and orders me back to shore.

"A man," I say between gulps of air. "Three men. On the boat. They've all gone overboard."

A life preserver is tossed down over my head.

"Get back to shore," a woman shouts at me. "This is no weather for recreational swimming." In an audible aside, she adds to the man piloting the vessel, *"Americans."*

After an insult like that one, I'm tempted to keep swimming out toward the abandoned dinghy, but the last thing I want to do is make things worse. My *American* sense of duty tells me that the best thing I can do is find my way back to Liam.

This proves to be much more difficult than I realize. I make it back to the water's edge just fine, but I can't find him among the faces of the crowd that's gathered there. People look shocked and horrified and—some of them, anyway—far too excited than they should be, given the nature of the crime, but none of them are familiar. I'm torn between staying put to watch the drama unfold and going in search of my brother.

In the end, my brother wins, and I head back toward the hotel. I'm dripping wet, chilled to the bone, and more shaken than I'd like to admit, but the Brighton Luxe is nothing if not upscale. A tall, neatly tuxedoed doorman who looks as though he just stepped off the set of *Downton Abbey* hands me an oversized towel and says, without a touch of irony, "Nice evening for a swim."

I nod my head in agreement and open my mouth to ask after Liam, but he's ready for that, too.

"I believe your brother can be found near the back of the lobby," he says. "He asked me to tell you that he's feeling rather . . . indisposed."

I bite back a groan. Of course he is.

"He managed to get a call out for help, though," I say with a nod out the revolving glass doors, where more and more people are shuffling through to take in the spectacle of death and drowning.

"Ah, no." The doorman sniffs. "That was me, I'm afraid. I saw the whole thing from here."

Sure enough, when I take a step back to the post he normally occupies, I have a clear view out to the ocean. In fact, the angle here is better than it would have been from where Liam and I stood on the shore. The doorman must have seen everything.

"I notified the authorities as soon as that poor man jumped."

"Jumped?" I echo. A large puddle has started to form underneath me by this time, rendering the marble tiles treacherous, but the doorman is either too polite or too well-trained to say anything. "What about the two other men on the boat?"

The doorman turns to me with a look of blank inquiry. "What two other men?"

A shiver moves over me that has very little to do with my current body temperature. It's a feeling I often get when something supernatural is headed my way—a tactic I used to fake in order to convince people that their houses were haunted, and that I now regularly experience as part of my whole Eleanor-can-speak-to-the-dead thing.

"Winnie?" I ask, since it's the only thing I can think of to say. "Birdie?"

At first, I get no response from either of my ghosts, but the sound of my sister's voice hails me before I give up hope.

I don't know yet, Ellie, she says, sounding grim. *Something's not right.*

The doorman is watching me with a slightly wary expression, but I ignore it. I'd ignore an earthquake if it hit right now, even if it was wrapped up in a tornado with a volcanic eruption on the side.

I don't like my sister's tone, and I don't like my sister's words. Mostly because she's not wrong.

Something *isn't* right here. And, if history has any intention of repeating itself, it's going to be up to me to figure out why.

Chapter 5

❧

Liam sleeps late the next day, snoring through the morning as though he hasn't a care in the world. That's one of the perks of not being in direct communication with the supernatural side of things. He might be able to witness a murder and/or suicide and drift off into contented slumber afterward, but I have far too many questions.

None of which Birdie or Winnie deigns to answer, by the way. Not even after I bribe my cats with some crab patties I swiped from the breakfast buffet and make an altar out of my wet clothes from last night.

"I don't see what a few candles and your ratty old shawl are supposed to do," Vivian says as I start to unwind my clothes from around the vase I'd used to hold my offering. Since I'd wanted to let Liam rest in peace—pun intended—I'd put my cats in their basket and held my session in Vivian's room. It's enormous, the kind of hotel suite that's normally reserved for rock bands and families of twelve. In addition to a separate bedroom and a bathroom with the most gorgeous claw-foot bathtub I've ever seen, there are two sitting rooms decorated lavishly with ornate furniture and long brocade curtains.

"It helps to ground the spirits in this world," I explain. "So they have something to hold on to. Like following a rope through a snowstorm."

She nods as though this makes perfect sense—which, if you know anything about witchcraft, it does—but her next words are anything but conciliatory. "If you ask me, you'd be better off sacrificing one of your cats."

"Vivian!" I can't help but grab the nearest animal—which happens to be Freddie—and drop a kiss on the downy fur of her forehead. "What a terrible thing to say."

"I didn't *invent* the practice," she retorts. "That's how they do it in the movies. The devil likes to make deals."

I can only stare at her and continue petting my cat. Vivian has chosen to dress today in what appears to be hotel cosplay, by which I mean she's hearkened back to the age of its construction and decided to go full Victorian matriarch. I have no recollection of packing a shirtwaist, but she's somehow acquired one and layered it over one of her longer evening gowns. The sapphires, I'm disappointed to note, are on full display around her neck and dangling from her ears. Armand is going to take one look at those and lose his greedy little mind.

"Vivian, you don't think I'm a Satanist, right?" I ask, since it suddenly seems important to make that clear. After what I witnessed last night—those two dark figures disappearing into thin air—the distinction is an important one. "I don't make deals with the devil. I occasionally talk to my sister. It's not the same thing."

She waves her hand as though the disparities between the two is a matter of indifference. "I never cared for labels."

"Yes, but the things I do—making potions and putting ghosts to rest—it's good work, important work. I help people more than I harm them."

"Do you?"

In light of all the emotions Armand Lamont's return to my

life has brought to the surface, this feels suspiciously like a personal attack. I'm about to open my mouth to defend myself when a loud series of knocks on the door startles us both.

"Ellie, open this door!" The pounding sounds again. "This isn't funny. You're not funny."

Since this is supposed to be the posh floor, I jump up to quell my brother's rage. Any relief I might feel at his being awake and dressed to face the day vanishes as soon as I see what he's talking about.

"Did you pay someone to do this?" He shoves Brunhilde at me. The doll looks to be no worse the wear for her adventure yesterday, with the same fixed stare and cracked smile from before. Apparently, our waiter couldn't find it in him to do away with her. "There's something seriously wrong with you, you know that?"

I take the doll, but only because he's shoving her at me and storming his way into the room. For some strange reason, I'm reluctant to touch her again.

"Where did you . . . find it?"

He casts me an accusing glare. "She was sitting in the hallway. Looking at me. Taunting me. I could almost swear that she's staring into the depths of my soul."

Technically, there's nothing funny about the events of the past twenty-four hours. Between Liam's indisposition, Armand's arrival in Brighton, this creepy-as-all-get-out doll, and the death we witnessed, most women would be packing up all their belongings and hightailing it home. *This* woman, however, laughs. It only takes a few seconds before Liam joins me. He might have a flair for melodrama—it's a trait we Wildes share—but he's also self-aware about it.

"Well, what would *you* have thought?" he grumbles as he makes his way into the room, with a courteous nod for Vivian and a warm welcome for the cats. He flings himself onto the couch. Like Vivian, he's chosen to dress up for the day, although he's in a more time-period-appropriate pair of tailored slacks and a polo shirt. I can only assume that he took one look out the window and decided that the continuing storm would make sunbathing difficult. "There's something wrong with her eyes. Everywhere you go, they look like they're following you."

It's true. Her eyes do tend to follow, but that's easily explained away. Artists have been doing it for centuries by using trompe l'oeil—a sort of optical illusion accomplished by the way the shadows of the doll's face are painted. It's the same reason the *Mona Lisa* will watch wherever you go. Renaissance painters were exceptional at freaking people out.

"It was probably Armand," I say, and set the doll on the nearest table. Freddie jumps up and starts tentatively sniffing around, but Beast wants nothing to do with it. "He got it back from the waiter and put it outside the door to try and scare you. The best thing you can do is pretend it never happened."

"I liked that young man," Vivian says. "He told me I look like a well-aged Hedy Lamarr."

Which just goes to show how dangerous it is to believe a word out of his mouth. Vivian looks more like Miss Havisham than anything else. "Well-aged makes you sound like a Christmas ham," I point out. "If I were you, I wouldn't believe a word he says. And you might want to put those sapphires back in the safe. He has a weakness for things that sparkle."

None of this seems to unsettle Vivian. "We all have a weakness for things that sparkle," she points out. "It's what makes us human."

The irony is that Armand would be the first to agree with her. Things that sparkle—pocket watches, wineglasses, crystal pendants—are his favorite tricks of the trade. Nothing draws the eye and clears the mind like a low, crooning voice and something shiny swishing back and forth.

"Just don't make any major financial changes without talking to me first, okay?" I say. "And if he starts telling you that you're feeling sleepy, run. Run as fast and as far as your legs will take you."

She only laughs. "What makes you think he's the first charming young man to seek me out in a place like this? Eleanor, dear, you're such an innocent lamb sometimes."

Liam and I can't help but share an incredulous look at this. No one has ever accused me of being innocent before.

"Just bear in mind that he's not everything he appears to be. I don't . . . I haven't always . . ." I sigh as I seek for the best way to put this. I want to put Vivian on her guard, but I also don't want to damage a relationship and a woman I've come to treasure. "I've done some things in my life, Vivian. Terrible things. Things Armand knows about. I'm not sure yet what he's doing here, but he might use those things to try and get to you."

Beast winds elegantly through Vivian's legs, the cat's fur brushing against the long hem of her skirt. Unthinking, Vivian picks the animal up and begins negligently petting her. "Excellent," she says. A smile touches her lips. "And here I was afraid I wouldn't find anything to do in Brighton."

I'm forced to accept this decree at face value—and strangely enough, I'm okay with it. For all her air of eccentricity, Vivian is as sharp as they come. Another woman might want to know the sordid details, to hear from the horse's mouth what kind of mischief it got up to, but not Vivian Hartford. Either because she's too kindhearted or, as is more likely, because she simply doesn't care, she's willing to overlook whatever nefarious deeds lie in my past.

I turn my attention to Liam. "In that case, we're supposed to go down and meet with the police as soon as you're ready. They need our statements about last night."

He pulls a face. "Is that really necessary?"

"Unfortunately, yes. The other option is to put on disguises and flee from the hotel before anyone knows we're missing, but that sort of thing has a way of casting suspicion. We're better off telling them what we saw."

I can tell Liam isn't enamored of the plan, but there's little he can do to stop the hand of the law from poking around. After extracting one last promise from Vivian that she'll keep an eye on my cats—and on her jewels—Liam and I head out.

As an afterthought, I grab Brunhilde and shove her into the wide black corset belt I'm wearing today. It's not as handy as having pockets, but you'd be surprised how much you can hide inside well-crafted leather.

"Really, Ellie?" Liam asks as we head toward the nearest elevators. "Does that thing have to come with us? She gives me the creeps."

"All the more reason to keep an eye on her, don't you think?"

He doesn't think. After a slight tussle in which Liam's gym teacher experience once again gives him an advantage, he manages to not only extract Brunhilde from my belt, but to toss her into a gilded garbage chute next to the linen room. She clanks and jangles all the way down.

"There." He gives a self-satisfied swipe of his hands. "That'll show her."

"She could have been useful," I protest. "Maybe someone is trying to tell us something. Maybe she has secret messages rolled up and carried inside her head."

He's not fooled by this. What I'm really saying—and what he already knows—is that I'm a lot more scared of that doll than I'm letting on. Not because I fear she's some mystical being who walks on porcelain legs at night, but because she's part of a larger puzzle that I don't yet understand.

I don't know what Armand wants from me. I don't know what we witnessed on that boat last night.

And I really don't know why trouble like this always seems to follow wherever I go.

* * *

The investigation for last night's death has been set up in a conference room on the first floor of the hotel, where we're escorted as soon as we set foot in the lobby. I'm not sure when we became so notoriously recognizable that the entire staff knows us by sight, but there's little we can do about it now. Public infamy isn't new to me, and Liam, at least, seems to appreciate the attention. Especially when we walk inside the conference room to find coffee and pastries waiting for us.

"Thank the caffeine gods," Liam says as he pours himself out a cup of coffee and takes his time deciding between a cherry Danish and some kind of scone oozing cream and jam. From the way he's eyeing them, I can only assume that yesterday's tea has run its full course. He ends up taking both. "You may now lead me to the slaughter, Ellie. My body is ready."

His body might be ready, but I doubt his nerves are. The woman waiting for us at the other end of the room doesn't look like the sort to accept stories of dark, disappearing men on boats in the middle of a storm. Part of it is her size—she's tall and solidly built, the sort of woman who was probably born playing rugby—but there's more to it than that. Her eyes are light blue, almost eerily so, but there's no sign of life in them. Her gray, ill-fitting suit, the tight knot of hair at the base of her neck, and the flat line of her mouth indicate that she's not a woman who cares about making a warm impression on others.

"Sit," she commands with a curt nod at the two chairs set up for us.

"Sorry to keep you waiting," I say as though I'm used to being ordered around by prison matrons who look as though they've never cracked a smile. "As I'm sure you understand, we had a bit of trouble getting to sleep last night."

"Eleanor Wilde," she says by way of answer, my name like the rap of a ruler on my knuckles. "And brother, William Wilde. Both Americans, here on holiday."

It takes me a moment to realize that she's speaking to the person seated behind her, a deflated, browbeaten man who looks as though he's been used as this woman's rugby ball once or twice. He barely glances up as we settle ourselves in our seats, but that's mostly because he's busy jotting down notes.

"According to reports, they were two of the three witnesses of last night's suicide," she continues. "They—"

I hold up a finger to prevent her from continuing. "I beg your pardon, but it wasn't a suicide."

The look she casts on me is unlike any I've ever experienced before. I don't believe in the power of the evil eye or the ability to turn people into pillars of salt, but if I did, she's absolutely who I would cast in the role. There are shards of ice coming out of her gaze, I'm sure of it.

"He was pushed," I say, hoping to clarify matters. "Well, pulled and tossed, really, but—"

The ice shards start pelting me anew. "Which is it?" she asks. "Pushed or pulled?"

I can't help casting a helpless glance at my brother. "Um, both? Neither? It was too dark to make out all the details, but there were two other men on the boat. They took him by the arms and sort of . . . *hefted* him overboard."

I nod, liking the way that sounds. Hefted is exactly what they did.

"And you can confirm this?" The woman turns to Liam. "There were three men in total?"

"I don't know that I'd call them men," Liam admits with a hunch of his shoulders. "They were more like . . . figures."

"Figures?"

"Dark forms."

"Dark forms?"

"Apparitions, if you will."

"Liam!" I jab him with my elbow. He's not helping us make our case in front of this drill sergeant of a woman. "You don't know that they were apparitions."

"They disappeared into thin air. I don't know what else you'd call them."

I do my best to appear like someone who's accustomed to dealing with belligerent law enforcement officers, which, to be fair, I am. "Regardless of who—or what—they were, we saw three beings on the boat. We're in consensus about that."

The officer in the chair diligently continues taking notes, but the woman has yet to so much as blink up at us.

"This isn't your first time seeing *beings*, is it, Madame Eleanor?" she asks.

That use of my professional nom de plume—something I've been careful not to advertise here in Brighton—has me making a double take, and then a triple take. There's always a chance that Armand or even Vivian has leaked the information, but something about the way the woman looks at me feels off.

That isn't the intent look of a law officer who's heard a few rumors. That's the intent look of a law officer with insider information.

"What did you say your name was, again?" I ask, scanning her gray suit for a badge. She's not wearing one, but she doesn't hesitate to answer all the same.

"I didn't," she says, "but you may have heard of me. I'm Gillian. Gillian Piper."

This is the first time I've ever heard this woman's name spoken out loud, and it's the first time I've ever seen her face, but I know her well. Piper is the surname of a certain police inspector back in my village—a certain police inspector who has me to thank for solving several different murder cases that have fallen in his lap. If anyone knows exactly how many *beings* I've seen in my lifetime, it's Inspector Peter Piper.

He doesn't believe that I see anything but cast-iron clues, of course, but that's part of the game we play. He pretends he doesn't need my help solving difficult cases, and I pretend he doesn't secretly consider me his best friend.

A best friend who, by the way, knows all the intimate details of his divorce. *And* how desperate he is to get his ex-wife back. He even quit smoking last year in an effort to ameliorate her.

I eye the policewoman—*Gillian*—with renewed interest. She's a good head taller than Peter and could probably crush him between her thighs, but I can totally see it. He's the exact sort of man to be attracted to a woman substantially stronger than him. After all, he and I are friends, and I'm much smarter.

I allow a smile to curve my lips. "No, Mrs. Piper. This isn't my first time seeing things from the great beyond. It's something of a specialty of mine."

I can see her bristle at my use of that *Mrs.*, which is why I keep going. Depending on how much her ex-husband has shared with her, this might be the only chance I'll have of gaining the upper hand.

"In fact, my ability to discern the supernatural is what makes my eyewitness account so valuable. The men on that boat weren't anything out of the ordinary. They were men, period."

My upper hand doesn't last very long. "You're very confident in yourself. How do you know they weren't women?"

Well, drat. She has me there.

"I can't," I admit. "But they were human, that much I know for sure. What makes you so sure it was a suicide? I'm assuming the body was recovered last night. Did you check his upper arms for antemortem bruising? That would confirm what we saw."

"Gross, Ellie," Liam says.

"Despite your previous work with my ex-husband, it's not customary for officers to share their findings with witnesses." She pauses and reconsiders. "But in an attempt to prevent you from spreading unfounded rumors around the hotel, I will mention that he left a note. It was found in his room."

"A suicide note?" I echo, slightly disconcerted. That doesn't fit at all with what Liam and I saw. "What did it say?"

Instead of answering, she nods at the man with the notepad.

"That will be all, Bertram. We're not going to get anything useful out of these two."

I resent the implication, but since this new Inspector Piper and I are just starting to get to know one another, I don't let it hurt my feelings. "You might as well tell me. I have a way of finding these things out one way or another." Pointing a finger straight up in the air, I add, "I have friends in high places."

Gillian narrows her eyes. "Is that a threat?"

"Just an observation. You'd be surprised how easy it is to get confidential information when you can call on the powers of the dead to access it."

In case you can't tell, this is a full-on bluff. As my failed invocation this morning proves, I can't control Winnie or Birdie to any useful degree. Fortunately, Gillian Piper doesn't know that.

"Fine." She heaves a sigh. "But I want to hear exactly what happened to the two extra men—I'm sorry, *beings*—on the boat last night. You said they disappeared into thin air, yes? No, not you. I want your brother's account. In his own words."

Liam casts an anxious look at me, so I give him a reassuring nod. For once in my life, there's no way this crime can be pinned on me. I wasn't in that boat last night, and I have no personal connection to the man who fell from it. We might as well tell the truth.

"That's all of it, honestly," Liam says. "One second, they had him by the arms and were throwing him into the water. The next, *poof*. They were gone. Almost like they hadn't been there at all. I've never seen anything like it."

Gillian nods in a way that's meant to aggravate me, as if she believes him. I could rant and rave about vanishing visions for days, and I'd come out looking like a delusional liar. Liam, however, is taken at his word.

"Could you make out any distinguishing features on these

two men?" Gillian prods further. "Anything at all—clothing, hair color, build?"

Liam thinks about it for a moment, his dark brows drawing closer together the longer he tries to come up with an answer. I wish I could say that his response baffles me, but it doesn't. For the life of me, I can't come up with anything. Not about their clothes or hair color, which would have been undistinguishable at that distance anyway, but not about their build, either. I should at least be able to tell if they were taller or shorter than the man in the bright yellow slicker.

"I'm sorry," Liam eventually says. "I can't remember. Can you, Ellie?"

I don't want to admit my ignorance, but I'm not about to fabricate facts to help make my case. "No," I admit. "That's weird, isn't it? We should be able to remember something."

"On the contrary," Gillian says, "if what you saw were shadows—and I suspect they were—then it's perfectly natural that you can't recall the details. Shadows shift and move with the light, which makes them especially unreliable."

But there was no light, I want to point out. I almost do it, too, only one of the employees from the front desk comes running into the conference room just then. Her hair has become loose from its ponytail, her burgundy-painted lips parted with exertion.

"I'm so sorry to interrupt, Inspector," she says, holding a hand to a stitch in her side, "but I had to come at once. There's been an incident."

Gillian instantly becomes a body in motion. As I suspected, she must have quite a bit of rugby in her past to be able to move like that. One second, she's a belligerent bulwark staring me down. The next, she's out the door and flying to the rescue. She's so quick, in fact, that she doesn't notice when I trail behind her.

"I'd normally call the local police in for something like this, but since you're already here . . ." The front desk clerk, one of those timeless, dark-haired women whose age might be anywhere between twenty and forty, rounds a corner with a clip of her high heels. "I'm sorry. He's a little overwrought. I tried to calm him down, but he won't listen to anyone."

"You're darned right I won't listen to anyone!" comes the response. The man who utters it isn't familiar to me on a personal level, but I know his type well. It's my calling to dissect people at a glance, and this man is as common as a housefly. The expensive but poorly fitting suit, the red and bulbous nose, the much too-shiny shoes . . . this is a man who wants to impress but doesn't know how. And a man who blames the world for that inability. "Are you the fancy police inspector she promised me?"

Gillian Piper takes these words exactly as one might expect. Which is to say, not well at all. "I am *a* police inspector, yes."

"Then I'd like to file a report." The man stabs one of his equally red and bulbous fingers at the front desk clerk. "She won't take me seriously, but I've been robbed. Robbed, I tell you."

By this time, Gillian has noticed that I'm standing right behind her and that Liam, with nothing better to do, is standing right behind *me*. She angles her body to shield the man from us, but it's an exercise in futility. The crowd that's gathered by now is almost equal to that on the beach last night. Apparently, people in Brighton have a hard time finding anything to do when the sun is behind a cloud.

"They took my watch. A Breitling Navitimer. *And* my opal cuff links. And a diamond tie pin and my signet ring. That last one is irreplaceable. It's been in my family for generations. They broke into my room safe and took them."

Gillian looks to the front desk clerk as if for confirmation. The woman nods slightly.

"These items were taken just now?" she asks. "While you were in the room?"

"That's what I keep saying!" the man cries. "I had just closed my eyes for a little rest, but I must have fallen asleep. I heard the sound of flames crackling and woke to find two men hunched over the safe. At least, I *thought* they were men."

I can't help but intrude. Mention of crackling flames and the two men is too coincidental to ignore. "I'm sorry—did you say you heard flames?"

He turns his fulminating eye on me. "Who are you supposed to be?"

I extend my hand before Gillian can stop me. "Madame Eleanor Wilde, paranormal investigator." This last bit is added at the last minute, but I like the way it sounds. It's official enough to get me answers but not so official it'll get me run out of town with pitchforks. "Tell me more about these flames you heard. Are we talking leaping bonfire, or like, a gentle hum in the background?"

"I don't see what that has to do with anything," he protests.

He wouldn't, but that's only because he didn't spend six months of his life working alongside a hypnotist. When you want to mask the sounds of an activity you'd like to go undetected—breaking and entering, for example—white noise is the way to do it. The constant and repetitive state lulls the brain into thinking all is well, especially in the deep recesses of slumber.

Armand loves white noise almost as much as he loves dangling a pocket watch. In fact, it's one of his signature go-tos. However, that bit about there being two men is unlike him. And, given last night's events, unsettling.

"What happened to the two men, if you don't mind my asking?"

He waves his hands in a vague, airy gesture. "Poof. They disappeared. Vanished. Puffed into thin air."

I can't help looking at Gillian. As I hope, she glances back. She doesn't like this new information any more than I do, but she can hardly refute a witness's evidence as he gives it.

"What about their distinguishing details?" I persist. Taking a page from the inspector's book, I add, "Anything at all—clothing, hair color, build?"

Gillian won't admit it, but she approves of this line of questioning. I can feel it in the way she leans forward for the answer, her whole body expectant.

The man blinks, slowly at first and then gaining speed until all he can do is shake his head. That action, more than the words that follow, convince me he's telling the truth. He's more surprised by his own revelation than we are.

"I don't know," he says. "I can't remember."

Behind me, Liam lets out a small squeak. "It was them," he says. "It was the same figures from last night."

Not surprisingly, this piece of news does little to calm the irate man down. Now, instead of blustering about his missing valuables and thieves lurking about, he starts going on about missing valuables and *figures* lurking about. Neither of those things are good for a hotel as expensive and classy as this one.

Of everyone here, I'm the most qualified to help calm the man down, but Gillian loses no time in getting rid of me. And she does it without even pretending to be polite, which leaves me feeling both annoyed *and* impressed.

"Get these two out of here," she commands the front desk clerk as she strides away, her hand clamped on the angry man's arm as she drags him behind her. "I don't care how you do it as long as you do it quickly. And find a way to shut them up about those shadow figures. The last thing we need is for people to get hysterical."

"That sounded rather ominous," I remark to no one in particular. Mostly because no one in particular is paying much attention to me. The crowd has followed the sound of the shouting, leaving me and Liam standing awkwardly at the desk. "How does she want you to shut us up? With duct tape? A knife? I should warn you—we don't go down easy."

The front desk clerk grins her appreciation. The lines around her mouth deepen from an etching to a groove, placing her age closer to forty than twenty. "Bribery, actually. I'm at liberty to tell you that the Brighton Luxe is prepared to comp you for the rest of your stay with us. For any emotional pain from what you witnessed last night."

This gets me to perk up in a flash. "Really? The whole stay?"

The woman starts to nod, but Liam bursts in before she can finish. "Does our emotional pain also include a room upgrade? Two vanishing bad guys seem like they're worth at least a suite."

"Liam!" I cry, only half protesting. It's wrong to benefit from a man's death, I know, but we *did* witness something terrible. And our room is so small. . . .

The woman's grin deepens. She's susceptible—as so many are—to that particularly wheedling smile of my brother's. He could have made an incredible fake medium, had he ever decided to take up the trade. With a tap of her fingers on the keyboard, she says, "Let me see what I can do."

As she busies herself comping us all kinds of perks and bonuses, I nudge Liam with my hip. "Can you really not remember what those guys looked like last night?" I ask, careful to keep my voice low. "Nothing at all?"

He shakes his head. "No. The whole night is kind of fuzzy. It felt so sharp and real at the time, but now . . . I don't know. It's like someone went inside my head and rubbed an eraser over it."

I absorb this comment with a sinking heart. If that bit about the crackling flames hadn't already cast suspicion on the dear, departed Armand Lamont, then our muddled memories would be sure to do the trick. There's only person in the world—or, at the very least, this hotel—capable of that kind of mind control.

I'm going to kill him, I think with a grimace. *Again.*

Chapter 6

⁓

"You, there. The pale woman who just walked in. Guess a number between one and a hundred."

I pause on the threshold of the pub I've just entered, giving my eyes a moment to adjust to the lights and my throat a chance to bite back its groan. Thanks to the inclement weather and the fact that a man recently died in the water, it's more crowded than it would usually be at two o'clock on a Tuesday afternoon. It's also more intoxicated than it would usually be at two o'clock on a Tuesday afternoon. Armand must be desperate if these are the sort of people he's working nowadays. It's practically highway robbery.

Or, as is more likely the case, *hotel* robbery.

"No, thank you," I say in my most damping tone. "I don't do magic tricks."

I recognize this remark for a mistake almost immediately. The first rule of dealing with a mentalist is not to deal with him at all.

"Oh, but this isn't a trick, little lady. I can read your mind. I could read it the moment you walked in the door."

I narrow my eyes and run my gaze over Armand's attire. I know this ruse well. He probably has several different numbers written on his body right now, as the many layers of his elegant clothing indicate. The bottoms of his feet, the back of his knees, inside his elbows—even his neck probably has a few, carefully concealed behind the crisp white ascot he wears. He'll have chosen numbers that end in a nine or a seven, as those are the most commonly picked random digits. Sixty-nine, seventy-seven, thirty-seven . . . people are painfully predictable when it comes to this sort of thing. All he has to do is find the most average-looking person in the crowd, ask them to pick a number, and voilà. He can roll up the matching sleeve or take off the designated shoe and pretend that he knew their choice hours in advance.

"Fifty," I state baldly. My time with Armand wasn't wasted. Very few people pick fifty. Statistically speaking, it's the number he's least likely to have written on his person.

"Aha!" A self-satisfied smile curves his lips. "I knew you'd choose that one. Where's the man I gave that slip of paper to when I first came in the bar? Could you tell me what it says?"

The man in question gets up from his stool and digs in his back pocket until he pulls out a slip of lined yellow paper. "Well, I'll be," he says as he unfolds it and brings it close to his face. "It says fifty."

Of course it does. I'm not as shocked by this as the rest of the pub's patrons seem to be. It just means Armand has been expecting me and, knowing that I know what he knows, guessed I'd pick the most difficult number. The man with the piece of paper has the bloodshot eyes and hunched posture of someone who spends most of his time on that bar stool. All Armand had to do was keep buying him drinks and rest assured that I'd show up eventually.

"How exciting," I say, my voice devoid of inflection. "You read my mind."

"I can read a lot more than that, if you'll give me a chance," he replies.

I don't intend to give him any such thing. Since I came here with the express purpose of finding him, however, I slide into the darkest booth in the darkest corner and wait.

Although I try to tune Armand out, I can hear him finishing his performance in the background. From experience, I know this will take quite some time, so I pull out my phone and start playing a colorful game of lining up baked goods. I'm in the middle of demolishing a row of snickerdoodles when he finally joins me.

"I hope I didn't alarm you with my ability to see deep into the recesses of your mind," he says, as though speaking to a stranger. "Can I buy you a drink to make up for it?"

I keep up the pretense by agreeing, but as soon as no one is paying attention to us, I kick him under the table and hiss, "Cut the crap, Armand. Where are the goods?"

He knows the kick is coming, drat the man, and neatly dodges. Mentalists really are the worst of all the magicians, tricksters, and charlatans out there. They take the fun out of everything.

"I've been at this pub for three hours," he says by way of answer. He lifts a hand and signals to the bartender, who must have been prepped ahead of time because he has two pints of something golden and liquid ready to go. "I didn't think it would take you so long to find me. What held you up?"

Meeting at the local watering hole is something of a tradition of ours. Back when we worked together, it was sometimes necessary for us to pretend not to know one another. Reluctant families that refused to be swayed by one psychic could often be moved by two pretending to work independently of one another. When that happened, we'd meet in the most remote bar in the immediate vicinity to compare notes.

These memories don't make me feel any warmer toward Armand. Although I don't regret most of the choices I've made in my life and in my career, I do regret falling so far under his spell. When I worked with him, I agreed to cases that I might otherwise have passed over, took advantage of people beyond what they could afford. The loneliness of my life back then could be blamed for part of why I let him in, but it doesn't explain everything.

In truth, I liked how invincible Armand made me feel, how superior we were to everyone else. Pride has always been my besetting sin, and this man knows it. He can sniff out a person's weakness in the same amount of time that Beast and Freddie can find a recently opened can of tuna.

"You know why it took me so long," I say, refusing to let myself get pulled in. It's easier now that I have people in my life who accept me as I am, but the temptation is still there. "What did you do with that man's watch and tie pin?"

His look of surprise seems genuine, but I know better than to trust it. "What man are we talking about? If it's that guy I hypnotized on the elevator, I used my own watch. I always do."

As if to prove it, he tugs on a long gold chain that dangles from his waistcoat. He allows it to swing like a pendulum in front of my gaze, but I swiftly shut my eyes. I don't *think* I'm susceptible to that sort of thing, but I'm not taking any chances.

He laughs. "Relax. I'm not going to do anything to you." He pauses and adds, "Not yet, anyway. How's Vivian doing this afternoon?"

I pop one eye open. "You stay away from her. She's not the feeble old woman you think she is. She'll chew you up, spit you out, and dance on the remains."

This only causes him to laugh harder. "You always did love a challenge, didn't you?" He leans earnestly over the table. Neither of us has touched our beers, but that makes sense. Intoxication doesn't suit our particular game very well. "How much does she know about you?"

"Enough to render your plan useless, so don't even think about it. Nothing you say to her will hurt me." I pause. "What happened to you, Armand? Blackmail? Robbing hotel safes? Since when are you so desperate that you'll resort to such out-and-out villainy? I thought we had a code."

It takes a moment for my words to sink in, but I can tell the exact moment they do. It's evident from the way a grin splits Armand's face. "Isn't this rich?" he says, leaning back in his seat and eyeing me with interest. "This is a clear case of the pot calling the kettle a villain."

"I beg your pardon?"

"If you don't want me messing up your scheme, then I want in on it. I can help." He hesitates and adds, "Well, not with the safe-robbing part. I don't know what that's about, but I'm disappointed in you. Burglary is so pedestrian."

"I'm not the one robbing safes. *You* are."

"Afraid not, little bird. Not my style."

I can almost believe him. There's a lack of finesse to that kind of crime, a sort of smash-and-grab quality that's beneath a man of Armand's experience.

"How much do you plan to take the boyfriend for?" he continues. "You're a fool if you get less than a million."

I bolt upright. "What? A million? *Dollars?*"

"You're right. Nicholas Hartford the Third is a plump pigeon for the plucking." He tucks the pocket watch away and rubs his hands greedily together. His palms are so dry, it almost sounds like the crackling of . . . what else? Flames. "If we play this correctly, we could get double that. How in love with you is he?"

"That's none of your business."

"Of course it's my business. Why do you think I came all this way?" His smile takes a decided turn toward a smirk. "Come on, Eleanor. Out with it. Are we dealing with Taj Mahal levels of devotion, or is it more of a Grace Kelly/Prince of Monaco sort of situation?"

"I don't know what you're talking about," I say, but it's a lie. I only *wish* I didn't know what he was talking about. It seems I wasn't entirely correct when I suspected this man of coming all this way to blackmail me. Blackmail isn't on his mind at all. If he's imagining the palaces and kingdoms that Nicholas might be willing to lay at my feet in the name of love, what he's after falls more along the lines of extortion. "It isn't like that. We met on the job. We liked each other. We started dating. There's nothing devious about it."

"Of course not," he agrees.

"I mean it, Armand. I'm not the woman you used to know. I don't play the game anymore."

He knows exactly what *game* I'm referring to, and he doesn't believe me for a second. With a gaze that's both insulting and appraising, his takes in every inch of my apparel—the corset-style belt and the flowy paisley dress it covers, the hair and makeup that haven't changed, the jangling moonstone bracelets up my arm.

"So I didn't update my wardrobe. Big deal." I sound much more defensive than I'd like, but I can't help it. I *feel* defensive. This is precisely why I refuse to let Nicholas pay for anything above and beyond the ordinary, why I'm willing to accept Vivian's generosity only as long as it's accompanied by her eccentric demands.

Past Eleanor would have seen Nicholas Hartford III and his family as a blank check for the cashing. In fact, Past Eleanor *had* seen him that way. I made an inordinate amount of money when I cleansed his house of the not-ghost that had been plaguing them. The moment we started dating, however, I put my foot down and my scruples up. I'm not that woman anymore. I make potions and cast spells and investigate paranormal crimes, but I don't take advantage of people.

As if on cue, my phone rings. I attempt a discreet glance at the screen, but Armand leans over and reads it alongside me. Old Nick. It's the name I used for Nicholas back when we first met, a playful nod to the devil inside him.

"Aren't you going to answer that?" Armand asks with an arch curve to his brow.

I don't want to, but getting hold of Nicholas while he's traveling is always a difficult task. I might not get another chance to hear his voice for a while.

"You could give me some space," I point out.

"I could." He crosses his arms. "But I don't think I will. Two million dollars, Eleanor. Any less than that and you're wasting your talents."

That remark sets the seal on what happens next. It would serve Armand right if I were to pick up the phone and divulge every last detail of his extortion plan while he sits and listens in. It will serve Armand much, *much* worse if I do things my way.

"Dearest, darling Nicholas!" I say in my best Grace Kelly impression. I ooze class and blond flawlessness, a hint of the siren underneath it all. "It's been ages since I heard the sound of your delicious voice."

As I hope, Nicholas picks up on the subtext almost immediately. I don't call him Old Nick for nothing.

"Are you being held hostage right now?" he asks.

"You could say something like that."

"Do I need to call the authorities?"

"Don't be absurd." I release a trill of laughter that's only partially faked. "We're settling in quite nicely, thank you. Your mother complains about everything, my brother is learning to make her drinks exactly the way she likes them, and—oh! I almost forgot—we witnessed a murder last night."

Nicholas pauses. "Are you joking about that last one?"

"It was just terrible, Nicky-poo," I say, forcing myself to sound like a damsel in distress. The damsel part is fine, but the distress bit sticks in my throat. "I almost fainted when it happened. The police think there's nothing to worry about, but if you only knew how scared I was . . ."

"I'll have my assistant cancel the rest of my trip."

"All I wanted was my big, strong man to hold me."

"I'm catching the next flight out."

"No, no. There's no need for you to put yourself out. Just hearing your voice makes me feel better." I pause, aware that with every word I say, Armand is listening for dropped clues. "It would only cause an uproar if Nicholas Hartford the Third were to arrive here out of the blue. You know how people are. I wouldn't get a moment alone with you."

"Only you could find murder and intrigue at the most fashionable resort in all of England," he says with a sigh. "I'll come under an assumed identity. What's the likelihood that we're all going to end up in prison after this?"

I'm too delighted that he figured out my angle to take offense at his question. "You dear man. I don't know what I'd do without you."

"I know exactly what I'd do without you," he returns. "And it doesn't involve flying halfway around the world in the dead of night to not-rescue you. Keep my mother safe until I get there?"

"I always do," I promise, and make a series of kissing noises into the phone. I feel slightly nauseated by the time we hang up, but I've accomplished my goal, and that's the most important thing.

"Not playing the game anymore, eh, Ellie?" Armand asks.

I shrug. "What can I say? Rich men find me irresistible."

Since there's plenty about me that's resistible to men of all incomes, Armand looks doubtful.

"I can be alluring when I put my mind to it," I protest. "But now that I've told you the truth, it's only fair that you do the same. Did you break into that man's safe?"

"Of course not."

"Did you have anything to do with what happened on the boat last night?"

"This is the first I'm hearing about it."

"You came all this way just to try and get what you can out of the Hartfords?"

He makes the motion of a cross over his chest. "On my honor."

I don't believe him on any of those counts. Murder isn't Armand's style any more than burglary is, but the coincidences are too glaring to ignore. Unfortunately, I have no proof that he's anything more than a nuisance. Unless I can find more to go on, there's little I can do to have him arrested. I can warn Vivian and Liam away, and I can drop hints in Gillian Piper's ear, but I have no real authority.

"He sounds like an idiot, by the way," Armand says as I start gathering my things up to leave, my beer untouched.

"What do you mean?"

"Your pretend boyfriend." He nods at the phone. "He really fell for all that? The *darlings* and the *Nicky-poos*? That works?"

Of course it doesn't work—not when the man in question is Nicholas Hartford III. Armand Lamont, however . . .

"Oh, it works," I say with a snap. "Men are rarely as intelligent as they'd like the rest of us to think."

Chapter 7

"Absolutely not. Out of the question. Not a chance."

I clasp my hands together and press them against my chest. "*Please*, Inspector Piper? I won't touch anything, I swear. You can even cuff me before I go in. I just want a quick look around."

I nod my head at the very closed and very inaccessible door to Leonard Mayhew's hotel room. That's the name of our dead man from the boat—Leonard. So far, it's the only information I've been able to glean about him other than the basics. Age: fifty-four. Profession: vacuum cleaner salesman. Likelihood of something strange afoot: high. No one sells vacuum cleaners door-to-door in this day and age. If that isn't proof of foul play, I don't know what is. It's all the hotel staff can talk about.

Gillian Piper doesn't appear to be moved by my promise any more than she was moved by my pleas, my persuasions, and, I'm not ashamed to admit, my tears. Unless I resort to bribery, I'm out of options. The woman is immovable.

Rather, she's *mostly* immovable.

"You could bring me on as a consultant," I say, preparing the ace up my sleeve. "Peter does it all the time. Just ask him. Let me call him up right now, and he'll tell you all about it."

That gets her attention. She pinches the bridge of her nose and exhales, long and slow and deep. "Is that a threat, Madame Eleanor?"

I mean, it's not not *one. . . .*

"Of course not," I lie. "Five minutes is all I ask. If I don't find something your team missed, then you can have me kicked out of the hotel for good. Word of a witch."

Apparently, a witch's word carries as much weight with this Inspector Piper as it does the other one. She rolls her eyes toward Bertram, the deflated-looking officer from before. His shoulders are rounded in a way that signals defeat, and he's unable to make eye contact with either me or Inspector Piper, but he clears his throat and finds the nerve to speak.

"I believe it's allowed with discretionary permission." He takes a step backward until he's literally pressed up against the wall. "What I mean is, it's not out of the realm of possibility. In investigations such as these, psychics are sometimes brought in to provide ancillary—"

"Thank you. I'm well aware of the rules regarding criminal consultations."

The chill in Gillian's voice—and in her eyes—is enough to transform the entire floor into an ice castle, but Bertram appears to be made of sterner stuff than his hunched form would indicate.

"I could get the paperwork started for you," he offers. "You wouldn't have to do anything but sign it. What could it hurt?"

From the way Gillian grimaces, I'm guessing it hurts quite a bit. "I cannot believe I'm doing this," she mutters. "Five minutes, Madame Eleanor. Not a second more, understood?"

I can't help but share an involuntary and delighted look with Bertram, who allows a light smile to touch his lips. Despite his receding hairline and terrible posture, that smile makes him appear almost young. With a start, I realize he's probably much closer to my age than Gillian's. Working next to that woman every day must be hard on a person.

"You won't touch anything," Gillian commands in a tone that brooks no argument. Since she's pulling out the key card to Leonard's room while she does it, I keep my mouth shut. "You won't call upon the powers of the universe to guide you. You won't invoke or chant or do anything else to annoy me. You will simply—and quietly—look."

I nod, too busy crossing the threshold into Leonard's room to take offense at the implied insult. When I'd sought Inspector Piper after my interview with Armand, it was to ask about the man and the missing jewels from the safe, not last night's death. Imagine my surprise—and delight—to find her skulking around outside this room. According to what Gillian says, they were merely finishing up so they could rule his death as a suicide and move on, but I know better.

She believes me about the two men in the boat. She believes me about the two men in the boat, and she *hates* it.

In a show of good faith, I put my hands behind my back before I step into the room. We're on the fourth floor, so the square footage and views aren't as nice as my fancy new upgrade, but it's a decent enough space. The architecture is all intricate scrollwork and pastel floral wallpaper, but the furnishings and details are modern. It's also surprisingly chilly when compared to the relative comfort of the hallway. The kick of an air conditioner in the background hints at the reason.

It also hints at a timeline.

"Has anyone touched the thermostat in here?" I ask.

A click of what might be approval sounds from the back of Gillian's throat. "No. I've asked that everyone leave the room intact. This is precisely how Leonard left it."

"Then he must have left before the storm rolled in." I risk a peek over my shoulder. "That wasn't the universe speaking to me, by the way. Just an observation."

Her lips form a flat line, but there's approval in the tilt of her head.

There's little enough else to illuminate the case. The bed is made and the toiletries are lined up, but there are tissues in the wastebasket, so there's a good chance Leonard was in the room after it had been made up by the cleaning staff.

"Before the storm but after maid service," I muse aloud. I'd normally keep my thoughts to myself, but I'm showing off a little. I want Gillian to recognize that I'm not the dunce she believes me to be. "Did you find anything interesting in his luggage?"

Gillian shakes her head. "Nothing noteworthy. Bertram can get you an inventory list, but there wasn't much except for his clothes, a few toiletries, and a vacuum cleaner repair guide."

"Some light reading before bed?" I venture.

Gillian doesn't so much as crack a smile. "That's not for me to say. Well, Madame Eleanor? Your five minutes are just about up."

I'm being tested, I know—and I'm fairly sure I'm being found wanting. "Anything in the safe?" I ask.

"It hasn't been touched."

"Anyone on the floor hear anything odd?"

"Not a peep."

"And where was the note found?"

She gestures toward the spot with a tilt of her head. There's a small, round table by the window, where a pad of hotel-monogrammed paper and a pen lie where they were dropped. The indentation of words on the pad are so deep that I can read them from where I stand.

"*Tell my mother I'm sorry.* That's it?"

Bertram gives a squeak of surprise, but Gillian's eyes have been following mine since I entered the room. She knows exactly how I figured this one out. "That's it," she confirms.

"Not much of a suicide note," I say. "He could have been sorry for anything. Maybe he forgot to pay her cable bill this month. Maybe he accidentally ran over her cat."

"Given that there were no signs of trauma on the body—antemortem or otherwise—it's enough. Especially since we have an eyewitness account of him jumping from that boat."

Ah, yes. The doorman—the one who saw nothing out of the ordinary, who summoned help long before Liam or I could make the attempt. I didn't catch his name, but I'm definitely going to seek him out. Now that I'm not dripping with seawater and jittering with adrenaline, he and I need to have a conversation about last night's events.

"Where did the boat come from, by the way? Was it a rental?" I don't wait for her to answer before defending myself. I can already tell that she's not likely to enjoy my line of questioning. "I'm just curious why he would have taken it out under those kinds of conditions. It was hardly ideal weather for a sunset cruise."

Her answer is disappointingly straightforward. "From all that we can make out, he stole it from a marina down the beach. As to why he took it, I think suicide would have been sufficient justification, don't you?"

Yes, unfortunately, I do. In fact, if anyone were to present the facts of this case to me as a hypothetical situation, I'd reach the same conclusion as Gillian: a man, traveling alone and out at sea on a terrible night, who left a suicide note and was witnessed by a doorman, almost definitely took his own life. As for the pair of crackpots who claim to have seen him pushed overboard by two disappearing figures . . . well, they were either mistaken or in search of the drama and fame that inevitably follows such an accusation.

But I *know* what I witnessed. I *know* Liam and I didn't make it up.

"Murder would be a pretty good reason, too," I point out. I turn toward Gillian, prepared to defend my theory to my last breath, but my world goes suddenly black. Instead of feeling fear, a thrum of anticipation floods through me. I've experienced this enough times to know what comes next.

It's Winnie. Or Birdie. Or some deeper, darker force that is yet unnamed. Whoever is responsible, it takes only a second before the vision kicks in.

I'm in this room, but it's early in the morning. I can tell from the bright lights streaming through the curtains, which flutter in the breeze of the open window. It's warm, no sign of a dark storm in sight, and I feel happy—optimistic. This is a good morning. The scent of eggs and a carafe of coffee at the foot of the bed could be the reason for my positive mood, but I think it's more than that. A knock sounds at the door, and I turn, straining to see who it is. Unfortunately, my vision clicks out before I have a chance—but not before I catch sight of several pastel blue cases lined up against the far wall.

"Where are the vacuum cleaners?" I ask as soon as I'm back inside myself. I jab a finger at the wall where they'd been located in my vision. "There should be three of them. Test samples, probably. The kind a salesman would carry to someone's house and show off."

No one answers me. For a moment, I think I must be alone—that Gillian and Bertram ran out the moment I entered my vision—but they're still here. And by *here*, I mean they're staring at me as though I've recently sprouted a second head.

Bertram is the first to speak. "What just happened?" he asks, his eyes and mouth agog. He looks like a fish pulled straight from the sea. "Did you have a psychic vision?"

I did, actually, but I can tell from the taut lines around Gillian's mouth that to confess as much will result in my immediate and irrevocable expulsion from this room. My visions don't happen very often, and when they do, they're not always trustworthy. They only show one small part of a larger picture—and in a way that ends up misleading me more than it helps.

But there were three cases against that wall at one point. I'm sure of it. And if my love of all things vintage taught me one thing, it's what vacuum cleaner cases from the sixties look like.

I draw close to that section of the wall and crouch. Without breaking the sanctified not-touching rule, I point at the indentations in the carpet. They're faint but unmistakable, easy to overlook but impossible to ignore now that I've noticed them.

"Well, I'll be," Gillian says as she falls into a crouch next to me. She whips a pair of latex gloves out of her back pocket and snaps one of them over her left hand. After poking at the edges of one line, she waves Bertram over. "Photograph these, Bertram, and from several different angles. I don't want anyone else coming in here until you've got these catalogued, understood? And I want a test of the carpet fibers under each of these, cross-referenced with the fibers from the carpet by the far wall over there."

"Yes, ma'am."

"And you." At this, she turns toward me. There's a quelling look in her eye, but I'm too excited to pay heed to it. This is it. This is the moment I've been waiting for. Finally—finally—I've found myself a police inspector with what appears to be unlimited resources at her disposal. Peter Piper refuses to give me anything fun like carpet fiber testing or body-sniffing dogs on account of his "budgetary restraints." His ex-wife must be much higher up on the food chain than he is. "How do you know these impressions were made by vacuum cleaner cases?"

Since I'm not about to upset a woman who embodies all my law enforcement hopes and dreams, I don't tell her the truth. Instead, I take the second latex glove from her grasp and slip it over my hand. She balks but doesn't stop me.

"See this here?" I ask, indicating twelve distinct impressions that are slightly wider and deeper than the rest. "Those are where the wheels were sitting. Two on each side."

"So? Plenty of regular suitcases have wheels."

Once again, her perspicacity delights me. "Yes, but look how much deeper these ones in the back are. Regular suitcases would have an even distribution of weight. Vacuum cleaners—

especially the old-school ones that a salesman might drag door to door—would be bottom heavy."

Gillian stares at me for a long, drawn-out moment before whipping the glove off her hand and turning to Bertram. He has a camera out and is furiously taking photographs of my discovery. "Find the porter who brought up Leonard's bags when he checked in," she says, her tone curt. "I want to know what luggage he had with him at the time—if either of them remember seeing what might be vacuum cleaner cases."

I nod along, happy to find my vision being taken so seriously.

"We should also contact his employer," Gillian continues. "If he's here for work, as our records seem to indicate, there's a chance he sold the vacuums and that's why they're not here. We could be looking at nothing more than a successful business trip."

It's on the tip of my tongue to point out that he could hardly have sold the test samples, but I don't. For one, I don't know nearly enough about the world of cleaning supply sales to state that as a fact. For another, Gillian grips me by the upper arm and yanks me to a standing position.

"And you," she says, her eyes examining me with a minuteness that makes goose bumps break out on the surface of my skin. "You're coming with me."

"To receive a medal of honor?" I guess.

Her breath chuffs out in a blast of indignation. "You know more about this case than you're letting on, Ms. Wilde. I want to know how. And why."

I can already tell that I'm not going to enjoy this next part. Mostly because although the *how* is easy—visions from beyond the grave—the *why* is much more difficult to pinpoint.

Murder and death just have a way of following me around. Whether I'm the cause or the effect, however, her guess is as good as mine.

*   *   *

In what might be the cruelest stroke of fate yet, Vivian happens upon my interview with Inspector Gillian Piper.

I call it an interview, but it's more of an interrogation. There's no light pointed at my head, and I'm not handcuffed to the conference room table, but there's no denying that the heat is on. There aren't even any pastries to take the edge off this time. Only tea.

"I'll ask you one more time, and you'd better start telling me the truth." Gillian lifts the silver teapot as though she's about to pour the scalding brew into my lap. At the last minute, she shifts the spout to hit a porcelain teacup instead. "What do you know about Leonard Mayhew that you're not telling me?"

"Nothing, I swear. I only know what's being discussed around the hotel. Anyone paying attention could tell you the same thing."

"Who have you been talking to?"

I haven't been talking so much as eavesdropping, but it hardly seems like a good time to point that out. Fortunately— or unfortunately, as the case may be—I catch sight of Vivian sliding in through the open doorway at that exact moment.

"Can we do this a little later?" I ask. "This is technically my holiday, and—"

"Eleanor!" Vivian calls. She's still wearing her shirtwaist outfit, but one of the sleeves is rolled up to the elbow. Vivid lines of red stand out on the veiny white of her forearm. "Eleanor, you've got to do something about those cats of yours. They've gone feral."

Gillian turns to stare at me, so I busy myself with the tea. "Cats?" I echo. "I can't imagine what you're talking about. Why would I have cats in a swanky beachside hotel?"

Vivian thrusts her forearm under my nose. When I don't react, she shoves it under Gillian's nose instead. "Do you see this?" she demands. "Do you see what they've done?"

"Ma'am, I'm sorry about your injuries, but I'm afraid you're interrupting—"

"Don't be absurd." Vivian interrupts further by scraping out a chair and lowering herself into it. She jabs a finger at me. "Your little friend managed to wrangle them into the bathroom, but I don't know how long that will last. I left him watching guard. They didn't seem to care for him much."

"My little friend?" I ask, my heart sinking. Does the woman listen to nothing I say? "Vivian, please tell me you didn't leave Armand alone in your hotel room."

She smiles in a way that confirms my worst fears. "He volunteered, dear. Such an obliging young man." She turns to Gillian. "Eleanor seems to think he's going to try and rob me, but that's absurd. Have you met Armand yet?"

I gulp my entire cup of tea at once. It's much too hot, and I can feel it burn all the way down my throat, but the loss of my esophageal lining is the least of my worries right now. I don't trust Armand, it's true, and I'm fairly certain he's more connected to recent events than he'd like me to believe, but I'm not ready to hand him over to the authorities just yet. There's no way to highlight his iniquities without shining a spotlight on my own.

"Of course she hasn't met him," I croak. "Inspector Piper is investigating the murder from last night, but you were having dinner with Armand when it happened. He can't be a suspect. Besides, I never said he was going to *rob* you. Just that you should be careful who you befriend in a place like this."

My attempt at deflection fails. Vivian and Gillian sense kindred spirits in one another almost at once. Vivian turns to her junior and murmurs, "Inspector Piper?" just as Gillian echoes, "Armand?"

There's nothing for it but to create a distraction. With a sigh, I fall back on the only thing I can think of that will put the attention back where it belongs.

"If you must know, Bertram was correct." I speak as though the words have been physically wrested from me. "I had a psychic vision. That's where I'm getting all my information, and that's how I knew there were three vacuum cleaner cases in that room. I saw them lined up against the wall. They're pastel blue and about yea high. I don't know why they're important or what they mean, but I wouldn't have seen them if they didn't matter. Find those cases, and you'll find what happened to Leonard Mayhew."

For the longest moment, I think Gillian might actually believe me. My emotions are real and therefore convincing, and that's something she can detect at a glance.

Until, that is, Bertram comes rolling into the room. He's pushing a gilded luggage cart containing—what else?—three pastel blue vacuum cleaner cases that are exactly *yea high*.

"Nice try, Ms. Wilde," Gillian says as she glances over her shoulder. "How long has he been standing there? You almost had me fooled."

As Bertram's arrival takes some of the heat off me, I don't bother correcting her. She rises to her feet to help him into the room. "Where did you find them?" she asks. "I didn't expect it to be this easy."

"Housekeeping." There's a wariness in Bertram's voice and in the way he stands, as though protecting his internal organs from an incoming blow. I wince in silent sympathy.

"Housekeeping?" Gillian echoes. She whips out her ubiquitous latex gloves and slips one on. Oddly enough, she puts it on the right hand this time. "What made you look in housekeeping?"

"That was where Laurel—the front desk clerk—told me to go."

Gillian's glance is sharp. "She saw someone put them there?"

"Something like that."

Gillian points that sharp glance at me. "Care to tell me what I'm going to find inside here?"

I shrug. Even if I *did* know what Leonard was hiding, I'm

not sure I'd choose this moment as my big reveal. Vivian must share some of my sentiment because she releases a sniff of disdain. "What on earth do you want with all these vacuum cleaners?" she asks. "If I'd have known you were keen on them, I'd have asked the maid to leave hers behind."

Gillian's hand is poised to open the clasp on the top of the case, but at Vivian's words, she pauses. "What do you mean? I don't want the maid's vacuum cleaner. I want these three."

"If you say so," Vivian agrees. "But they all look the same to me. Antiquated and far too heavy. The poor girl in my room could barely lift hers."

"Bertram?" Gillian's voice is careful—*too* careful. "What is she talking about?"

Bertram nervously clears his throat. "It seems that this particular line of vacuums is what the hotel has been using for decades." He rolls an apologetic eye over the gilded cart. "They said there are probably fifty of them in housekeeping, but they only let me take these ones. The rest are in use."

For entirely unfair and unwarranted reasons, Gillian Piper places the blame for this on my head. "What game are you playing, Madame Eleanor? Is this supposed to be funny?"

It's not *supposed* to be funny, but I can't help being amused. "Oops. I had no idea they belonged to the hotel—honestly, I didn't. I just assumed they were Leonard's."

"I can't believe this," she mutters.

I can. This is the exact sort of trick that the spirits like to play on me. "Maybe he's the one who sold them to the hotel in the first place," I suggest. "Or he was coming to offer them the latest in pastel blue vacuum technology. You should probably check with whoever buys supplies for the hotel."

Although this is a sound piece of advice, Gillian ignores it, opting instead to reach for the nearest vacuum cleaner case and flick it open. Sure enough, it contains . . . a vacuum cleaner. The thing is oversized and industrial, as one might expect when it's being used to clean hundreds of rooms every day. Gillian pokes at the buttons and opens the top to peer inside the mechanics, but it all looks very technical and straightforward.

"You're Inspector Piper's wife," Vivian says suddenly.

Nothing could have been more calculated to push a woman already teetering on the sharp edge of annoyance. Gillian stops in the middle of slicing open the vacuum cleaner bag. "I *am* Inspector Piper," she counters, and in a voice that dares Vivian to continue.

She does.

"It's small wonder why it didn't work out between the two of you." Vivian releases a light tsk. She begins rolling down the sleeve of her shirt. "It must have been terribly confusing whenever someone called the house."

"Is there a reason you're both still here? Bertram—please escort our guests out. I think we can continue this part of the investigation without their services."

"Or at parties," Vivian continues, blithely ignoring her. "'Delighted to meet you, Inspector Piper.' 'Leave your coat right here, Inspector Piper.' 'Inspector Piper, what can I get you to drink?' It's enough to make anyone's head spin."

"A man is *dead*, Mrs. Hartford."

"Not to mention what it must have been like in the bedroom—"

I don't wait for Gillian to react to that one. Without managing to suppress my choke of laughter, I grab Vivian by the elbow and direct her toward the nearest exit. It doesn't look as though Inspector Piper means to give chase, but I don't doubt her ability to catch us should the urge take over.

"That was a close one," Vivian says as soon as we leave the conference room and move through the maze of hallways to the lobby. "She looked as though she had all manner of unpleasant questions to ask you."

"Vivian, did you say all that on purpose?" I demand. "To get us away?"

"Well, someone had to. She was going to use that vacuum cleaner hose to tie you to the chair." She gives a thoughtful pause, her finger just touching the dimple in her chin. Nicholas has a similar one. "That was why they separated, you know."

"Because she tied Peter to chairs using household items?" It's not a difficult thing to imagine.

Vivian chuckles. "No, dear. Because Gillian always was the better investigator. I only knew her by reputation, but, oh, what a reputation it was. They call her in for the big cases— she's the one who caught that serial killer in Kent a few years back. You'd best be careful, or you're going to find yourself in difficulties."

I think of the dead man, the stolen items from the safe, Armand's pub tricks, and the fact that there are fifty identical vacuum cleaner cases inside this hotel and laugh.

"Sorry to disappoint you, Vivian, but I think it's safe to say I'm already in them."

Chapter 8

I find the doorman exactly where I expect him. At the door.

He looks the same as he did when he handed me a towel last night, tuxedoed and straitlaced and with the kind of face that makes it impossible to know what he's thinking. He's implacable and impassive to the highest degree, and would have been perfect as the butler of some grand estate where everyone cheats on their spouses and asks for highly questionable favors in the night.

"So, about that murder we witnessed last night," I say as I walk up.

He pauses at my less-than-subtle approach but doesn't blink. "You mean that suicide we witnessed last night?"

"Po-tay-to, Po-tah-to." I give an airy wave of my hand. "I assume our good Inspector Piper has already grilled you about the details?"

His answer is to doff his hat. At first, I think he's replying with a formal assent—and that our entire conversation will include curtseys and elegantly scraped bows—but he pulls open the door and nods to an elderly couple shuffling through.

"Good evening, Mr. and Mrs. Janis," he says, his voice low and unobtrusive. "That wind is something, isn't it? Let me take your bags so you can warm up by the fire. I'll have one of the bellboys take these up to your room."

Their response is a smile and a discreetly slipped bill into one of his gloved hands. The red glint of Queen Elizabeth's face indicates that it's a fifty-pound note—no small perk for what looks to be two shopping bags and a pink box of pastries.

"This must be a pretty sweet gig," I say as the Janis party moves toward the fire. Mrs. Janis, I note, is wearing an impressive set of emerald earrings that would give Vivian a run for her money. "Does everyone tip you that much?"

The doorman casts a very obvious look over me. "No, not everyone."

I don't take offense at this. If he gets a note from every well-dressed couple who walks through these doors, then he takes home a heck of a lot more money than I do. He can afford to let my lack of generosity slide.

"I didn't catch your name, by the way," I say. "I'm Eleanor. Eleanor Wilde."

"I know who you are. Room 113, recently upgraded to suite 28A. Your brother ordered room service for lunch. Steak, medium rare. A plate of chips. He asked for a salad, too, but he sent it back untouched. You have three bags between the two of you and a mysterious basket containing lobsters." He turns a glinting eye on me. "Do you really eat them raw?"

Well, well. It seems we have a budding investigator on our hands. Gillian must love this guy.

"Actually, I set them free in the ocean," I say. "I felt it was time they went to their forever home."

He accepts this lie without so much as a twitch of his well-groomed eyebrows. "How nice. You must be an animal lover."

I am, although my feelings on shellfish aren't up there with my feelings on, say, my cats. However, this isn't the conversation I was hoping to have with this man, and there's yet another couple straggling down the sidewalk through the blasts of wind. That's fifty more pounds this man plans on pocketing and five more minutes of my time he plans on wasting.

I take a more direct approach. "You know all of my secrets, but I know none of yours, James."

As I hope, this catches him off guard. "My name isn't James. It's Uli."

"And have you had your interview with Inspector Piper yet, Uli?" I ask. "My brother and I had ours this morning. That's why he needed the steak and chips. It was brutal."

"Yes, I've spoken with her. Just one moment, please."

He uses his moment to open the door for the next couple. They're much younger than the last pair and don't seem to care about the weather conditions. From the moony-eyed way they look at each other and the laughing way they try to get their umbrellas un-inside-out, I'm guessing their relationship is of recent origin. Uli's next words confirm it.

"Mr. and Mrs. Lund. You made it back. The honeymoon suite is ready for you now. I'll call Neville to take you up."

He does this with what appears to be a genuine smile for the newlyweds. In another lifetime, I imagine I might also enjoy this sort of job. Uli is in the thick of activity, his nose in everyone's business, his eyes on watch for anything out of the ordinary.

Including, it seems, a sleek black cat sauntering up the sidewalk as though she hasn't a care in the world.

It takes all my training as a faux psychic-turned-witch not to jump at the sight of Beast enjoying the sights and sounds of Brighton like a seasoned traveler. It's been a few hours since I popped up to Vivian's room to check on the cats, but the last I saw, they'd taken up residence in the huge, queenly bathroom, each claiming one of the plush white bath mats as their own private domain.

I turn my head and my attention to Uli as he sends the happy couple on their way. "So," I say, struggling to keep my voice level. "Want to compare stories? Inspector Piper mentioned a suicide note, but my brother and I are sure we saw two other people on that boat."

Uli frowns. It's brief and it's controlled, but it's still a frown. "And I'm sure I didn't. Does the inspector know you're talking to me about this?"

Beast is drawing closer, her body swaying like a lady of the night. Wherever she's going and wherever she's been, it hasn't forced her into unseemly haste. My cat *never* undertakes unseemly haste. She's far too regal for that.

"I'm helping the inspector with her investigation," I lie. "I have experience with this sort of thing, and the two of us have a personal history. Did you see Leonard take the boat out?"

"No. I already covered all this with the inspector."

I'm sure he did, and I'm equally sure that Gillian has no intention of sharing the information with me. I've also started to realize that there's something in Beast's mouth. Like all micropredators wandering around England, she has a love of mice, birds, and other helpless creatures who wander into her path. I can only hope that she plans on passing us by. This is *not* the time for her to present me with one of her "gifts."

"Did you see him leave the hotel?" I persist.

"No, I didn't. I saw him in the lobby a few times, and once in the elevator, but I don't recall noticing him yesterday. If you ask the other staff, they'll say the same thing. He was quiet and kept to himself. No one saw him before his . . . accident."

A thought occurs to me. "Did he tip well?"

Uli blinks. "I beg your pardon?"

"Leonard Mayhew. Did he tip well? Grease palms? Sweeten the pot?"

By this time, Uli has noticed the black cat approaching the gilded hotel doors. He blinks but doesn't show any sign of surprise, which means he's either the most amazing doorman ever to stand his post, or this isn't the first time she's done this. He drags his gaze from the cat to meet my eyes. "Yes, actually. He was very generous. That's why one of us would have noticed him had he been around yesterday."

I nod, satisfied that Uli is telling the truth—on this score, at least. I open my mouth to ask about Leonard's luggage, but there isn't a chance. It seems that Beast has no intention of making her way discreetly to a side entrance. She stops a foot away and plants herself on the ground.

It had been my intention to disclaim any and all knowledge of Beast's existence, but she chooses that moment to drop the item in her mouth. As soon as I catch a glimpse of that cracked porcelain face, I'm done for.

"What in Tartarus?" I jump forward, my hand dashing out to grab Brunhilde before Uli can beat me to it. The doll looks none the worse for her trip down the garbage chute, her clothes and hair as filthy as before, her eyes just as vacantly staring.

"I wouldn't touch that if I were you," Uli says, joining me in front of my cat. "It could have rabies."

"This cat doesn't have rabies. She's probably someone's pet." And a master escape artist, but that part goes without saying. Beast has always been exceptional at worming her way through tight spaces.

"Then why is there blood on its collar?"

Uli's question takes me by surprise, but not nearly as much as the fact that he's correct. Although Beast won't let me draw close enough to pick her up—she's a smart one, that cat, and knows better than to acknowledge me in public—she does brush up against my leg in a brief show of affection. Blood, fresh enough to leave a mark, transfers itself from her collar to the hem of my dress.

"Oh, no!" I cry. "Is she hurt?"

She isn't. At least, not that I can tell in the brief second before she dashes down the sidewalk. I want to chase after her to make sure she knows how to find her way home again, but if there's one thing I've learned in our time together, it's that Beast can take care of herself.

"I can throw that thing away for you," Uli offers with a nod toward Brunhilde. I thank him but don't take him up on the offer. Something very strange is going on around here, and I don't just mean a dead vacuum cleaner salesman and the two mysterious men who threw him in the water. There's no way this doll should still exist in this condition. Even if Beast *had* made her way into the garbage chute and back out again, the doll should be broken, cracked, or, at the very least, covered in mustard stains.

"I'll hold on to her for now," I say, and return to the subject of Leonard's vacuum cleaners. "When Mr. Mayhew arrived, what kind of luggage did he bring in? Did you see three light blue cases?"

"I wasn't here when he checked in, unfortunately."

I frown, wishing my vision had been a little bit more clear about those cases—and why they might be so important. As far as I can tell, Uli has no reason to lie about this, but there's no saying what people will do when backed into a tight corner.

Almost as an afterthought, I ask one last question—probably the most important question of all. "There's a man here," I say. "He's very . . . hypnotic. Wears a purple velvet jacket and too much eyeliner. Do you know him?"

"Of course." He gives a slight bow in acknowledgment. "Armand Lamont. Room 619. Checked in two days before you did."

Two days, huh? That was presumptuous of him. Even if he had somehow learned about the reservation Nicholas made for his mother, there was always a chance I'd have decided to stay home instead of coming along. Or stayed at a smaller and more affordable hotel farther away from the beach.

"Isn't it against the doorman law to give people's room numbers out?" I ask.

"Yes." Uli winks. "But he told me you'd ask and gave me permission ahead of time."

Of course he did—and of course I played right into his hands. I really need to stop acting like a predictable fool. I'm only helping Armand look good.

"If you happen to see him milling around, keep an eye out for anything that strikes you as off, would you? See who he approaches? Talks to?"

I wish I had a surplus of fifty-pound notes to bribe Uli with, but I have to make do with a winning smile. I'm not sure it's successful, but at least I make an attempt. Besides, if it doesn't work, I can always resort to dire warnings. With evil dolls popping up out of the blue and death around every corner, those will be easy enough to believe.

Chapter 9

"Kill it. Crush it. Burn it with fire."

I dive after my brother, barely managing to grab hold of his shirt before he makes it to Brunhilde. She's resting in the center of the mantelpiece in our new hotel suite. The fact that we're steeped in luxury, awash in regal draperies and overstuffed furniture, doesn't appear to have alleviated any of Liam's anxieties.

"Ellie, I love you—I really do—but if you don't do something to get rid of that thing, I'm getting on the first plane home and never coming back."

Instead of attending to the doll, I hand him Beast's collar, careful to highlight the section with a crusted blob of blood on it. "What do you make of this?" I ask.

He immediately throws it across the room. Against all odds, it swings like a horseshoe around the post of the nearest bed. Even this, apparently, is to be laid at my door. Liam turns to me with an accusing glare. "This is like that time you convinced me that my homework was being eaten by the neighbor's dog, isn't it? *You* were the one who kept chewing up the edges and leaving it in weird places, but you had me convinced that Nelson was some kind of evil sorcerer."

I laugh. Ah, the early days of my delinquency. Poor Liam was my trial-run victim for years.

"It's not Beast's blood." I know this for a fact because I gave my cats a thorough going-over when I retrieved them from Vivian's room, both of them curled sleepily on their respective bathroom mats. I have no idea how Beast got in and out of that room so quickly, but I'm less concerned with her journey than I am with her destination. I don't know where she got Brunhilde, and I don't know why she had to wade through blood to get there, but I'm guessing the answers aren't good ones.

"She brought the doll back from whatever hell it escaped and ran into something bleeding along the way. Human? Animal? Your guess is as good as mine."

Liam casts a glance down at Beast, who is calmly licking her paw near the window. "I thought you said that cat is a conduit to Winnie."

"She is."

"So Winnie is the one bringing us that cursed doll?" He doesn't wait for an answer. Instead, he glances up at the ceiling and shakes his fist. "Stop it, Winnie. It's freaking me out and putting a serious damper on my vacation. Go find mice instead. Or a ball of yarn. Live your best cat life."

He doesn't think I'm inside *the cat, right?*

A giggle escapes my throat. "He might. He's never really understood this whole sister-cat connection."

Liam whirls on me. "Is she talking to you right now?"

I nod happily.

He doesn't seem to share my joy, his face blanching white. Stepping backward, he presses his palms against the wall. "What is she saying? What does she want?"

The fear in his eyes causes me a physical pang. My chest squeezes once and holds tight, my heart aching at the thought that anyone—least of all our brother—could fear the things

Winnie says and does. She's my light, my beacon, my hope of something good in this world.

Don't fret, Sister mine, Winnie says. *I know he loves me, in his own way.*

She's right, of course. All my brother has ever wanted is the nice, normal life that was taken from us the same day as Winnie. It's not his fault that a nice, normal life is the one thing neither of us will ever be able to give him.

I pause just in case Winnie has more to add, but she leaves as quickly as she arrived. With a sigh, I return my focus to the task—and the bloodied cat collar—at hand.

"It might be a message." I hook the collar around my finger and lift it from the bedpost. Not for the first time, I wish I had full access to a DNA lab. "The blood and the doll both. Someone might not like me poking around in last night's murder."

Liam shudders but allows the subject change. Apparently, cold-blooded murder is less daunting to him than the otherworldly voice of the woman with whom we once shared a womb. "Maybe that doorman was right. Maybe it was our imagination."

"Liam!"

"What?" He rolls his shoulder in a hunched shrug. "It was dark. It was raining. My intestines were tied up in knots. It's possible that I imagined the whole thing."

"Yes, but *I* didn't." I twirl the collar around my finger. "And don't forget that guy with the safe. He said the same thing as us—that there were two men who disappeared, and he has no memory of what they looked like."

Liam is stubborn enough to hold fast to his resolution. "That could have been a coincidence. A fluke. For all we know, that guy heard us talking about the two disappearing figures and stole his own jewelry, figuring he could blame it on them."

I give a jolt, the collar dropping suddenly. The sound of it jangling against the carpet causes Liam to cry out in surprise.

"What now?! Help! Gah!" He makes a move as if to dive under the nearest bed. "Ellie, you can't do things like that. I don't have the nerve for this lifestyle."

"You're absolutely right," I say, ignoring the bulk of his commentary.

This sentence is so rare coming from my mouth that Liam loses his fear. Curiosity takes its stead. "I am?"

"It's the perfect crime." In fact, I'm a little irritated at how neatly it fits—and that I wasn't the one to realize it first. Liam is turning out to be annoyingly good at this crime-solving stuff. "I bet every piece in that safe was well-insured. *If* they were even in there in the first place. A guy like that wouldn't put a seven-thousand-dollar watch in his safe. He'd wear that sucker on his wrist until the day he died."

Liam visibly swells. "I solved a robbery?"

"I wouldn't start updating your resume just yet, but, yeah," I admit. "Everything about it fits."

With one mystery well on its way to being solved, I pluck the cat collar from the floor and set it aside. Liam's gaze follows it before darting nervously toward Brunhilde. "That still doesn't explain how or why that doll keeps coming back," he says.

"No, it doesn't."

"Or what we saw out there on the water."

"Agreed."

He swallows heavily. "Maybe we should have stayed in your boring little village, after all."

My heart—and my guilt—give a small twang. I forget sometimes that as much as I enjoy the intrigue and excitement of all things ghostly, it's not a pastime Liam enjoys. "Do you want to go back?" I offer. I mean it, too. As much as I'd hate to leave before this thing is over, I'd do it for my brother.

I've done a lot more than that in the name of sibling affection.

He pulls in a breath and lets it out again. His gaze, when it lands on me, is fond. He knows how important this is to me—how much I'm enjoying myself.

"No, it's fine," he says. "Despite everything that's happened, no one has tried to harm us."

True. As long as he doesn't count Armand's extortion attempts . . .

"Besides," he adds as he summons up a smile, "after everything that's happened, how much worse could things possibly get?"

Chapter 10

❦

I'm almost disappointed to awaken the next morning without any further intrigue. I'm not saying I *want* people to be robbed or killed, but it would have been nice for some new information to push its way to the forefront of my investigation while I slept.

Instead, I yawn and open my eyes to find Liam tucking gleefully into a stack of room-service pancakes the size of his head. People are similarly enjoying themselves when I head down to the lobby—coffee and tea and chitchat are the order of the day. Even the weather seems to be cooperating, with a hazy sun promising a few rays of cheer before the day is through. It's almost as though everything that's gone wrong on this vacation is nothing more than a figment of my imagination, as if death and despair exist only in my head.

Then I catch sight of Armand. He's standing near a potted ficus and holding a well-dressed older woman captive with a crystal pendant that dangles from his fingertips. Since the last thing I want to do is talk to that man—or get sucked into whatever con he's trying to pull right now—I duck out the nearest side entrance.

And immediately jump in alarm.

"Oh, good. Eleanor. There you are." Vivian is standing outside the hotel, a cigarette holder dangling from her fingertips. I've never known her to smoke before, but from the assured way she stubs the gold-tipped apparatus into the nearest wall, I assume this isn't her first time. "I've been waiting for you for hours."

"Here?" I glance around to find that we're in a quiet, discreet alleyway nestled between the hotel and a shop selling what my nose indicates is fish and chips. "Whatever for?"

"A breath of fresh air, naturally."

Between the cigarette smoke and the fish-scented oil, I don't see how anyone could make such a claim. Several butts litter the ground, indicating a popular spot for hotel employees taking their breaks.

"I left Armand inside doing parlor tricks for my friend Marian," she says as she kicks over several burgundy-lipped stubs that form a pile near her feet. "Imagine running into her after all these years—she and I used to go to boarding school together. We used to steal sweets from the kitchen and trade them for cigarettes. I hope you don't mind that I recruited her for our mission."

My heart sinks. Anyone Vivian went to boarding school with—and genuinely liked—is going to be wealthy, influential, and very, very odd. In other words, the exact kind of woman Armand seeks out as his victims.

"I hope you warned her about him," I say. "He outright admitted yesterday that he's here to use me as a way to get money out of you and Nicholas."

She has the audacity to laugh—a sound that quickly turns into a cough thanks to this new smoking habit of hers. I wonder how much of it has to do with running into her old schoolmate. As my own situation attests, a direct encounter with your past can have quite an impact.

"How?" she cackles. "Is he going to kidnap you and hold you for ransom?"

She needn't be *quite* so amused by the prospect. "Blackmail is more likely, but there's no saying what he's capable of. Why? How much would you pay for my safe release?"

Vivian thinks about it for a moment before nodding once. "Ten thousand pounds."

Ten thousand is a far cry from the two million that Armand seems to think he can extract from the Hartfords, but I'm still moved by her generosity. Vivian never spends a penny of her own money if she can help it.

"You're a treasure, and I thank you." I get up on tiptoe to press a kiss on her cheek. "I had no idea you felt that way."

"Yes, well." She's pleased by my show of affection, but she gathers up her bag and her long skirt—another of her grand gowns, this time in midnight blue—in an attempt to cover the sentiment. "You've far too much energy for a woman of your size, and your brother isn't much better, but I'll say this for you. You don't nag."

I take this comment as it's intended, which is not to mention the cigarettes to Nicholas, and smile. I have no idea what she and Marian have planned for Armand, but I'm sure it will keep him on his toes and out of my way.

Which is helpful for a lot of reasons, not least of which because I've got a marina to visit and a murder to investigate. In that order.

"Oh, for the Lord's sake. What are you doing here?"

When I walk through the cheerfully jangling door of the marina, it's to find that no one has plans to rent a boat today. Whether because the choppy waves promise seasickness or—as is more likely—because a man recently died in one of their vessels, Gray Seal Boat Rentals is empty save for one woman.

"Inspector Piper," I say, making a good show of being delighted to see her. This is mostly due to the fact that I *am* delighted to see her. She looks grim and tired and as though she'd like nothing so much as to throw me out the door—all signs that I'm making good progress on this case. "Fancy running into you. I'm here to rent a boat."

"A boat?" she echoes, disbelief pulling at the corners of her mouth.

"A boat!" cries the man behind the desk. He claps his hands and whips out a brochure from under the counter. "What can I get you? A clipper? A skipper? A yawl?"

I have no idea what any of those things are, but I appreciate his enthusiasm. The poor man is probably ecstatic at the thought of making any money today.

"I'd like the boat stolen by the gentleman who was killed, please," I say, not mincing matters. At the man's look of alarm, I add, "I'm interested in the macabre. I thought it might be fun to take out so I can re-create his death."

Gillian speaks up before the man can give way to his full horror. "She can't have it. It's evidence."

"But it is here, yes?" I make a show of peering out the nearest window to where the rental boats jostle and dance against the dock. "It's that white one, right? It doesn't look like evidence to me. Anyone could walk up and start poking around. There isn't even any police tape."

Gillian positions herself near the door leading to the dock, her rugby-strengthened frame blocking my access.

"It's not very big," I say, ignoring her. From this close up, the boat in question resembles a kayak—the sort of thing a couple might rent for a quick tool around the pier. I turn to the man. "How many people can it carry?"

"She's made for two," he replies. "You could squeeze in a third if you were desperate, but I wouldn't recommend it. Not in this weather."

As the conditions are considerably better than what we experienced the night Leonard Mayhew died, this remark gives me pause. It also gives Gillian pause, her eyes briefly catching mine. I know, without quite realizing how, that her thoughts coincide with my own.

"If it was carrying three passengers the night Leonard took it out, what would have happened?" she asks.

The man gives a nervous twitch of his shoulders. "I'm not liable if my property is stolen. I'd never rent it to that many. For safety reasons."

"What would have happened?" she repeats, more firmly this time. She even moves away from the door, which goes to show which of us she considers of more immediate interest. I could head outside and steal that boat right now, and she'd be less concerned with my movements than this man's response.

"Any number of things." He flutters his hands in front of him. "The engine might have stalled at the extra capacity. The imbalance could have caused her to capsize. Like I said—not my fault. They wouldn't have even made it out of the harbor."

My heart sinks with each word the man utters. "But it's possible, right?" I persist. "That there could have been three? Or that someone swam out and joined them on board once the boat reached its destination?"

Even as I ask the questions, I realize how silly they are. Even if the murderers *had* boarded the boat after it was already out to sea, why would Leonard have been there in the first place? A vacuum salesman that no one seems to recall as anything other than a well-tipping, nondescript nobody would hardly have been out on a pleasure cruise at that time and in that weather.

"You searched it already?" I ask Gillian, although I'm fairly certain I know the answer to that, too. "You didn't find anything out of the ordinary?"

"Leonard Mayhew was a man who made very little impression on the world," she says. "He left no family, no friends, and no secret clues wedged inside the boat floorboards for an amateur psychic to uncover. Sorry."

I ignore her sarcasm. "What about his mother?"

She shakes her head. "There isn't one. She died in 1989."

"Aha!" Latching on to a woman's death like it's a lifeline isn't my finest move, but at least it's something. At this point, even *I* am starting to question what Liam and I saw. "Then why did he direct his suicide note to her?"

"As you said, that could have been anything. A memory. A phone message. He might even have been writing out the first line to a novel."

This is a piece of utter nonsense, and I'm about to point out as much, but the man behind the desk speaks up. He looks, in a word, devastated.

"Does this mean you don't want to rent a boat?" he asks.

I feel guilty for leading him on when he was clearly hoping for some business, but not so guilty that I'm willing to venture out on the ocean in one of those rickety-looking vessels. I'm still not sure what a yawl is, but I'm pretty sure those things docked outside aren't it.

"Unless I can have the murder one, I'm afraid not," I say.

He casts a pleading glance at Gillian only to have it immediately shut down. Stifling a sigh, he makes one last attempt. "There is a boat where a woman had an appendix burst last year."

Gillian barely tamps down her snort in time. For a brief moment, I hope this is the break I've been looking for—a crack in her exterior that I can use to my advantage—but she gains mastery over herself using nothing but her iron will.

"Thanks, but I'll pass," I say. And, since I can't bear the crestfallen look the man gives me, I add, "But I'll buy some of those postcards before I go."

The postcards adorning the rack on the edge of the counter are indifferent at best. Faded, dated pictures of the pier, sketches of the waterfront as seen from the sea, and an aerial shot of the hotel are hardly worth the two-pound sticker price, but I grab one of each. Worst case scenario, I can send them to the villagers back home. Gillian Piper might consider me unworthy of helping with her investigation, but her Peter will get a kick out of a holiday souvenir.

Especially if I happen to mention on it that I found a way to solve this murder before his ex-wife. *That's* something we'd both enjoy.

Chapter 11

❦

When I return to the hotel, it's to find a stranger in Uli's place at the door and Bertram pushing a luggage cart towering with blue vacuum cleaner cases toward the conference room. As interesting as I find the former, it's the latter I address.

"Oh, dear." I cluck my tongue in sympathy as I bustle forward. The sag of Bertram's shoulders has become a veritable slump by this time. "That doesn't look fun."

Bertram jumps at the sound of my voice, but not very high. He's too exhausted for that. "Oh, hello, Ms. Wilde. You scared me."

"That happens more than you'd think." I take up a position on the other side of the luggage cart. I start pushing and immediately understand his pain. These things are *heavy*. "Did you get put on vacuum cleaner duty all by yourself?"

He pauses to rub a hand on the back of his neck. "The precinct sent down a few helping hands, but it's slow going. Each one has to be catalogued as evidence."

"One of the many benefits of being a paranormal investigator instead of a real one. No one checks my paperwork trail. Want a hand?"

He does—if his eager expression is anything to go by—but this is a man who's accustomed to taking orders from a very capable, very commanding superior. No doubt he needs to run it up the ball and chain of command first. Considering where and how I left her, I'd rather skip that particular step.

"I won't tell her if you don't." I make the motion of a zipper over my lips. "I can be very discreet."

"She did say she wouldn't be back for a few hours. . . ."

"That settles it." I begin pushing the cart with renewed vigor. "While the boss is away, the minions will play. You're a braver man than I, Bertram. I don't know how you spend every day of your working life with that woman. She terrifies me."

He casts me a sideways glance. "But I don't spend every day of my working life with her."

"What?" I'm startled enough that I almost trip over a snag in the carpet. "She's not your boss?"

"For this job she is, but they only bring Inspector Piper in for the big cases. Or when she specially requests one."

This makes the second time that someone has mentioned how high-ranking Gillian is. Since one measly murder that's not even classified as a murder yet isn't "big," she must have requested this one.

We've reached the conference room by this time, so there's no opportunity for me to verify this. "Nothing but vacuum cleaners in this last lot," a woman announces as we walk in. Like Bertram, she's dressed in low-ranking-officer blue. She peers up at me through a pair of thick, plastic-rimmed eyeglasses. "Hello. Who's this?"

"Eleanor Wilde," I say, extending my hand. "I'm helping Inspector Piper with the investigation. I'm a consultant."

This isn't strictly true, but Bertram doesn't contradict me, so the woman accepts me at face value.

"Then you can get started with that batch over there. Open 'em up, take 'em apart, look for anything that might be a clue."

She tosses me a pair of gloves. "Are you familiar with vacuum mechanics?"

I shake my head. That particular worldly knowledge has never come my way before.

The woman sighs. "Of course not. You're going to end up being as helpful as that psychic crackpot who started us on this wild goose chase in the first place. Just shout if anything seems off, and that'll be good enough for me. I'm supposed to be the tech expert, but I'm used to taking computers apart. Vacuums are new for me."

Bertram clears his throat, looking embarrassed, but I don't correct the woman. Psychic crackpot or not, I'm just happy to be in the room.

I sit down in front of a row of blue cases and get to work. The task is much more boring and tedious than it looks, which is to say, a lot. When I pointed these cases out in Leonard's room, it was with the expectation that they'd be holding millions of dollars in cash or evidence of Leonard's depravity and debauchery—or, at the very least, a murder weapon. I didn't expect we'd have to examine every tiny screw of every single one.

They look like screws. End of story.

"So," I say after about ten minutes of poking around and finding nothing. "What's the word on yesterday's safe robbery? Any leads?"

At this not-so-subtle line of questioning, both police officers glance up from their work. "What do you know about the robbery?" Bertram asks.

"I have a theory, that's all. A good one."

He drops all pretense of work, his voice taking on a warning tone. "If you know something that directly impacts this case, you're legally obligated to share it."

I'm fairly certain that's not true, but I go ahead anyway. "I just wonder how trustworthy our victim is, that's all." I mentally apologize to Liam for stealing his theory. What he never knows won't hurt him. "Are we absolutely certain that he was robbed? Insurance fraud is a real problem in this day and age— for all we know, he took those items himself and tried to blame them on the same men who killed Leonard."

Instead of the admiration and awe I expect, the female police officer laughs so hard that she's forced to nudge her glasses up her nose with the back of one gloved hand. "Is she for real?"

"She's American, Billie. It's hardly her fault. She can't be expected to recognize him."

I look back and forth between them—Bertram and Billie, officers and compatriots at law—and swallow. "What?" I demand. I hate not knowing obvious things. "Who is he?"

Instead of answering, Billie turns to me with renewed interest. Her eyes, which had seemed owlish and imperceptive behind those thick glasses, suddenly turn sharp. "Why is an American consulting with Inspector Piper on this investigation? What exactly is your role here?"

"I'm Eleanor Wilde," I say as though it's the most obvious thing in the world. "Paranormal investigator."

Billie shows every urge to throw me from the room right then and there. She might have attempted it, too, only a scream from the direction of the lobby halts us all in our tracks. It's a feminine scream, sharp and piercing, and we leap to our feet as one. Abandoning the vacuums and sending screws flying, we dash in the direction of the noise.

"Someone please help!" a woman cries as we enter the lobby. She's standing at the far end of a parted crowd, as though the guests are afraid of drawing too close for fear of contamination. "They broke into my room! They went for my safe!"

Billie and Bertram don't hesitate. They might look better suited for a desk than danger, but they're well-trained when it comes to emergency situations. They both rush to the woman's side.

My own assessment is slightly slower. The woman is around

fifty years old, dressed in a disheveled linen dress. Her carefully curled locks are flat on one side, and her lipstick is smeared along one edge of her face, giving her a clown-like grin. She looks like one unhappily awakened from sleep—which, from the sound of it, is precisely what she is.

"Ma'am, are you hurt?" Billie asks.

"Ma'am, I'm going to need you to take a deep breath," Bertram adds. "Who broke into your room?"

I don't wait to hear what she says. Call it a premonition. Call it intuition. Call it common sense. No matter what name it goes by, I know who she's referring to: two figures, shadowy and intangible, intent on robbing her while she took a restless, trance-like nap.

In other words, *Armand.*

I waste no time hightailing it for room 619.

Bypassing the elevators, which are untrustworthy when time is of the essence, I aim for the stairwell instead. Six floors are no small feat when you're already breathless with outrage and anticipation, but I fly up them all the same. I wait only until I reach the door before I start making noise.

"Armand, you'd better be in there," I call. "Innocent and fully alibied."

There's no answer.

"Armand Lamont, I swear on everything you hold dear, if you don't come out right now, I'm turning you in. I'll tell Inspector Piper everything I know about you, even if it means I'm signing my own warrant in the process."

Still nothing.

"Armand! Armand!"

"For the love of everything, Eleanor, must you make all that racket?" The door swings open to reveal Vivian Hartford, dressed in the same blue gown from before. It's much lower cut than I realized outside, the neckline so plunging that it dips below her sternum. It's perfect for showing off her diamonds, which glitter heavy and tempting against her chest.

"Vivian?" I say, blinking at all that glitz. "What are you doing in Armand's room?"

She winks and takes a long drink from the martini glass in her hand, ignoring my question and the outrage that accompanies it. "Come in, come in. Armand and I were just discussing our plans for tomorrow. Apparently, there's a jewelry store in town that's not to be missed. They have a tiara that exactly matches these diamonds. Wouldn't that be lovely? I've never owned a tiara before. Marian and I are all agog to go."

My relief at finding Armand in his room—and therefore not currently robbing that woman downstairs—is replaced by a feeling of profound mistrust.

"I don't understand," I say as I walk in to find Armand and Marian sitting on the chaise longue at the end of the bed, smoke from Armand's long, thin cigar curling around their heads. They're joined by Liam, who sits in a chair near the window. My brother isn't smoking or drinking, but his favorite electronica music is playing in the background. He looks more relaxed than I've seen him since this vacation began. "You guys are having a party? Without me?"

Vivian laughs. "You were busy gadding about town, dear."

Yes, because *some* of us are trying to solve a murder. "You could at least have had the decency to invite me," I say. And, since there are bigger issues right now than my exclusion from the Armand Lamont Fan Club, I add, "Besides, there's been another robbery."

That gets their attention, everyone suddenly talking at once.

"Another one?"

"Are you absolutely sure?"

"If it's those two shadow men again, I'm not surprised. You are aware that this hotel is haunted?"

The last one comes from Marian, and it has the effect of silencing all other conversation in the room. I turn to the woman eagerly, taking in her full appearance for the first time. My initial assessment had been that she was around the same age and income level as Vivian, and that holds just as true now as it did this morning. She's dressed much more sensibly than Vivian in a pink tweed suit, her jewelry limited to a pearl brooch on her lapel and a wedding band that would be the envy of a queen. She's not precisely handsome, and I doubt she ever was, but there's something about the slow, confident way she speaks that's more arresting than mere beauty.

"Haunted?" I echo. "What do you mean?"

She rolls her eyes my direction. I don't know if it's the fact that I'm dressed in a faded herringbone romper that makes me look all of twelve years old, or that Vivian has been telling stories about me, but she doesn't seem impressed by what she sees. "I mean precisely what I said, young lady. Strange things have always happened here. It's an old hotel—a hundred and fifty years, at least—and it's seen its fair share of tragedy. Anyone who's anyone knows about it."

From the loftiness in her tone, I take it to understand that I'm not considered *anyone*. "Why am I just now hearing about this?" I demand of the assembled crowd. "Did you guys know?"

"It's not common knowledge, but yes," Armand admits. "They say the shadow men walk at night, possessing the innocent and maligning the damned."

"Please. You're just making that up to mess with us."

It's the exact sort of thing he *would* do, taking advantage of our collective fears to spin a narrative that suits his purposes. In fact, it's the exact sort of thing we *did* do, manipulating local lore for the sake of making a quick buck. Every city has its ghost stories, if you dig hard enough.

"The hotel has put a lot of money and resources into burying the rumors." Marian shakes her head and sighs. "Alas, it's to no avail. Every few years, they crop up again. The shadow men are new. When I was a young woman, it was a ghost maid who roamed the halls."

"If you're such an expert, then who are the shadow men?" I demand of Armand. "And what do they want?"

"I don't know, Ellie. Communicating with ghosts was always more your thing than mine."

I'm not buying it. "I thought your brush with death made you some kind of ghost-savant."

"It wasn't a brush. I literally died. I have a death certificate and everything."

Yes—one that *I* forged. Unfortunately, there's no way to refute his claim without sharing my part in it, so I clamp my lips shut. The moment the silence takes over, Birdie arrives to fill it.

He's not wrong about this hotel being haunted, she says. *I always made it a point to stay here whenever I traveled through Sussex. It has such a nice, dark aura about it, don't you think?*

I wish I could dismiss Birdie's claims as easily as I do Armand's and Marian's, but I can't. During her lifetime, Birdie claimed to know the exact shape and scope of every haunting and possession—real or fabricated—in the United Kingdom. It was sort of her superpower.

"Why didn't you mention this before?" I ask Birdie. Armand, thinking the question is for him, opens his mouth to answer, but Vivian gives him a slight shake of her head. She's seen me talk to my sister enough times to recognize when I'm communing with the dead. "That's the sort of information I like to have *before* I arrive at a place."

"At least the hotel being haunted explains the cursed doll," Liam says.

"And your dead man." Armand nods. "I've been meaning to tell you, Eleanor. . . . If you'd like to try and resurrect your memories of that night, I'd be more than happy to help. I might be able to reach in and erase some of the haziness that you and your brother seem to be experiencing."

"Oh, no, you're not." I clamp my hands over my ears. "You're not getting inside this head."

"He already tried me, but it didn't work," Liam offers. He puffs up with something like pride. "Apparently, I'm unhypnotizable."

"No one is unhypnotizable," Armand corrects him with a gentle cough. "You're spiritually blocked. It's different. With Eleanor, however . . ."

I shake my head. "Nope. No way. No how."

"I don't see what the big fuss is," Vivian says. I'm starting to feel very ganged-up on, not to mention disappointed. Vivian and Liam are supposed to be on my side, not ranging themselves next to a man I trust as much as a snake. "We'll be here the entire time. We won't let him do anything untoward."

I almost snort out loud. Armand's *untoward* actions aren't what I fear while I'm under his spell. It's the subtle ideas he'll plant in my brain, the way he'll wiggle his hooks under my skin so he can tug at a future date of his choosing. I've seen this man work before. His ruthlessness is secondary only to his charm.

"Come on, Eleanor," Armand says, his low voice already entering its most silken state. "You have questions. I have the key to unlock the answers. What is there to lose?"

Other than my moral high ground and the complete control of my own mind? Plenty. While there's no way I can place recent events at Armand's door, since he's obviously been in this room for some time, there's no denying that he came to Brighton with malicious intentions. To give him control of my mind and body would be insanity.

Don't they always say there's a fine line between genius and insanity? Birdie asks. *Who's to say which side you stand on?*

I wish I could discount Birdie's words, but she's once again hit the nail on the head. It *is* strange that we can't remember the details of those shadow figures. Whatever is going on around here—murder and theft and who-knows-what-other-crimes—

is somehow tied to them. Until I can recount my own memories with confidence, there's not much I can do to convince everyone else that I'm genuine.

Besides, it's not as if I actually *believe* in Armand's ability to hypnotize people. . . . It's not magic. It's the power of suggestion.

"Fine," I say, throwing up my hands. "But, Liam, you need to go downstairs and see what's happening with that woman who was attacked. I left before I got all the good details."

He looks disappointed. "I wanted to watch you get hypnotized. I was going to ask you questions about that time you 'accidentally' washed my lucky jacket. To this day, I'd swear on my life that you did it on purpose. You wanted my team to lose the basketball championship so I wouldn't get to go to Florida without you."

I laugh. "Let me save you the trouble. Yes, Liam. I washed it on purpose. It was disgusting."

His response is a deep scowl, but I pretend not to see it. After extracting a promise from Vivian and Marian to record the entire experience, he lopes off to discover what he can about the woman downstairs.

I'm secretly glad that Liam's the one to initiate the recording. I'd also prefer to have a detailed account of what's about to happen in this room, but I don't like being the one to ask for it. To do so would only make me look scared.

I'm not scared. I'm suspicious. It's different.

As soon as Liam leaves, Armand makes a big show of getting everything prepared for the sitting. Unless it's for the benefit of my two audience members, I'm not sure why he bothers. I've seen this happen enough times to know that the dimmed lights and the low hum of the air conditioner in the background aren't necessary. They can help, yes, particularly when the person being hypnotized is nervous or being put under without their knowledge, but I'm fully consenting and this isn't my first rodeo.

"What really happened when you put Liam under?" I ask as Armand tugs out the chaise longue at the end of the bed and has me stretch myself out on it. "He's one of the most gullible people in the world—he believed in Santa and the Tooth Fairy well into his preteen years. He's not unhypnotizable."

Armand smiles, his teeth glinting down at me. "I told you. He's spiritually blocked."

Vivian releases a cynical harrumph. "Balderdash. That boy couldn't sit still long enough to get put under. He fidgeted and asked questions and couldn't stop blinking."

I laugh. That does sound a lot like my brother, and I can't help but feel proud of him. We Wildes don't go down without a fight—even in our subconscious minds.

"Unlike Liam, I promise to be at rest the whole time." I place my hands over my stomach, allowing them to rise and fall with the steady movements of my breath. I feel a little silly, but I know how this is supposed to work.

I'll breathe and relax.

I'll let myself be lulled by the soothing tone of Armand's voice.

I'll follow the perambulations of his pocket watch until it's the only thing in the room.

And then . . .

Chapter 12

I awaken to the end of times.

That's what it sounds like to my addled brain, anyway, with blaring sirens and the pounding of footsteps in the distance. The world around me is loud and disorienting, especially when combined with the bright lights overhead and the sudden splash of water over my face.

Cold water.

"What the—?" I splutter and force myself into a seated position. I'm on the chaise longue in Armand's room, surrounded by anxious faces and a scene of mass destruction. I rub my eyes with the back of my hand, but it doesn't do anything to put the lamps upright or fix the curtains hanging askew over the window.

"There you are. *Finally.*" Armand wraps an arm around my waist and hoists me to a standing position, sending all of my senses reeling at once. "We're being evacuated. I tried lifting you, but you're a lot heavier than you look. Are there weights in your shoes or something?"

I'm not so disoriented that I don't know an insult when it's being leveled at my head.

"It's not my fault you're a ten-pound weakling," I retort. To my surprise, my voice is hoarse and scratchy, my throat raw. As alarming as I find this, I'm more concerned with our current predicament. From the way everyone is carrying on, the entire hotel must be on fire. "Where's Liam?"

"Already on his way out, most likely," Vivian says, and in a much more maternal tone than I'm used to hearing from her. "Come, dear. We're supposed to make our way to the beach."

It takes a moment for this to penetrate the haze of my brain. "Wait—the hotel's not really on fire, is it?"

Instead of answering, Vivian and Marian share a look over the top of my head.

Planting my oh-so-heavy feet on the ground, I force my raw voice to start working again. It feels as though someone forced broken glass down my throat. "I'm not going anywhere until someone tells me what's going on. What happened? How long was I under?"

"Ten minutes, twelve minutes, tops," Armand says in his most reassuring tone.

"I've never seen anything like it," Marian adds. *Her* tone is more excited than anything else. "One minute, you were lying there and muttering about what a fool you were for agreeing to this, and the next . . ."

"What?" I demand. "What came next?"

"Things started flying," Vivian supplies. She gestures around her. "The lamps, the curtains, the dresser drawers. We thought it was confined to the room, but then you screamed as though the devil himself was after you. The lights flickered and the alarms started sounding."

I don't have to fake the heaviness in my feet after this. The entire purpose of the hypnosis exercise was to clarify my memories, to turn those two hazy figures into something—or someone—I can remember. Instead, there's a gaping hole where the past ten minutes should be.

I don't like it. I don't like it, and I certainly don't trust it.

"Let's get going. I don't think there are any actual flames, but you never know. You were . . ." Armand shakes his head. "If I didn't know better, Ellie, I'd say you were an actual witch. How did you do that?"

I don't have an answer for him. What he wants to hear—that I rigged this room with magnets or disguised pulley systems— might explain our current surroundings, but it would take a lot more coordination than that to cue the fire alarms and electrical system. I mean, it *could* be done, don't get me wrong.

The thing is, I didn't do it. And the only other person who might be capable of such a thing is the one staring at me with a fearful look in his deep, rich eyes.

"You guys head down," I say, forcing myself to start moving again. "I'm going to get my cats."

"Your cats?" Armand echoes.

Vivian clucks her tongue. "Oh, Eleanor, really."

I don't heed either of them. "If there's an actual fire, the authorities won't let me back inside to rescue them. It's now or never."

Although my sluggishness makes it feel as though I'm walking through a funhouse, I make it out the door and to the emergency stairwell. I have to fight the downward traffic in order to make it up to the suite, but everyone is so caught up in their own safety that they don't bother with the disheveled woman going in the wrong direction.

It's eerily quiet when I make it to my floor. Doors are flung open and the alarm lights flicker, making it look as though I'm on the set of a zombie apocalypse movie. Worry about my cats is at the forefront of my mind, but I'm also driven by the knowledge that something very odd is happening inside this hotel—haunted or not.

I can hear Freddie's frantic mewling before I even reach my door. My heart gives a lurching pang at the sound, but a blur of movement catches the corner of my eye before I manage to pull out my key card. Acting mostly on instinct, I whirl and press my body flat against the closed door so I'm not visible to anyone peeking down the hallway.

And then I do some peeking of my own.

At first, I think that Vivian has followed me up here—to help save my cats or because curiosity got the better of her—because the person who appears in the frame of the emergency stairwell is dressed as antiquated as she is. I only catch a quick glimpse, but what I see is a tall, gaunt frame covered by a long, dark dress and hair that's pinned up in a knot on top of the woman's head. Her skin is preternaturally pale and what looks like blood is dripping down the side of her face.

Just like, you know, a ghost maid.

My heart leaps to my throat, but only momentarily. This isn't a moment for fear—it's a moment for logic. All I have to do is follow her, and I'm sure her presence will be explained. She could be a member of the staff. She could be a guest making her unhurried way to the beach.

Unfortunately, Freddie chooses that moment to begin mewling in earnest. By now, the poor animal is well aware that I'm standing outside the door, and she isn't happy to be trapped on the opposite side of it. If I could be sure that Beast is in there to take care of her, that the dratted animal hasn't run off again in search of evil Victorian dolls, then I might be able to get away without too much guilt.

But I'm not sure, and as much as I'd love to indulge in my instinct to investigate, Freddie comes first.

With a pang of regret, I give up on the idea of chasing the ghost maid. A swipe of my key card later, and I'm through the door.

Our suite is a bastion of calm in the upheaval of the rest of the hotel, the lights off and the beds made, everything neat and tidy. That's more due to Liam than me, since he's better at organization than I am. Even the cat food has been laid out on a towel to prevent spills, their litter box discreetly hidden in one corner of the bathroom. Beast is equally calm, though Freddie pounces on me with enthusiastic relief.

"Some help you're turning out to be," I mutter to Beast as I fold Freddie in my arms. The low rumble of her purr does much to soothe us both. "So far, you've done nothing but make my work ten times harder. I could be chasing a ghost right now."

Beast's only response is a haughty twitch of her whiskers.

"Where's your survival instinct?" I demand. "Where's your deep, profound need to protect your offspring?"

Again, I get no answer . . . which is all the answer I need. In my time with Beast, there's no denying that she's displayed an uncanny sense of self-preservation. She knows she only has nine lives and is fiercely protective of each one. If there was a fire blazing somewhere in this hotel, she'd be the first to hightail it out that door.

Calm for the first time since I awoke from my hypnotic trance, I inhale deeply. I detect nothing but the scent of clean linens and a slight tinge of eau de cat. A quick peek out the window further assuages my fears. Most of the people congregated on the beach below are annoyed rather than scared, and the fire brigade isn't carrying axes or lifting hoses.

"I guess it was a false alarm," I say, more to soothe Freddie than because I believe it. As much as I'd like to believe otherwise, the alarm itself wasn't false. It *did* go off, and it *did* instigate a hotel-wide panic—and all within ten minutes of my hypnotic trance that sent every object in Armand's room flying.

Because of an unfortunate coincidence?

Because this is just one more trick Armand is using to bend me to his will?

Or because I saw something truly and deeply terrifying while under that spell?

Chapter 13

The next morning dawns sunny and bright.

Okay, so the temperatures are still a good ten degrees lower than they should be this time of year, and my weather app promises much more of the same, but there's no denying that the elements have taken a turn for the better. The fact that my brother is clad in swim trunks and slathered in sunscreen as we head toward the beach is proof of that.

"I'm going to read this entire book from start to finish," he announces with an almost defiant air as he makes his way toward the line of beach chairs that have been set up optimistically near the water's edge. The paperback he holds up is thick and covered with women in improbable armor. "I won't come inside until every last dragon is slain and the maiden's virtue recovered. Is that understood?"

"You deserve it," I say as I lean forward to press a kiss on his cheek. He's surprised by this show of affection—and by my sincerity. "I'm sorry this has been such a rotten vacation for you. I promise not to summon any demons or poltergeists until you're fully relaxed."

"That's not what I meant."

"I know. But until I get to the bottom of all this, it's the best I can do."

Now *he's* the sincere one. He pulls his completely unnecessary sunglasses down to the end of his nose and stares at me over the top of them. "Are you sure you can, Ellie? Get to the bottom, I mean?"

I nod, unwilling to give this particular lie a voice. I haven't yet failed to solve one of the mysteries that life always seems to be throwing at me, but there's no denying that the task ahead of me is a daunting one. The size of this hotel alone—not to mention the number of people inside it—is enough to set anyone back a few paces.

"I'm heading in to talk to Gillian now," I say. That, at least, has the benefit of being true. I've been summoned to speak with Inspector Piper and have been told, in no uncertain terms, that to fail to show up will result in my immediate arrest. "I'll send a waiter out with cocktails as soon as it strikes noon. Enjoy your morning, Liam."

I lope off in the direction of the hotel before Liam can say anything more. By this time, Uli's shift has started. He opens the door for me, his eyebrows arching up to his hairline as I step into the marble interior.

"It sounds like you had quite an interesting time of things yesterday," he says, sweeping me a light bow. "I'm almost sorry to have taken the time off."

It *is* rather odd that a man who appears to live at this post by the door should have been missing during one of the most exciting events of the past few days, but I don't mention it. For one, everyone is entitled to their downtime. For another, there's still that niggling matter of his pretending not to have seen the shadow men on that boat.

Uli knows more about the comings and goings in this hotel than anyone. He sees everyone who walks in and everyone who sneaks out. He knows about ghost maids and shadow men and everything else that might happen inside a building with fifteen floors and hundreds of five-star reviews on Yelp.

That makes him a highly valuable witness . . . or something else entirely.

"Inspector Piper is waiting for you in the conference room," he says, unaware of the suspicions I'm currently heaping on his head. "If you want to put her in a good mood, take her a strong tea. Milk and two sugars, and make sure you stir it well. She's looking none too spry this morning."

I nod my thanks and make a move toward the complimentary tea table before hesitating. While I'm grateful for the information Uli provided, I can't help but feel that it's one more mark against him. He knows an awful lot about how Gillian Piper takes her tea. It's the sort of information someone like Armand—and someone like me—would be sure to pounce on and tuck away for future use. Insignificant as it may seem, small tidbits like that can be used for all sorts of nefarious deeds. They lower guards and grease the wheels of trust.

I retrace my steps back to him. "Could you do me a favor?" I ask.

He gives another slight bow. "Of course."

I reach into the pocket of my black capri pants—paired today with a floaty tank top in a color that can only be described as "witchy purple"—and extract the stack of postcards. In addition to the one for Peter, I've scrawled two off for my friends Annis and Oona, the vicar and local doctor, respectively.

"Could you pop these in the mail for me?" I ask. "I'm not sure where the nearest post office is."

"I'd be delighted," he says. Even though I don't tip him for the service, I know his delight is real. As soon as my back is turned, he's sure to read the entirety of my correspondence. I've written nothing noteworthy to either Annis or Oona, but

I'm mightily curious how he'll take the information that I know a second Inspector Piper—and that I've cheerfully informed said man about my chance meeting with his ex-wife.

If that's not something a nosy doorman will use to his advantage, I don't know what is.

I lose no time in fulfilling Gillian's tea order and heading toward the conference room.

"Here." I hold out the paper cup as I enter the now-familiar room. All the vacuum cleaners have been cleared out, but the feeling of industriousness remains. "You look as though you could use this."

Uli's advice fails. Gillian takes one look at my peace offering and snorts. The sound matches her aesthetic, which is so buttoned up and pulled back that she looks like nothing so much as an oversized horse jockey. "What I need is a double whiskey neat, but until this dratted case is solved, I'm a teetotaler. Sit down."

Such is the command in her voice that I instantly comply. I also start drinking her tea. Gillian Piper isn't the only one feeling none too spry this morning.

"What got taken from that woman yesterday?" I ask. Liam didn't manage to secure any information before the alarms started going off, but I didn't have the heart to berate him for it. It was a bit of a strange day for us all. "Let me guess—empty safe, stolen jewels, two dark figures that she can't quite remember?"

Gillian's scowl confirms everything, which is when an additional thought occurs to me.

"Was anything else taken? During the fire alarm, I mean? If there are thieves—or, uh, demonic visions—prowling around, that fiasco would have been a perfect cover."

In other words, maybe the alarm going off had nothing to do with my being hypnotized at all. Maybe it was an opportunist, plain and simple.

"Not to my knowledge, no, but I wouldn't be surprised if you're correct. Strange that the thought should have occurred to you but not to any of my team."

I sit immobile, aware that I'm being carefully watched. "I can't help it. I'm very astute."

Her lips, which had remained tightly pursed throughout this interview, twitch. "From our sole confirmed victim, they got two diamond necklaces, several rings, more bracelets and brooches than any woman needs to own, and something called a chatelaine."

I release a soundless whistle. "That sounds like a jackpot."

"Indeed." She unbends enough to lower herself to the chair opposite me. She sits ramrod straight, no sign of friendliness or kindness in her demeanor, but it doesn't put me off as much as it might have a few days ago. This rigid control of hers is an act—I'm sure of it. Somewhere, somehow, this woman and my Inspector Piper fell in love. Yes, they also fell out of it, but from the way Peter moons and sighs and doodles in his police notebook, it's obvious that his feelings remain.

If I want this woman to loosen up toward me, I need to use those feelings as a means to an end. Where fear, intimidation, and ghosts won't work, love is one of the only options left.

"If I promised to leave here today, would you accompany me home?" I ask. "I'll get out of your way, clear your path and all that, but only if you drive me to the village yourself."

Her eyes are the only part of her that react to my offer. The ice in them expands until it cracks. "What makes you think I want to get rid of you?"

"Call it an educated guess. Is that a yes?"

Her response is to reach to the table behind her, where a black leather knapsack sits upright. I watch, curious and wary, as she opens the flap and extracts something contained within it.

And then I laugh.

"Oh, dear." I don't bother to hide my reaction at the sight of—what else?—Brunhilde. According to Liam, he threw her in the ocean yesterday. Walked her down to the beach, tied a rock to her neck with his shoelace, and threw as hard as his gym-teacher arm could muster. From the dry, sprightly look of those cracked lips, Brunhilde seems none the worse for her swim.

"Do me a favor and hide this from my brother, would you? He's terrified of that thing."

"He's terrified of a doll?" Gillian's disdain matches my own.

"It, um, keeps coming back. We've given her away, thrown her down a garbage chute, and tossed her into the ocean. Yet she always ends up back in this hotel." I pause just long enough to change the subject back. "I'm sensing you don't want to take me up on my offer to leave. I can't imagine why. Peter would be happy to see you again."

The use of her ex-husband's given name doesn't soften the inspector in the slightest. "Someone left this doll outside a room on the thirteenth floor."

"Someone also left it outside mine the day I arrived. So far, it hasn't presaged anything catastrophic." Unless, of course, you count Armand Lamont re-entering my life, a man thrown off a boat, two robberies, and the hypnotic trance I can't recall. "Do you mind if I hold her? I want to try something."

Gillian complies and watches as I drop Brunhilde to the floor and grind her under the heel of my strappy black sandal.

She's surprisingly strong for such an ancient, delicate-looking thing, but I manage to crush her head into several large pieces. Her hands and feet remain weirdly intact.

"I'm no expert in the art of porcelain, but this looks pretty new to you, right?" I exhibit the largest head-chunk to Gillian. Although the exterior is still as decayed and spooky as before, the inside looks solid and clean.

She takes the shard from my fingers. "Hmm. Interesting."

"Not really." I shrug. "I'm pretty sure it's just an old friend of mine messing with me. Relationships are so hard, you know?"

Once again, my bait fails to entice the good inspector. Apparently, getting her to open up about her ex-husband isn't going to be easy. She does, however, lift an interested brow. "This would be the Armand Lamont I've heard so much about?"

I nod, but without enthusiasm. I don't want Gillian peering too closely at that man or his past. I did a little Google searching into the electronic trail Armand has left behind over the years, and although there doesn't appear to be anything incriminating, you never know what kinds of files a full police force has access to. For all I know, he's been robbing people around the world since we parted ways and is now wanted by Interpol.

"If it helps, he was in his room yesterday when that woman was robbed," I offer. "It's why I left so quickly. I wanted to see if he had an alibi."

"Which he did?"

I shrug helplessly. "I don't like the guy, but he's neither your murderer nor your thief. Sorry."

"Then what is he doing here?" she asks.

I see no reason to lie. "He's trying to extort my boyfriend's family for two million dollars." At Gillian's sudden start of surprise, I hasten to add, "I'm not going to *let* him, obviously. But I'm not ready to let him off the hook that easily, either. I'm waiting to see how everything plays out."

"You are aware that extortion is a punishable crime in the United Kingdom?"

I shrug again. "Technically, he hasn't done it yet. He's only hinted at it. Is hinting at extortion illegal in the United Kingdom, too?"

It's not, as we both well know, though I can tell she'd like it to be.

"Is your boyfriend's family aware of what's happening to them?"

They're not *un*aware of it, so I do my best to assuage her

concerns. I'm not sure how successful I am at it, but I hope I've at least given Gillian a reason to leave Armand—and his past—alone.

"By the way," I say as I prepare to take my leave of her, "did Bertram and that other police officer find anything in the vacuum cleaner cases yesterday?"

Inspector Piper shakes her head. "No, unfortunately. It's starting to look as though the cases might be a dead end. Or a false lead. I haven't decided which."

I can't help but laugh. A false lead, in this instance, would mean that *I* was the one to give it to her. "You saw those marks in the carpet. What else could they be? Especially in a room where the hotel's vacuum cleaner salesman was staying?"

Her gaze sharpens into twin ice picks. "Who said he was the hotel's vacuum cleaner salesman?"

I pause, suddenly feeling a lot less sure of my ground than when I walked into this room. I thought that was a fact we'd already established. "He had to be," I say before I fully realize what it is I'm giving away. "The cases in his room were the same color blue."

She smirks in a way that makes me feel the full weight of my slipup. I forgot that I'm not supposed to know what color those vacuum cleaner cases were, that the information was given to me in a vision. If I'd *really* used my powers of deduction, I'd have no way of knowing if the cases were black or brown or covered in rainbow sparkles.

"Couldn't someone on the staff confirm it?" I ask, trying to backtrack. I know Uli wasn't working when Leonard arrived—or so he claims—but there's a whole roster of employees who must have seen something. "The person who checked him in must have taken his luggage up."

"Strangely enough, no one can recall seeing anything out of the ordinary."

"But what about his employer?" I persist. I'm not wrong

about this. I know I'm not. "He must have had business cards somewhere in his room. They'd surely know what brand of vacuum he sold."

"Apparently, the company listed on all his documents is a fake," she says as though informing me about the color of the walls. "I don't suppose you're able to randomly come up with the answer to that, too, are you?"

I'm not going to lie—I give it a real college try. Closing my eyes, I reach out to Winnie and Birdie, hoping one of them can give me an edge over Gillian Piper and her infallible logic, but I don't feel or hear anything out of the ordinary.

"Sorry," I say with real meaning. "I'm not a magician."

"But you are a psychic?" she asks doubtfully.

I resent the implication. A psychic can't just pull answers out of thin air. As a fake one, I could bring about all kinds of miracles and manifestations—and on my own timeline. As a real one, I have much less influence than I'd like.

"*And* a palm reader," I say, knowing it's the one thing that will get me out of here without further questioning. "So when you're ready for me to take a look at that love line of yours, Mrs. Piper, all you have to do is say the word."

Chapter 14

❦

It had been my intention to spend the afternoon questioning the staff and guests at the hotel for news of hauntings both past and present. I even dressed for the occasion by going full Madame Eleanor, with pinned braids coiled at the nape of my neck, blood-red lipstick, and a gothic sundress with lacy skulls stitched onto the collar.

Unfortunately, I only get as far as talking to a waiter who clearly has more important things to do before I notice something strange.

And by something strange, I mean my brother laughing it up with a tall, striking man he appears to have picked up on the beach.

I'm in the second-story bar, which boasts a terrace overlooking the hotel lobby. From my vantage point, I can just make out the top of Liam's head as it bobs and weaves in what can only be termed a *flirtation*. Not that I'm judging him for it—the man he's flirting with is well worth the attention. Broad of shoulders and graceful of person, the man radiates confidence in every movement of his long, strong limbs. In white linen slacks that

billow as he walks, a cheerful teal shirt open one button too many at the throat, and blond-tipped hair above a pair of browline glasses, the man looks wealthy and relaxed.

He also looks an awful lot like Nicholas Hartford III in disguise.

Unable to prevent the happy thump of my heart at the sight of my beau, I force myself to take a deep breath and appear outwardly calm. I don't see Armand skulking around anywhere, but that doesn't mean he isn't watching. It would be unthinkable to blow Nicholas's cover after he went to such painstaking lengths to secure it. In the two years I've known this man, I've never seen him go anywhere near a bleach kit. He must have pulled out all the stops to make this transformation happen.

I take the stairs at a much more sedate pace than I normally would and approach my brother as though his arrival—and not Nicholas's—is the one I've been waiting for.

"Liam, there you are," I say. I lean in to kiss both his cheeks. "I have good news."

"So do I," he returns with a hiccup. His words, I note, are slurred. "The hotel dinn't just comp us a room. They comped us drinks, too. No limit."

"Oh, I think you've reached your limit." I don't bother to hide my sigh. An intoxicated Liam isn't going to be of much use for the rest of the day. He's a happy drunk but intolerable once the hangover sets in. "What are the chances I can convince you to head up to the room to take a nap?"

He ignores the question. "Whass your good news?"

Now is decidedly not the time to produce the shards of Brunhilde's head for his inspection. "It can wait." I turn my attention to Nicholas, who's been standing and watching this interaction without a sign of the amusement he certainly feels. "Are you going to introduce me to your friend?"

"My friend?" Liam echoes, his brows pulled tight across his

forehead. "Oh! Yes! My friend. Ellie, this is . . . Piers. Piers Pierson. Yeah. Thass it."

"Piers Pierson?" I echo. Liam must have been hitting the mai tais even harder than I expected. "That's not a real name."

"Alas, it's too true." Nicholas—or Piers, it would seem—turns to me with a slight bow. "Piers Pierson, at your service. I met your—ah, brother, is it?—on the beach and thought he could use a helping hand back to the hotel. You should probably get some nonalcoholic fluids in him."

"Isn't he handsome?" Liam demands. "He's very handsome. *And* a doctor."

Nicholas clears his throat and adopts what I assume is supposed to be a doctoral air. He mostly manages to look condescending, but that's pretty much the same thing when it comes to members of the medical profession. "It's really quite dangerous to mix sun and alcohol," he says, his usual urbanity flattened to a monotone. "Heat stroke, for example, is one of the most common outcomes. Dilation of the blood vessels and—"

"A *doctor*, Ellie."

"Yes, thanks. I believe you."

"He said I remind him of someone. I bet it's Clark Gable. Everyone loves Clark Gable. He's taking me to dinner tonight." Liam hiccups again. "But I need an eensy-weensy rest first. Doctor's orders."

I can't help but catch Nicholas's gaze. When I'd hinted that he needed to come here under disguise, I'd assumed he'd fly under the radar, make himself somehow a part of the backdrop. I should have known better. Like his mother, when he does a thing, he does it all the way.

"You look exactly like Clark Gable," I agree. "And an eensy-weensy rest is just the thing."

Nicholas gives a slight bow. "As I have yet to check in to my room, I'll leave you two to, ah, hydrate." He pauses just long

enough to take Liam's hand and hold it in his own. "It was an absolute delight to meet you, Liam. I sincerely hope to see you at dinner. Seven o'clock in the lobby restaurant. Don't forget."

Liam grins delightedly and slurs something about the chicken piccata being excellent. As he loathes capers and has never gone anywhere near the dish in his life, I can only assume the liquor is starting to seep into his intellect.

I take my leave of Nicholas and drag my brother toward the stairs. He blanches at the sight of all those steps but draws a resolute breath. "You're right," he says with something approaching clarity. "I need to work off all those carbohydrates. You never told me that your friend Armand can *drink*."

I trip on the bottom step, the strength of Liam's arm the only thing keeping me from falling flat on my face. "Armand? He was on the beach with you?"

"Wouldn't leave my side." Liam starts dragging me up the stairs but has to pause on the first landing to close his eyes and let a dizzy spell pass. "I lost count after the sixth round. I don't know where such a small man puts all that liquor."

"Down his sleeve, most likely," I say. Worry pings the pit of my stomach. Getting someone intoxicated as a way of extracting information isn't unheard of in our line of work, but it's sloppy—cheap. It's the sort of tactic Armand would only resort to if he was starting to get desperate.

But why would he be desperate? And why use a trick he knows I'd be able to see right through?

"What did you tell him?" I ask, though I doubt I'll get a rational answer.

In this, I wrong my brother. He starts on the second set of steps, clarity coming a little closer with each one.

"Nothing, I think. He kept asking me personal questions, so I distracted him with stories about the kids in my fifth-grade class. Lily and Theodora and Aiden B. and Aiden Q. and Aiden G.—"

I interrupt him before he starts telling *me* about all those kids. "That was smart thinking. You're sure you didn't let anything else slip?"

His brow wrinkles. "I got close. He wanted to know about Nicholas and you."

"I'll bet he did. What'd you say?"

"Just the basics. How long you've been dating and how he's always traveling for work. That's when my umbrella—the little one in my drink, I mean—blew away, and Piers brought it back to me." He sighs and places his free hand over his heart. "He's a doctor, Ellie. A rich one. Did you see his glasses? Gucci. I'm sure of it."

We've reached our floor by this point, but I like the privacy of the stairwell, so I force Liam to halt before we move through the door. I peer into his eyes, waiting until the pupils fix on mine before I speak. "Liam, you know that wasn't really a doctor named Piers Pierson, right?"

Liam heaves a wistful sigh. "He told me I have a soulful way about me."

"Listen to me. He's not—"

"And a noble brow." He strikes a pose so I can see him in profile. His brow looks the same as it always does. "What do you think? Could I be a marble bust?"

"Liam. Snap out of it." I give his shoulders a shake. "I appreciate that you didn't have a choice when it came to all the drinking, but that wasn't some random stranger hitting on you at the beach. It was—"

He giggles. "Relax, Ellie. I'm not an idiot. I know that was your boyfriend."

He says this last bit loud enough to reverberate up and down the stairwell. With a hiss of disapproval, I tug my brother through the door. "Careful. We don't want anyone else to know." I pause as a thought occurs to me. "*How* could you tell it was him, by the way? Did Armand suspect anything?"

Liam grins. "If he did, Piers quashed that theory flat. He talked about Mohs micrographic surgery for twenty minutes. *Twenty* minutes. If I didn't have an extra mai tai to tide me over, I'd have fallen asleep on the spot. How does he know so much about skin cancer?"

I take my lip between my teeth to keep from laughing. "I have no idea, but if anything is going to throw Armand off the scent, it's long, rambling medical dissertations. He hates anyone with a background in science. They're always the first to see through his tricks."

They're always the first to see through *my* tricks, too, but whereas I embrace the challenge, Armand prefers to work on the unsuspecting.

The cats are napping when we enter the room, the pair of them forming an ouroboros on the end of my bed. The sight of them—behaving themselves, for once—reminds me of the Brunhilde shards in my pocket.

"Oh! I almost forgot to show you. Check this out." I hold up the largest piece for Liam to inspect. "I don't know why we didn't think to crack her open before."

Liam flails his every limb in an attempt to get away from me. "Gah! Have you lost your ever-loving mind? Where did you get her? She should be at the bottom of the ocean."

"Someone went and retrieved her." I turn the piece around so he can see how clean and crisp the interior is. "I, for one, am glad, because it turns out she's not nearly as old as she looks. This had to be manufactured sometime in the past decade."

"So? That doesn't explain how your devil-cat found her and brought her up here. Or how she clawed her way out of the ocean."

"Well, no," I admit. "But it's a step in the right direction."

"I'm not staying in the room with her broken head pieces."

"I'll give her a proper burial," I promise.

"No—we're exorcising her. Right here and now. With fire."

Liam is still tipsy enough that playing with flames isn't a great idea, and the commotion of last night's fire alarm is still fresh in my memory, but I go along with him anyway. After all, this is supposed to be his holiday. If burning bits of porcelain is how he wants to spend his time, I'm not going to stop him.

As I watch him throw scraps of paper and debris into the metal wastebasket, I can't help but ask, "It's weird, right? How the fire alarm went off last night while I was under hypnosis?"

Liam barely represses his shudder. "I'm just glad you sent me out of the room so I didn't have to watch. From what Vivian and Armand said, you went feral."

An unsettled feeling creeps through my stomach, but I press it down. "Vivian exaggerates and Armand has an ulterior motive," I say. "Anyone could have pulled that alarm."

Liam pauses in the act of lighting a match to look at me. "Yes, but could anyone have thrown furniture and lamps through the air?"

I'm not sure how to respond to this, so I don't.

"And you really don't remember anything?" he asks. "Anything at all?"

I close my eyes and will myself back into that room, but it's no use. Like my memory of those dark shadows on the boat, there's something odd about it—a piece missing, as if it's been surgically removed from my brain. "Nothing," I admit. "What happened when he tried to put you under?"

"Nothing," Liam echoes. He casts the match into the wastebasket, jumping a little as the paper catches fire. He gestures for me to toss the rest of Brunhilde in. I'm hesitant to damage what amounts to evidence but comply. The porcelain pieces hit the bottom with a ping. "A different kind of nothing, though. I could hear him just fine, and I knew what he wanted me to do, but I didn't feel like doing it."

That's hypnosis in a nutshell, really. You hear the command, you understand the command, and—if you're like most people—you comply with the command. Not because you *have* to, but because of how good it feels to relax and put someone else in the driver's seat for a change. You become a vessel, a vassal. All responsibility for your own decisions disappears in a flash. The thing that's important to remember, however, is that there's always an element of choice. No one can be forced to do anything against their will. They can be strongly convinced, that's all. And Liam, who is much more stubborn than he looks, is difficult to convince of anything.

So are you, Winnie points out.

"I know," I tell her. "That's what worries me."

Not unsurprisingly, Liam assumes I'm talking to him. "Did you want me to go along with him and pretend to be hypnotized?" he asks, his brow raised. "I can, if you think it would help."

I shake my head. Considering the lengths Armand went to in an attempt to spin my brother into a drunken confessional, I'd rather limit their time together in the future. Liam was able to hold out today, but only because of Nicholas's timely intervention.

"She's charring quite nicely," I say as I peek inside the wastebasket. Porcelain has to get to like three thousand degrees before it melts, so I doubt the damage will be lasting, but the strands of her hair and scraps of her dress are toast. "Are you really going to have dinner with Nicholas tonight?"

"Of course." Satisfied that Brunhilde will no longer torment his waking hours, Liam gives a sleepy yawn. "It's not every day a rich, handsome doctor offers to buy me a steak. I might go all in and add a lobster tail or two."

I roll my eyes. He probably will, too. "I'll warn Nicholas to sell a few priceless heirlooms so he can afford you. I don't suppose he found a discreet way to tell you what room I can find him in?"

Liam yawns again, this time adding a rub of his eyes. He throws himself onto the nearest bed—mine, and my cats are none too pleased about it—before stretching himself out. "No. But he did mention that he spent seven years in medical school and ten months in residency and then stepped on my foot really hard, so that might have been a clue."

I laugh. That was a clue, all right. Trust Nicholas to take my game of espionage and boost it to the next level.

Leaning down, I press a kiss on my brother's forehead. He's warm from the sun, and there's a tinge of pink that I fear is going to turn into out-and-out sunburn later, but he's already gently snoring. With any luck, he'll sleep until his dinner date.

I, unfortunately, have a lot more work to do.

After leaving a pot of aloe and lavender next to the bed and dousing the smoldering wreckage of Brunhilde's sacrifice with a glass of water, I lose no time in making my way out the door.

And head directly to room 710.

As delighted as I am to see Nicholas again—and as a blond, no less—his embrace isn't the first thing I run toward when he opens the door to let me in.

"What's that doing in here?" I demand. A familiar blue case sits against the back wall. "How did you get your hands on—?"

"I'm almost done in here," a female voice interrupts. I stop myself short as a slight, red-haired woman comes bustling out of the bathroom. Her black-and-white uniform and gloved hands—not to mention the spray bottle she carries—denote her one of the cleaning staff. "I apologize again for the delay. You should be all good to go now."

"No worries," Nicholas says easily. "It was my fault for surprising you by coming back so soon."

He extracts a bill from his pocket and hands it to the woman.

Her start of surprise indicates that it's a much bigger bill than she was expecting, so I lose no time in using Nicholas's generosity for my own ends.

"Leave the vacuum cleaner," I command. Upon seeing her jump, I add a belated "please."

Nicholas sighs and takes out another bill. "Whatever the lady wants."

The cleaning woman clearly thinks I'm about to do unfathomable things with that vacuum, but I let it pass. I wait only until the door closes behind her before pouncing on the case.

"Delightful to see you, too, my love," Nicholas murmurs.

"Shh," I command as I unlatch the top. "I'm looking for clues."

The vacuum cleaner is, alas, just that. There are hoses and mechanisms and disgusting clogs of hair, but nothing that might indicate why a man would be pushed off the side of a boat. "I'm starting to think my vision was wrong," I say, disappointed. The police have already gone through every blue case inside this hotel and found nothing. I glance up at Nicholas. "This is just a stupid vacuum."

"A thing I could have confirmed for free, seeing as how she used it to clean the carpets not ten minutes ago."

I sigh and accept the hand he holds out to me. It's a trap, and he uses the leverage to pull me into his embrace, which is all strong arms and the briny scent of the sea. I remain ensconced by both for a good five minutes before I'm allowed a breath of air.

If you ask me, air is overrated.

"And here I thought you were chasing after my brother," I murmur as soon as my mouth is freed long enough to form the words. My head rests against his chest, and I note that his heartbeat thrums faster than usual, its cadence matching my own. "Don't be cruel to him, Piers. He's a lot more vulnerable than he looks."

"I'm glad to find that such a sentiment flows *somewhere* in the Wilde veins," he responds. He plants a kiss on the top of my forehead, his lips soft and pliable from their recent workout. "In my defense, I didn't have any other choice. Unless you want me to remain a stranger for the duration of this trip, I needed to find a way in. It came down to either seducing Liam or my mother. Forgive me for choosing the former. I caught a glimpse of dear Mama in a caftan and turban on my way in. There's no way I'm touching that."

I laugh so hard that he's forced to loosen his grip on me.

"By the by, who and what was that man getting your brother drunk on the beach?" he asks.

The laughter dies in my throat. To admit the exact nature of my relationship with Armand will mean admitting the exact nature of my past misdeeds. Nicholas is an understanding man, but even understanding men have their limits.

I can't let this be the thing that ends us. I won't.

"He's the reason you had to come here incognito." I toy with the cuff of his shirtsleeve. I glance up at his face only to look quickly away again. He's watching me with the intensity of the sun. "He's, ah. Well. Um."

The touch of Nicholas's finger under my chin is gentle but compelling. This time, when I look at him, I force myself to swallow and hold fast.

"He and I used to cleanse houses together." My throat feels dry, my tongue twice its normal size, but I manage to get the words out. "I didn't agree with some of his tactics, so we ended things . . . badly. But now he's back, and he's convinced that I'm only dating you as a way to take advantage of you and your mother. He came here in an attempt to get in on my extortion scheme."

Not by so much as a flutter of an eyelash does Nicholas betray any emotion whatsoever. "And what did you tell him?"

I shrug, but only because I need to do *something*. I've never felt less blasé in my life. "At first, I maintained my innocence. When that didn't work, I let him go ahead and think whatever he wants." When Nicholas's brows come down, I rush to add, "If you're worried about your mother, don't be. I already warned her that he's not what he appears, and she seems content to toy with him. She even recruited an old friend of hers to help."

"She would."

"There's just one eensy-weensy problem."

"Why am I not surprised?"

Mostly because he's an intelligent man who has never, for one instant, believed any of my fake mysticism. The *real* stuff he accepts with complaisance, but attempting to lie to him has never—and will never—work.

"Armand is a hypnotist by trade," I admit. "I don't know how much you know about the events at this hotel over the past few days, but everything that's happened carries a decidedly hypnotic flair. I don't think he's behind the murder or the thefts—he's been with one of us every time they've occurred—but there's a chance that Inspector Piper will latch on to him as a suspect and start investigating his past. And once that happens . . ."

At the mention of Inspector Piper, Nicholas lifts a brow. "Inspector Piper?" he echoes. "Oh, dear. I think perhaps you should start this tale at the beginning."

I'm more than happy to comply. The murder that Liam and I witnessed, the shadow men responsible for it, my vision of the vacuum cleaner cases, even Brunhilde—none of these things seem to surprise him. He remains stalwart and unblinking the whole time. The fact that the entire investigation is being run by Gillian Piper, however, causes consternation to settle over the heavily lined features of his face.

"What is it?" I ask, reaching out to take his hand. "What do you know?"

He shakes his head. "Nothing, really. But Gillian Piper isn't a woman to toy with."

A thing I've been aware of since the moment she introduced herself. "You know her?" I ask eagerly. "You've met her?"

"Not officially, no. But I know *of* her."

"And?" I prod.

I can't identify why I'm so excited at the prospect of Gillian Piper being a woman who inspires awe, but I am. I *should* be afraid of her—and in some respects, I am—but I mostly want her to consider me an ally worth having.

Nicholas must sense some of this, because he takes both of my hands and squeezes them. "There's a reason she left Peter the way she did, moving away to take a job in a bigger city, never quite feeling settled in our little village."

I can understand this perfectly. Whereas I embrace everything about the place we call home—how small it is, how connected the people are—it's hardly the launching point for a noteworthy career. "She wanted more," I suggest.

He nods. "She's an ambitious woman, Eleanor, and a smart one. Precisely how many laws did you and this Armand break in your time together?"

I can't help but laugh. "We didn't break them—we just bent them a little," I promise. "And if we did occasionally step over a line, it was hardly enough to warrant extradition. I'm sure I'll be fine."

He doesn't appear convinced of this, but it's hardly my most pressing concern right now. "I should warn you that Armand can be a very persuasive man when he puts his mind to it. No matter what he says or what he implies, you know that I would never do anything to hurt you or your family, right? And that it's never once crossed my mind to try?"

Nicholas's response to this is a kiss. It's a deep kiss and a long one, but it's not a real answer.

I believe you, that kiss says. *I believe* in *you.*

Unfortunately, if there's one thing I know in this world, it's that belief—like faith and hope and joy—are what people like Armand exploit every chance they get. Sometimes for fun. Sometimes for revenge.

And sometimes for two million dollars.

Chapter 15

The next time I see the ghost maid, it's in the company of Gillian and Bertram.

We're standing on the beach in the exact spot where Liam and I witnessed Leonard's drowning, the three of us working together to verify a set of facts that I've already sworn, five times over, to be true.

"I can get a doctor to confirm that my vision is perfect," I say, pointing out over the open waters of the English Channel. "There wasn't much of a moon, so there weren't any reflections off the water, and shadows would have been an impossibility."

Gillian falls into a crouch and squints out at the waves. As the sun hasn't yet set and there are several bobbing bodies as guests venture out for a spot of sea bathing, I don't know what she expects to happen. The shadows are hardly going to pop out and do a dance right here and now.

"There could have been a second boat farther out than the first one," I say, offering the only reasonable explanation that's occurred to me. "Out of the line of sight, I mean. Either that, or the two murderers scuba dived out, and—"

Pluralitas non est ponenda sine necessitate, Birdie says.

I flap my hand to wave her off, but it's no use.

That's Occam's razor, in case you were wondering.

"Yes, thank you," I say, but so low that my murmuring might be taken for the crashing of the waves.

In original Latin.

I glance quickly at Gillian and Bertram, but it's too late. They've heard me and are now intensely interested in what's happening inside my head. "That's not really helping, Birdie, but I'll take it under consideration."

I know Latin now. Isn't that fun?

I sigh and turn to face the two logical, skeptical officials whose respect I'm currently trying to court. Honestly, I don't know why I even bother.

"That was my spirit guide," I say, giving up with a shrug. "She's on your side. She pointed out that the simplest explanation is usually the correct one."

Bertram clears his throat in embarrassment and looks away. "I wasn't going to say anything."

"If it helps, I do have a second spirit guide, and she thinks there's something off about all this, especially since people keep getting robbed by the same two shadow men." This coincidence is, I assume, the entire reason we're out here in the first place. If it weren't for those robberies, I'd have been written off as a fraud days ago. "Who was the first robbery victim, by the way? Bertram said he was famous."

Bertram clears his throat again. "Not famous. Just . . . notorious."

"Notorious for what?"

I don't get an answer. Instead, Bertram jolts as though struck by a bolt of Armand's lightning, his eyes fixed on something in the distance. As I'm already tense and on edge, it only takes me a second to follow the line of his sight to see what startled him.

From where we stand, the higher floors of the hotel are fully visible. It's the only multistoried building for some distance, its windows overlooking the ocean to provide the best—and most expensive—views. On the upper levels, outdoor terraces offer even more incentive to spend money. Most of them are empty or boast fluttering towels left out to dry, but one contains a tall, dark figure staring out over the sea.

I jolt just as much as Bertram, even going so far as to reach out and grip his arm—though whether it's for his comfort or mine, I can't say. The figure looks as if she stepped out of the pages of a Victorian novel. Her long, dark dress flaps in the wind, and she scans the horizon as if seeking something out. To both my and Bertram's shock, she stops as soon as her gaze alights on us, her hand lifting as if in greeting.

"It's her." Since this isn't my first encounter with the ghost maid, I'm the first to lose my shock. I lose no time in hightailing it toward the hotel. "She's back."

Whether because of the unsteadiness of my nerves or because running on sand is really hard, both Gillian and Bertram outstrip me long before we make it to the walkway leading up to the hotel.

"Eighth floor," I pant as they whiz by. "Ten rooms from the right. Catch her. She knows something—I saw her yesterday during the fire alarm."

Gillian pauses long enough to cast a suspicious look over her shoulder at me before picking up the pace. Once again, I'm left to marvel at her physical prowess, at how easy she makes it look to dodge bystanders and dawdling families, and even take a flying leap over a ledge of potted plants that block the entry to the hotel.

"I think I might love her," I say as I take the long way around the plants. "Peter was a fool to let that woman go."

In my heart of hearts, I know there's no way the ghost maid will still be there by the time any of us make it to the eighth floor, but I push through the pain and dart up the stairs as quickly as I can. The growing stitch in my side and heaving of my breath aren't without their rewards—as soon as I step out onto the floor, it's to discover Bertram and Gillian in fierce conference.

"Of course I don't trust her," Gillian hisses. Assuming that the *her* in question is me rather than the ghost maid, I slip toward the nearest room and hold myself flat against the door. "She's a con woman, Bertram. She makes a living out of lying to people."

My chest gives a small heave at my hero thus reducing me, but I hold myself still. Rome wasn't built in a day, after all. It might take a few more than that to convince Gillian Piper that I mean her no harm.

"Just keep getting on her good side, accept whatever help she offers. Either she'll slip up and tell us something about what she's hiding, or one of those visions of hers will turn out to be correct."

My heart swells a little at that last bit. She must have *some* faith in my abilities if she's open to the possibility of my accuracy.

But then she laughs. It's a low sound, warmer and more infectious than I'd have guessed, but I can't enjoy it. I've been nothing but honest with her, a friend to her investigation from the start, but none of that matters. When she looks at me, she sees all the things I used to be: devious and sneaky and unreliable. She doesn't see any of the things I've become.

"And the paperwork?" Bertram asks.

Gillian releases a sound somewhere between a cough and a grunt. "Keep it back-burnered for now. Until she gives us something concrete, there's no reason to mention her to the powers that be. If things don't work out, it's not going to look good to have her on either of our records."

That hurts even more than the rest. Being infamous isn't my favorite thing, but it's better than being invisible.

I slip back to the stairwell door and make a big show of dashing through the door. Since my heartbeat is erratic and my chest is tight with emotion, I appear convincingly winded. "Did you catch her?" I ask, drawing forward. "Is the ghost maid still here?"

Gillian, who does an admirable job of looking innocent of having denigrated and demeaned me to her coworker, tilts her head at the closed door. "No one answered our knock. We were waiting for you before we go in."

"Oh." I pause. "That was nice of you."

"There's nothing nice about it." Gillian extracts what must be some sort of master key card from her pocket. "You're the one who claims to know this maid. You can be the one to question her."

It's on the tip of my tongue to point out that it's not a *regular* maid I'm hoping to catch inside that room so much as a *ghost* one. Bertram, however, catches my eye and gives a discreet shake of his head. I obligingly clamp my lips shut. He works with this woman more closely than I do. If he thinks I'm better off maintaining my silence, I believe him.

The door clicks open. Gillian pokes her head in and announces our presence, but there's no reply—human or ghost. Stepping into the room, she casts a triumphant look around. "Well, Ms. Wilde?" she prompts.

The room is, alas, empty. From the impersonal cleanliness of it, it doesn't even appear to have a current resident. We look under the bed and inside the bathtub and even on top of the closet shelves, but there's nothing to indicate that anyone was recently skulking around in here.

Until, that is, we reach the terrace. I'm half afraid of finding a woman clinging to the wall or trying to make a daring escape to the room below, but when I step outside, it's to find a different kind of terror.

There, sitting in the middle of the patch of cement, is Brunhilde. Her dress is bloodied, her hair is burnt off, and the cracked pieces of her face are glued together to reveal a gap where her mouth used to be, but there's no mistaking the evidence.

She's back. And if the screaming void of her nonexistent lips is any indication, she's none too pleased about it.

Chapter 16

The good news is that Brunhilde is no longer going to present a problem. Gillian took one look at the doll sitting in the exact location where Bertram and I saw the ghost maid and immediately catalogued her as evidence. The doll might be able to drag herself from the depths of the ocean, and my cat might be able to fish her out of a garbage chute, but I defy anyone to get past official evidence lockup.

Nothing purges a demon quicker than bureaucracy.

The bad news, unfortunately, is that I'm no nearer to an answer now than I was before. Someone took that doll from our room, pieced it back together, and put it on the terrace for me to find—I'm sure of it. We were lured upstairs from the beach for the sole purpose of discovering it. Why it was there and what it's supposed to mean, however, are entirely beyond my comprehension.

I'd love nothing more than to discuss this recent turn of events with Nicholas and Liam, but they're currently dining under the low lights of the lobby restaurant, the pair of them laughing it up over the bread basket. I'm much more nervous about this than I'd like to admit. Liam knows too much about my childhood foibles to make their conversation as innocent as it seems.

"I don't want to tell you how to go about your business, but casting jealous glances at your brother every two minutes isn't helping you maintain your cover." Vivian, who has yet to look at her son even once, delicately lays a napkin over her lap. She's dressed for dinner in a rucksack of a dress covered in every piece of jewelry she owns. Diamonds layered over sapphires shouldn't count as a fashion choice, but she's making it work.

Probably because of the brand new tiara glittering on top of her head.

"Neither is trying to lure Armand into clubbing you over the head in a dark alley," I return. I point my fork at her new acquisition. "How much did that set you back?"

"Didn't anyone tell you it's not polite to ask prying questions?" She grins and touches the center of the tiara, where a diamond the size of a walnut glistens. "It didn't cost me a penny. Apparently, the owner of the store and Marian go way back. He's letting me wear it as a loaner."

"Vivian!" My fork clatters to the table, Liam and Nicholas all but forgotten. "Have you lost your mind? You can't go around wearing tens of thousands of dollars that aren't yours. It's only a matter of time before Armand finds a way to get his hands on it, and then what will happen?"

Her smile doesn't falter. "I imagine your good Inspector Piper will hunt him down, and everyone will go about their business as usual."

I swallow my groan. "In case you haven't noticed, *my* Inspector Piper has yet to solve anything worth note. Don't put all your eggs in her basket. I thought she was supposed to be some kind of detective wizard."

"She's likely thinking the same thing of you."

Recalling the conversation I overheard between Gillian and

Bertram, I can't help but agree. I'm not sure what Peter told his ex-wife about me, but if she's expecting miracles to fly from my fingertips, she's going to be waiting a long time. My methods are similar to hers: I watch and listen and look at the facts.

Fact: A man in this hotel is dead, and no one—neither friend nor family nor foe—seems to care in the slightest.

Fact: He had three vacuum cleaner cases in his possession, all of which match this hotel's brand of vacuum cleaner and are currently missing.

Fact: He was killed by two shadow figures who have since been moonlighting as thieves breaking into safes while the unsuspecting victims nap.

Fact: A ghost maid—who is *much* more human than shadow—is also running about, leaving behind creepy dolls for me to find.

And therein lies the problem. As disparate facts, they stand on their own feet. As a collection of facts that lead to a plausible solution, they're pretty much useless.

"I'm not entirely sure why you found it necessary to beg Nicholas to come to our rescue," Vivian says as we continue to listen in on the chortles of laughter coming from my brother's table. "Hello? Eleanor? Are you listening to me?"

"I'm sorry." I force my attention back to my dinner companion. "I'm listening. And I didn't beg him. He offered. He was worried about you."

"About me?" Her laugh carries through the dining room. "Whatever for? I'm having a grand time."

She is, too. I've never seen her like this before—engaged and sparkling and happy. I don't know if it's her old school friend that's the cause, or if it's thanks to the heart attack she's trying to give me with all that jewelry on display, but she's like a child at a birthday party.

"I think my favorite part so far is when you threw things around Armand's hotel room with your mind," she adds as calmly as though she's discussing the dessert menu. "You ought to do that more often. The villagers back home would adore it."

To be honest, I think they'd be more likely to run screaming in the opposite direction, but perhaps that's just me. "Do you still have the recording?" I ask. "It's not that I don't believe you about the mind-throwing, but I'd like to hear it for myself."

"Of course." She digs in her purse until she extracts her phone. Placing it squarely on the table, she begins playing the recording. At full volume. "Just wait. It doesn't get good until about halfway through."

I'd much rather listen to this in the privacy of my own room, but Vivian refuses to hear reason. Like the borrowed tiara she's wearing on full display, she intends to make a show of it. I sit back in my chair, resigned to the stares and outrage of my fellow patrons, and wait.

At first, there's nothing extraordinary about the sounds coming from the phone. Armand sets up the scene, we have our little discussion about Liam being unhypnotizable, and I grumblingly accept my fate. There's a slight susurration in the background that I can't quite place, but it could be one of several things. The ocean in the background, the air conditioner that Armand had been careful to turn on, even the microphone function on Vivian's phone could be responsible.

I close my eyes and try to remember the exact conditions of the room. Yes, the air conditioner had definitely been on. Vivian was sitting to my right, Marian to my left, and Armand at my feet. Everyone was careful not to touch me or breathe too loudly, all concentration on the quiet of my own mind, and then . . .

When I wake up this time, it's not to find myself plunged into the end of the world. Instead, I'm standing in the revolving doors to the hotel, my nose pressed against the glass so hard that I leave a smudge of makeup and skin cell residue behind.

"Oh, dear." I'm not nearly as surprised as I should be to find myself in a new location and making a fool of myself. Stepping back from the glass, I survey my surroundings to find that I've been followed by Vivian, Nicholas, Liam, and a few bystanders who must have sensed that something exciting was about to happen. I only hope they're not disappointed by the show—or lack thereof. "How long have I been here?"

Of the assembled crowd, only Nicholas looks unduly worried by my actions. His brow is lowered but he's careful to hold himself back, his concern for that of a stranger rather than the woman he's dating.

"About five minutes." Uli, always alert and in attendance, nudges the revolving door. The sound of it brushing against the floor pushes me along until I pop out next to him. "You were going around in circles. I tried to stop you, but that doctor over there said it was better to let you keep going."

Nicholas clears his throat and forces the worried pucker from his brow. "It's important not to disrupt the brain activity of someone in a sleep state," he says, making a good show of sounding like someone who knows what they're talking about. "The natural rhythms of the REM cycle are key to good mental health."

I don't know about how REM affects my brain, but I'm starting to have a serious problem with what hypnosis is doing to me. Whatever trick Armand pulled on that recording is powerful enough to plunge me under even when he's not in the room.

"Did I say anything?" I ask, scanning the faces I know. "Throw anything? Scream?"

I hold my breath, half afraid of the answer, but all I get is a row of shaking heads. "You got up from the table and started walking toward the door," Liam says. "We thought you were going to the beach, but you just kept moving around and around in circles. You really don't remember?"

I really don't. I also don't feel anything coming from Winnie or Birdie, even though I strain every psychic nerve I have to reach them.

A hand grips me by the elbow, pulling me back into the moment. From the tender and familiar way those fingers press into my skin, I'm sure it's Nicholas. However, when I glance over, it's to find Uli smiling gently down on me.

"Let's get you somewhere you can be more comfortable, Ms. Wilde," he says. I recognize his most correct doorman voice—the same one he used with the couples pressing fifty-pound notes into his hands. "And a glass of water. Unless you'd prefer something stronger?"

"Water is fine, thanks," I manage. I also allow him to lead me over to a couch, which goes to show how shaken up and disoriented I am. "And if you could, ah, disperse the crowd a little, that would be great."

Something about the way he hesitates and refuses to let go of my arm until I'm fully settled in my seat has me on alert. I put my hand over his.

"What is it?" I ask in a tone low enough that only he can hear. "What do you know?"

He shakes his head until a lock of his pristinely oiled hair falls across his forehead. "Nothing—it's nothing. You were mumbling under your breath as you went through the doors, that's all."

"What did I say?"

His gaze catches mine and holds it. "Ask Inspector Piper."

Ask Inspector Piper what? I think, but there's no opportunity to voice the question aloud. The rest of my entourage is crowding around the couch with my glass of water, the stiff drink I turned down, and, in the case of Nicholas, a red-colored note to press into Uli's hand. At least now I don't have to feel guilty whenever I ask for extra favors. That should tide Uli over for a few days.

"I think we should play it one more time." Vivian holds up her phone, her finger hovering over the play button. I'm about to jump to my feet and physically wrest it from her hands, but Liam beats me to it. "What? We can tie her to the chair and put a gag over her mouth this time. Aren't you a little curious what will happen?"

"Not curious enough," Liam says. He looks as though he plans to smash the phone to pieces and thus prevent any more hypnotic wanderings, but he only holds it out of Vivian's reach. "Who knows what would happen if we weren't around to keep watch over her?"

I can't help a shudder from moving up and down my spine. I don't know the answer to that question any more than Liam does, but there's no denying that the recording is the least of our worries. As long as Armand walks and breathes, there's always a possibility that he can hypnotize me whenever he feels the urge.

"If my services are no longer required here, I think I'll return to my dinner," Nicholas says, bowing slightly. "Liam?"

Liam is unused to Nicholas's calm exterior in the face of danger, and is therefore understandably set aback by this question. "Oh, um. What? Dinner? *Now?*"

"My mistake. Naturally, you'll wish to be with your sister at this time." He takes Liam's hand between two of his own in what could be viewed as a gesture of affection but is actually a ploy to get his mother's phone into his own possession. I have to fight a smile at how neatly he does it, unseen by any eyes but my own. He turns his bow on me. "Miss, if you find that you experience any dizziness, nausea, or a headache, feel free to call on my services. Your brother knows where to find me."

And with that, he returns to his meal as though my wanderings mean nothing, Vivian's phone securely in his pocket. Liam watches him go for a moment before shaking himself and returning to the task at hand: *me.*

"You're going to be the death of me, you know that?" he says as he takes my hand and yanks me to my feet. Considering how tenderly Uli handled me, I find this disregard for my well-being rather rude, but my physical state appears to be unimpaired. "You're like a child who wanders off if left unattended for longer than five minutes. And you." He turns to Vivian, his hand still clasping mine. "What were you thinking, playing her that recording?"

Vivian studies the jagged edges of her fingernails. "How was I supposed to know a person could be hypnotized by a recording? If you ask me, she's making it all up. Not happy with setting off a fire alarm, she also had to go and—"

"The fire alarm?" Uli turns a sharp eye on me. "So that *was* you?"

I mentally curse Vivian for letting our secrets slip in front of a man I'm still not sure I trust and do my best to make a recovery. "It was an accident, I swear," I say. "I slipped and hit the emergency alarm with my elbow. I've already been issued a citation from Inspector Piper, so there's no need to make me feel worse. It's costing me a small fortune."

I'm not sure how much of my lie he believes, but he lets us go without further questioning. I have to elbow Vivian to keep her from continuing her commentary while he's in earshot, but that only has the effect of making her flounce away to finish her meal. I'm left alone with Liam, who's looking more and more concerned the longer we remain.

"Don't say it," I warn him, and not just because we're standing in a public place. The last thing I need right now is a lecture from Liam in full older brother mode. "I had no idea that would happen."

"I know," he says. His brow puckers, his dark eyes flashing with concern. "That's what worries me. The longer we stay here, the more it seems you don't know."

Chapter 17

Under the pretense of dizziness, nausea, and a headache—none of which I'm currently experiencing—Nicholas visits our room around eight o'clock. He carries a medical bag for authenticity and wears the resigned look of a medical practitioner forced to work on his holiday, but he drops both those things the moment the door closes behind him.

"I just spent the past two hours listening to the recording on repeat," he says. The bag falls open to reveal that it's filled with nothing but the crinkled pages of yesterday's newspaper. "Why the *devil* didn't anyone tell me how bad it was?"

I make a move to go to him, my arms outstretched and my sweetest smile in place, but he holds me back with one upheld hand. With a start, I realize he's angry. At *me*.

"Liam wasn't in the room at the time, and I—if you'll recall—was somewhat indisposed while it was going on. If you're upset, you should take it up with your mother."

"I intend to," he says through his teeth.

Since my embrace is obviously not going to do much good right now, I scoop Freddie up from the bed and hold her out.

Without realizing what he's doing, Nicholas accepts the bundle and holds her to his chest.

It's ridiculous—and difficult—to be angry while running a finger up and down the spine of a gently purring cat, so he sighs and lowers himself to the end of my bed. "I've never heard anything like it before," he says, more composed now. "That scream, Eleanor. It wasn't human."

I cast a nervous glance at my brother, afraid of how Liam will take this, but he looks more interested than alarmed. "I haven't had a chance to listen to it yet," he admits. "She screams and then the furniture starts flying, right? Or is it the other way around?"

I fail to see what difference it makes—and am about to point out as much—but Nicholas hands Liam the phone. "Take it into the bathroom and use headphones," he says. "And don't say I didn't warn you."

Liam handles the phone the same way he did Brunhilde—which is to say with extreme caution. "Don't be such a wimp, Liam," I say. "It's just a recording. It can't hurt you."

"No," he agrees. "But it can hurt you."

Nicholas and I sit in silence as Liam grabs his headphones and sequesters himself in the bathroom. Even with Freddie in his lap, Nicholas holds himself tense until enough time passes that he accepts I'm not going to go off into a trance by proximity.

"I was never in any real danger," I say. "It's strange, yes, and I don't fully understand what's going on, but—"

"I want to talk to that man."

I blink at Nicholas. That particular tone—of anger and hatred, of actual violence—is one I've never heard from him before. "To Armand?"

"Yes. Where is he?"

"I don't know," I admit. Even if I *did* know, I doubt I'd tell Nicholas right now. He looks as though he'd like to snap Armand in half using his bare hands. It's a sentiment I've shared myself, but only because the idea of my causing physical harm is laughable. Strength isn't my strong point, if you'll pardon the pun. "But it should be easy enough to rouse him. He's never far from this hotel—or your mother."

"Then make it happen. Find a way for us to meet. Tonight."

"Are you sure that's a good idea?" I make the mistake of reaching out to touch his forearm. It's the same arm I've touched countless times in the past, strong and supportive and always there for me to lean on, but there's so much rigid tension in it that I almost recoil. I don't, though. I wrap my fingers around his muscles and hold my hand there until he looks at me. "He wouldn't hurt me. Not like this. Not when it could so easily be traced back to him."

If the firm set of Nicholas's jaw is anything to go by, he doesn't believe me. "It'll have to be somewhere with a lot of ambient noise," he says as though I haven't spoken. "That way he can't hypnotize you without your consent. And somewhere we can all be without drawing attention to it."

Both of these things sound eminently sensible and not at all like what we should be talking about right now.

"He's greedy, yes, but not a monster. I'm not in any real danger."

I might as well not have spoken for all the attention Nicholas pays me. He drops his hand on mine and holds it there. "Promise me you won't be alone in a room with him, Ellie."

It goes against the pluck with me to give in when Nicholas is being his most autocratic—and not just because my kneejerk reaction to anyone giving me orders is to blithely and unapologetically do the opposite. As much as I wish I could give him what he's asking for, I can't. Armand is too much tied up in all this, too much a part of my past. I can't just dismiss him and hope he goes away.

I tried that once already. If there's one thing I'm coming to learn in all this, it's that the past will always find a way to catch up.

"I think we should hit the clubs," I say with a decisive nod. I pull my hand out from under Nicholas's. "That'll give you a sound cover and an excuse to be out with me and Liam. If we make sure your mother goes to bed early, Armand will be sure to tag along. He won't want to waste an entire evening sitting around the hotel, twiddling his thumbs."

"Did you hear one word of what I just said?"

"Yes. I heard several of them. You want ambient noise and a chance to meet with Armand face to face. Behold." I give an airy wave of my hand. "I deliver."

Nicholas doesn't go so far as to crack a smile, but he does relax slightly. It helps that Beast, sensing his distress, plants herself at his feet. They're shameless, my cats, but they know how to get results.

"I haven't gone to a club since I was in university," he says. "And to be perfectly honest, I didn't much enjoy them then."

"No kidding? You?" I force a light laugh. "You forget that I've danced with you before. You're not half bad when you put your mind to it."

I think he's going to reply in kind—offer a playful rebuttal of his moves or even show me a few of them right then and there—but he shakes his head. "I don't like what that man did to you," he says.

My throat suddenly feels tight. It would be easy to pretend he's only talking about the hypnosis and the unearthly scream, the way Armand entered my mind and planted something strange inside, but he and I both know that's only half of the story.

If we take my wayward youth into account, Armand had a lot more influence on me than that. As much as I'd like to pretend that he was an evil influence, and that I was an unwilling participant in his many different games, the truth is that I'm just as responsible—and just as culpable—as him.

And Nicholas, who has the uncanny ability to see all, knows it.

* * *

Nicholas Hartford III might not be much of a one for clubbing, but Piers Pierson has the lifestyle on lockdown.

"Save me," Liam gasps as he joins me at the bar. I'm nursing a cranberry vodka in hopes that it lends me an air of authenticity, but there's no denying that I'm hardly the target audience for a place like this. My skirt is too long and my makeup too gothic, and the repeated thumps of the music are starting to make my head pound. "I don't know how Piers can dance like that and not sweat. I might die if he keeps this up."

That makes two of us. Piers Pierson, who's wearing a tight T-shirt under a blazer as well as artfully weathered jeans, appears indefatigable. And, I need hardly add, gorgeous. His usual cashmere sweaters and well-cut suits have nothing on this new look of his. I can't believe he's been holding back on me all this time.

"Too bad," I say as I push a glass of water toward my brother. "You have to make it look as though you're enjoying yourself. Armand just walked through the door."

As I anticipated, it didn't take Armand long to get wind of our activities and rig himself out for a night on the town. And by *rig himself out*, I mean he looks a lot like me—as if he just stepped off the pages of *Emo Teen Monthly*.

"Thank goodness." Liam gulps the entire glass of water. He wipes his mouth with the back of his hand. "This is where I'm supposed to enact part two."

"There's a part two? Actually—scratch that. There was a part one?"

He holds up three fingers and ticks them off in succession. "Part one, party. Part two, snag a private table at the back. Part three, let your dear boyfriend loose on the enemy."

That plan sounds a lot more ominous than Liam realizes. "Liam, please make sure that Nicholas doesn't—"

There's no chance for me to issue my warning. Armand

catches sight of us and makes a beeline for the bar. Liam, who is turning out to be as phenomenal at acting as Nicholas, takes one look at him and falls drunkenly on his neck.

"Armand!" he cries as though he just guzzled vodka instead of water. "Good to see you, mate. Come dance with me and Piers. The party's just getting started."

From the looks of it, Armand would much rather sit next to me for a private chat, but Liam is nothing if not persistent. "You look like a man who knows his way around a dance floor," he says, dragging Armand away by the arm. "Show us what you've got."

Whether because Armand is trying to save face, or because he knows that any attempt to hypnotize me in this booming, blaring environment will be useless, he gives in. I waggle my fingers as I watch them go, torn between gratitude that I don't have to join them and annoyance at being left out.

"I'll have what she's having." A woman smelling of citrus and cigarette smoke sidles up next to me. It takes me a moment to place her. She's not wearing the crisp white shirt and black skirt of her hotel uniform, but those burgundy-painted lips and long waves of dark hair couldn't belong to anyone else. "I hope you don't mind if I join you. I was supposed to meet a friend, but she's not here yet. I hate being at clubs alone."

"Laurel, right?" I ask. I don't know the front desk clerk's last name, but I do remember that she was the one who upgraded our room. For that, she'll always have a place in my heart. "From the hotel?"

She nods, pleased to have been recognized. Although the low lights of the club are meant to make everyone look younger—and all the surfaces cleaner—I note the same lines around her mouth from before. I thought they denoted age, but her cigarette scent makes me think they might have a more direct cause. I double down on this theory when I recall the burgundy-lipped cigarettes from outside the hotel.

"I know." As if reading my mind, she grimaces. "It's a nasty habit, but I can't seem to shake it. I've been trying to quit for years."

"Green tea has been proven to help," I say, offering the same advice I once gave Inspector Piper of the Peter variety. "Chewing licorice sticks or taking skullcap can also do the trick."

She grimaces. "Thanks but no thanks. I'll stick to good old-fashioned vodka when I need a distraction."

As if to prove it, she lifts her drink in a mock toast and kicks it back. The burn of the alcohol doesn't faze her in the slightest.

"Rough day at work?" I ask.

"Something like that."

"Belligerent guests, or just the general mayhem of working in a place that's haunted?"

As I hope, she checks at that second bit. "Who told you the hotel is haunted?"

The truth—an aging society damsel who shares Vivian's love of all things eccentric—doesn't have the same ring as visions from beyond the grave, but I'm oddly loath to lie to this woman. She's been nothing but helpful.

"Oh, right." She taps her temple before I have a chance to say anything. "I forgot. You're a paranormal investigator. You must have known the moment you walked through the door."

There's no choice now but to accept my fate. I had been angling my body toward the dance floor so I could keep an eye on my unlikely trio out there, but I turn so that I'm fully facing Laurel instead. As long as this opportunity is presenting itself, I might as well take advantage of it—even if watching Nicholas dance circles around Liam and Armand is rapidly becoming my new favorite pastime.

"I've seen the ghost maid two times so far," I say.

Laurel nods as though this makes perfect sense. "Yeah, she comes and goes. She never hurts anyone—just sort of wanders the halls. They say she used to work at the hotel back when it first opened, and that she was murdered by a guest who walked away scot-free. Some rich toff with a penchant for violence. You know how it goes."

That rich people get away with murder? Yeah, I'm familiar with the tale. "You've seen her?" I ask.

She shrugs an uncomfortable shoulder. "Everyone sees her eventually."

"What about the cursed doll she leaves behind wherever she goes?"

Laurel's gaze meets mine with a direct, piercing quality I find unsettling. I'm not sure why, unless it's the surreal sensation of holding this conversation in an environment with so much going on. It's loud and hot and smells of too many bodies packed together in a confined space, undergirded with the sickly scent of sugary cocktails. Despite the swirling cacophony of sensations, Laurel's locked gaze holds me in place.

"I'm not the one you should be asking about that," she says. "I've only been working at the hotel a few weeks."

Uli, I think, but Laurel perks up and waves a hand before I can say his name out loud. Her friend, a tall woman wearing a silver shift dress that dazzles like a disco ball, has finally arrived.

And just like that, I'm forgotten. Laurel leaves me to dance the night away, Nicholas and Liam have enacted part two and disappeared to their private booth in the back, and even the bartender refuses to come back and refill my vodka cranberry. In other words, I'm alone and tired and a little bit sad.

Just like a cracked, broken doll left out for someone else to find.

Chapter 18

"I still don't understand how he knew I was going to pick a purple elephant." Liam enters our hotel room with the overloud, overbearing demeanor of a man who spent the better part of his evening somewhere he had to shout to be heard. "I know it's all fake, but *how*? I could have picked literally any combination of color and animal."

I sigh as Freddie shifts from my lap to greet the newcomers. I've been spending my own evening keeping her company. I came home early from the club to find that Beast pulled another disappearing act. Liam might be mystified by how Armand uses his powers, but I'm much more curious about my cat's movements. Unless the cleaning staff is ignoring the Do Not Disturb sign, I have no idea how she manages to slip in and out. Beast refuses to be contained by the laws of our physical world.

"He directed you to choose a purple elephant," I say. "That's the whole trick. If you'd have been paying attention, you'd have noticed that he was planting seeds the entire time he was with you. He probably asked for a bowl of peanuts from the waitress, right? And talked about his days as a circus performer? And then used a lot of alliteration about the peripatetic propensities of people from Portugal?"

I watch as Liam's brain works through everything I've just said. Nicholas must already have some idea, because he grins as Liam first displays incredulity, then realization, then outrage. Those are the usual three stages of being duped by a mentalist. Oh, how I know them well.

"Are you serious?" He looks back and forth between me and Nicholas. "He was playing me from the start?"

Nicholas lowers himself to the nearest chair, looking just as groomed and put-together as he had been back at the club. The only sign of exhaustion he exhibits is the way he leans his head on one hand. "I would have said a cerulean arthropod, but I suspect that's why he didn't ask me. Pity. It would have been entertaining to see him work his way out of that one."

Liam is crestfallen. "I had no idea I was so predictable. Ellie—why didn't you tell me? Am I really that basic?"

He is, but it would only hurt his feelings to say so. "Of course not," I soothe. "Armand is good at what he does, that's all. I warned you. He's a dangerous man for a variety of different reasons. What did you get out of him?"

"I don't know that we got anything." Nicholas runs his hand along his jawline, where another subtle sign of his exhaustion— his late-night stubble—is starting to show. "He managed to cadge a prescription for painkillers out of me, and I'm fairly certain he and Liam are promised to vacation in Aruba together next year, but he wasn't particularly forthcoming."

"Nicholas!" I cry. "You didn't actually write him out an illegal prescription at a nightclub?"

"I believe he was testing my backstory." He reaches into an interior pocket and extracts a pad of prescription paper that looks alarmingly realistic. "With any luck, the pharmacist won't be able to read the atrocious handwriting I used. I believe what I did is classified as a misdemeanor."

I take the pad of paper and study it, unsure whether I'm impressed or alarmed at Nicholas's foresight. I had no idea he was so resourceful.

"Don't ask where I got it," he says, smiling gently. "I wouldn't want to have to take you down with me."

I'm not fooled by that smile. Considering how determined he was to have this meeting with Armand—the emotion he barely managed to keep in check—there's no way he's letting this go so easily.

"What is it?" I ask. "What aren't you telling me?"

Liam kicks his shoes off and grunts. Lying back on his bed, he murmurs, "Don't mind me. I'm just going to rest my eyes."

I have no doubt that he'll be fast asleep in less than sixty seconds. Liam has always enjoyed the untroubled sleep of the innocent.

"Out with it, Nicholas," I say in a slightly lower tone. "What happened? What did he say to you?"

He shakes his head, his brow furrowed so that a line forms right down the center of his forehead. I long to reach out and touch it, to smooth that anxiety and annoyance away, but it wouldn't work. These things he's feeling—these things he's worrying about—can't be erased so easily. I know because I've been living with them for *years*.

"He didn't say much of anything to *me*," Nicholas admits. He glances at Liam and, noting the regular in-and-out movements of his chest, nods down at him. "But he was very interested in your brother."

"Of course he was. He's trying to pump him for information, remember? As a way to get to me and therefore to *you*."

"That wasn't it." The furrow down Nicholas's forehead deepens. "I don't think it's money he's after, Eleanor. Nothing about his actions signals greed."

Of course he's after money. He admitted as much to me that first day, threatening my livelihood for a chance at a few paltry millions. Money is the only thing Armand has *ever* wanted.

"Then what does he want?" I demand. My sudden increase

in volume causes Liam to stir but not to wake. More moderately this time, I add, "He has your mother and her friend walking around dripping in jewels. He's hanging around this hotel—which isn't cheap—and is following us all around like a puppy who's lost his bone. He all but begged me to let him in on my scheme to take you for all you're worth."

And none of that takes into account the fact that he hypnotized me into strange and uncanny actions. Armand is the most dangerous person I know, and that's counting the murderer currently on the loose.

"Has it ever occurred to you that he might want . . . you?"

"Your mother has already promised to pay ten thousand pounds for my release, should Armand take it into his head to kidnap me," I say. "So I think I'm safe."

Nicholas refuses to let himself be amused by this—or to increase his mother's offer, which I find highly insulting. I should be worth at least fifty thousand to him. "I don't mean he plans to lock you in his basement, Eleanor. I mean he *wants* you."

Only by clapping my hand over my mouth am I able to subdue my shout of laughter in time. Even then, I can't hide the grin that spreads across my face. That Armand Lamont would be the least bit romantically interested in me is preposterous in the extreme. Not only has there never been a spark of chemistry between us, but Armand is only happy when he knows himself to be the smartest person in the room. Since I *obviously* have him beat in that regard, there's no way he'd willingly place himself by my side for regular comparisons.

"I'm sorry, Nicholas. You're sweet—really, you are—but so very, very wrong. It's never been like that between us."

He doesn't answer my smile with one of his own. If anything, the furrow in his brow deepens. "You used to work together. Closely."

"Yes, but only because we were using each other. He needed my skills. I needed his experience. That was all."

"You dumped him without warning."

"I killed him off without warning," I correct him. "That's different. Have you ever fake murdered an ex-girlfriend? I think you'd find it hard to come back from that."

Even my attempt at levity doesn't work. "He came all the way to England to find you," Nicholas says, watching me. "And even though he's embroiled in a murder investigation, he refuses to leave. He's ingratiating himself with your family and friends using every means at his disposal. He's also influencing you with his powers in ways you can't explain."

Nicholas scrubs a weary hand over his face. He looks older than his years, and like he needs nothing so much as a good night's rest. "You're a beautiful, intelligent, fascinating woman in your prime, Eleanor. You have shared interests. You have a history together. Is it really that difficult to believe?"

I sit back, stunned at what Nicholas is saying—and how he's saying it. He's not kidding. He genuinely thinks Armand is here to do Cupid's bidding, to woo me with promises of a rosy future together.

In other words, he's *jealous*.

My ability to react to things like a normal person has always been questionable. I push when I should back away, laugh when I should cry, and dance with the devil every chance I get. In this moment, surrounded on all sides by murder and mayhem, all I can do is feel deep, unadulterated joy.

"You think I'm fascinating?" My lips curve in a delighted smile. If it weren't for Liam snoring gently on the bed next to me, I'd do a lot more with them than that. No one has ever called me fascinating before.

"I also said beautiful." Nicholas doesn't seem nearly as enchanted by this conversation as I am. He pushes himself to his feet and stares down at me. "The kind of beautiful that's not easy to forget. The kind of beautiful that could drive a man to do things he never thought himself capable of."

I can no longer tell if we're talking about Armand and his

hypothetical drive to enact murder or Nicholas and his hypothetical drive to . . . what? Follow me to Brighton for a non-holiday full of jealousy and intrigue? Pretend to woo my brother in the name of universal justice? Or remain in a committed relationship with a woman who's a witch, medium, psychic, and/or clairvoyant, depending on the day?

"He doesn't feel that way about me," I protest, but feebly, unsure what I'm supposed to do. I've never been in a situation like this before, where half my heart is soaring and the other half feels like it's just been overloaded with lead weights. "I'm telling you—this is something different. Something darker."

Nicholas casts a long, unreadable look on me that extends so long that I begin to feel uncomfortable. I fight the urge to squirm and adjust my hair, forcing myself instead to hold his gaze. If this is what being beautiful means, I'm not so sure I like it.

"Get some sleep, Eleanor," he eventually says, shaking himself off enough to plant a kiss on my forehead. He smells of his usual bergamot and mint, but this time with an undertone of those same sticky cocktails I detected at the club. It's as good an indication of any of what I've done to him—brought him down to my level, embroiled him in yet another affair not of his making. "And for the love of everything, be careful."

Chapter 19

"Ellie, we have a problem."

I awaken to my brother's terrible breath and even worse frown.

"Ellie, wake up. Ellie, we're in trouble. Ellie, are you listening to me? Ellie, I think we're going to jail."

That last *Ellie* is the one that finally gets me to roll out of bed. "Mother Goddess Almighty, I'm awake." I roll to escape my brother's breath and make a quick survey of the room. Not only does everything appear intact, but Beast returned at some point during the night. She's sitting at the foot of my bed and casually licking her paw. "What's the catastrophe now?"

"It's in the bathroom."

"What's in the bathroom?"

His answer is a long, convulsive shudder that matches his exterior. His hair is mussed and his clothes from last night are disheveled, his eyes ringed with purple bags. He looks like a man who spent the better part of last night partaking of vice—and who is now deeply regretting that decision. "I'm not saying her name out loud."

Brunhilde. Of course. My cat is determined to foist that unearthly being on us at all costs. I have no idea how she managed
to get into official police evidence, but I don't doubt that it
happened. The only question is why Liam is convinced that of
everything we've seen and done the past week, *this* is the thing
that will send us to jail.

Until I see her.

"Liam, is this a trick?" I stabilize myself with my hand on
the bathroom door frame, hesitant to step across the threshold.

"I told you." His voice is directly behind my ear, causing me
to jump. "I'm not seeing things, am I? Please tell me I'm seeing
things."

I only wish I could. Despite all odds—and all laws of our
physical world—Brunhilde is lying in the middle of our bathroom floor. Except instead of the cracked and burned shards of
her former self, she's been magically healed. Oh, she still looks
ancient and decrepit, the stains on her dress exactly how we remember, but there's not a mark on her.

And the worst part is, that's not the worst part.

"Don't touch her," Liam says.

For once, I comply. Not—like my brother—because I'm
scared, but because tangled up in the scraggly bits of her hair is
a gold chain interspersed with some of the largest pearls I've
ever seen in my life. I have no idea what a piece of jewelry like
that must be worth, but it's more than I'd care to part with.

"You're right." I nod once. Unless I'm mistaken, the owner
of that necklace didn't care to part with it either. At least, not
willingly. "We don't want to get any fingerprints on it."

Liam physically balks. "You're not going to tell the *police*
about this, are you?"

It had been my intention to head straight for the lobby and
demand that Gillian share in this experience with us. Not only
would she be keenly interested in the doll's apparent rise from
the dead, but there's a good chance that the necklace we're

looking at once belonged to the woman who was robbed the other day. If anything is a matter for official channels, it's this.

However, Liam's question is a valid one. The necklace is in our room. Attached to a doll that shouldn't be in our possession. Brought—one assumes—by a cat that isn't supposed to be sharing our hotel room.

And I thought Gillian was suspicious of me before. . . .

"Oh, dear," I murmur. "Perhaps you're right."

"Perhaps? *Perhaps?*"

"Fine, you're definitely right. We're going to want to keep this one in the family." Since I can hardly leave Brunhilde where anyone can walk in and find her, I pluck her from the floor. Physically touching her is the final straw for Liam.

"That's it," he announces. "I don't want any part of this."

"It's a little late for that, don't you think?"

He ignores me. "I'm going for a run on the beach. That monstrosity had better be gone when I get back."

Personally, I'd rather deal with the holy undead than willingly run on sand again, but I wave him off. It'll do him good to sweat out last night's vodka.

I barely register the sounds of him thumping around as he changes into his running gear and heads out the door. I'm too focused on untangling the necklace from Brunhilde's hair and allowing it to slide through my fingers. It's heavier than it looks, the chain links slipping through my fingers like frozen silk, the pearls gleaming and effervescent in the bright bathroom lights. I'm no jewelry appraiser, but this thing looks expensive. Whoever lost it is going to want it back.

Since leaving the necklace in the room where Beast can do goodness-knows-what with it isn't an option, and I'm definitely not keeping it in the safe, I tie it up in the end of a colorful shawl that I then I wrap around my waist. It's not ideal to walk around carrying stolen goods on my person, but at least this way, I can feel the reassuring weight of it against my hip.

"If I go downstairs for a few hours, can I trust you to stay put?" I ask my cats. They don't answer, but I do make a thorough check of all the room's potential exits just to be safe. I don't *think* there's any way for Beast to slip out, but I know better than to trust something as simple as sight. It's almost as though Brunhilde is calling to her. "And if you must leave, at least avoid committing any more crimes. It's going to be hard enough to explain this one as it is."

Options for a paranormal investigator are limited when one is carrying stolen goods through a hotel teeming with police officers while simultaneously trying to avoid a hypnotist and one's overly anxious boyfriend.

In this, as in all things, I manage.

"Remember that time we saw a random cat carrying a cursed doll down the sidewalk?" I don't bother saying hello to Uli, opting instead to take him by surprise. If his startled jump is any indication, it works.

He takes a moment to peer out the front door to make sure there aren't any incoming guests before answering in a low, hushed tone. "Of course I remember. What's the matter with you?"

"Lots of things, but the only one that need concern you right now is my dogged determination to see a project through to its conclusion. How much would it cost me for information?"

"That depends on the kind of information," he says. "If it's about that cat, I don't know anything. I haven't seen it hanging around."

That's something, at least. I feel much better about Beast roaming the hotel halls if she's doing it discreetly. "I'm looking for a visual description of all the items that have been stolen from this hotel," I say. "I already heard a list of what was taken from the loud, angry man and the older woman, but I need a more detailed—"

"Nadia Gordon."

I'm surprised to find him so forthcoming but am not about to look a gift doorman in the mouth. "That's the one. And the man, Mr. . . ."

My second attempt at extracting information free of charge doesn't work as well. Uli's eyes narrow.

"What's this about?" he asks with another furtive glance around. This time, he's not looking out the door so much as around our immediate vicinity. "What do you want from me?"

The answer to that is more complicated than I'm willing to go into right here and now. The truth is that Laurel wasn't wrong when she pointed the metaphorical finger at Uli last night. He's somehow tied up in all this. If his insistence that Leonard was alone on that boat when he died and his intricate knowledge of this hotel's activities aren't proof enough, then the fact that he wasn't at his post when both the gentleman and Nadia Gordon were robbed is.

There's only one thing to do in a situation like this one. With a quick movement of the knot at my waist, I open up the scarf to reveal the contents inside.

At first, Uli must think I'm about to flash him, because he starts to back away. As soon as he sees that glitter of gold and pearl, however, he leans in. *Very* closely.

"Where did you get that?" His head jerks up, his eyes no longer narrow. They're so wide that I can see every variation of the pigment in his eyes. Striations of brown and gold glint at me. "How did you find it?"

I don't say anything right away, content to watch Uli go through his emotions unchecked. He's wary yet interested, shocked yet not altogether surprised. Unless I'm very much mistaken, he's seen this necklace before.

The question is, did he see it hanging around Nadia Gordon's neck, or did he get a much more personalized glimpse?

"Give me the man's name, and it's yours," I say, waggling my hip so the gold chain dances in the light. "Who is he, and where can I find him?"

Uli reaches for the chain but doesn't make contact. His eyes dart up to meet mine instead. "Where's the rest of it?"

Since Beast is the least helpful witch's familiar of all time, I don't have the answer to that question. I'm guessing the rest of the stolen jewelry is somewhere on these premises, but until my cat takes me into her confidence, I'm not likely to uncover it. "The gentleman," I insist.

Uli's tongue darts out and touches the edge of his lips. "The baron, you mean."

"Baron?"

He nods. "Baron Gendry-Webber. He always stays here for a few weeks every summer. You can practically time the tide on his arrival."

"So someone knew he'd be here." I say this mostly to myself—and to Winnie and Birdie, should they chance to be listening in—but Uli answers.

"Yes."

"Lots of someones."

"If you mean the staff, yes. But other people would know, too. A large percentage of our guests are regulars." Uli pauses and casts another nervous look around. "Put that thing away, would you? People are starting to stare."

"You don't want it?"

He shakes his head, though I notice that he hesitates at first. He *does* want the necklace, but he's a lot like Liam in that regard. Crime is all fun and games until a stint in prison becomes a likely possibility.

"Suit yourself," I say as I tightly knot my scarf once again. "But one more thing I need to know before I go . . . How does the baron tip?"

Although it doesn't seem possible, Uli's nervousness ratchets up another level. "Not great. Why do you ask?"

No reason. Just that the baron doesn't strike me as a pleasant guest to have around. High demands and low compensation might not be a motive for murder, but they'll definitely do for theft.

Uli pieces together my meaning almost immediately. "I didn't rob him!" His whole body gives a convulsive twitch. "I would never do anything to jeopardize my position with the hotel. This place is my whole life."

Which is yet another hint that Uli knows more about the recent turn of events than he's letting on. I'm not sure what kind of loneliness would lead a man to spend his every waking hour in a hotel, but I'm guessing it's not the good kind.

"Where's the baron right now?" I ask.

"I—I don't know."

"Yes, you do. You know everything about everyone. If Baron Gendry-Webber is such a creature of habit that he vacations at the same time and the same place every year, then he probably sticks to a similar schedule every day. Where is he?"

Uli gives in, resigned both to his fate and to the fact that I know what I'm talking about. "The spa, most likely. He'll be finishing up his massage and heading to the sauna to sweat out his impurities."

"Excellent." I smile. "You've been most helpful this morning, Uli. Thank you."

My thanks are not accepted with grace. "I thought you were supposed to be some kind of *paranormal* investigator," he says. "A psychic—a witch. Not an interrogator."

"I am a psychic," I reply, nettled at being thus reduced. Can't a woman be more than one thing? "I also have enough common sense to know that you didn't really see that man jump from the boat all by himself. Admit it, Uli—you saw what we did. Two shadows, two figures. Leonard was pushed to his death. Who paid you to lie?"

"No one paid me." He seems genuinely insulted, but that

could just be because there's a woman and her young daughter heading our way. Before he opens the door for them, he lowers his voice to add, "I'd be careful about throwing around accusations like that. This hotel has been around for over a hundred years. It sees things. It knows things. It protects its own."

Narrowing my eyes, I study Uli anew. He's so long, so lean—in fact, if I was looking at him from afar, I might even call him gaunt. True, there's no knot of hair on the top of his head, and he's in trousers rather than a dress, but those things could be easily rectified.

"Is that a threat, Uli?" I ask.

He shakes his head. "No, Madame Eleanor. Just a warning. When a place is as old as this one, you never know what sort of monsters walk at night."

Saunas have never been my favorite way to relax and unwind. The dry heat makes my eyeballs feel like a pair of desiccated tangerines and my skin like parchment paper, but some things must be suffered in the name of truth. I wait only long enough to do a quick Google search of my quarry and slip into my blue one-piece bathing suit—the necklace now knotted in the towel at my waist—before I find my way to the spa.

As Uli foretold, Baron Gendry-Webber appears to be enjoying himself, heaving and sweating inside the wood-paneled box for much longer than I'm sure his doctor would recommend. His red, bulbous nose is the same as before, but instead of his poorly fitting wool suit, he's wearing his poorly fitting birthday suit instead.

"Hullo," I say, averting my eyes. There's a sign on the wall above his head stating that no nudity is allowed, but I don't mention it. Someone that unabashedly on display must not feel the rules apply to him. I breathe the air of a desert planet and try not to gasp. "This is lovely, isn't it?"

He grunts a noncommittal reply, so I find a seat and try

again. Although I don't go so far as to bar the door, I place myself close enough to it that he'll have to ask me to move before he can exit. "I'm heading over for a massage after this," I say. "There's nothing like a little rest and relaxation, is there?"

"Sure."

"After the past few days, I think we deserve it. This is some hotel, isn't it? Between the police wandering around asking questions and the fire alarms going off for no reason . . ."

He fails to take my bait. "Are you going to chatter the whole time?"

It had been my intention, yes. Men sitting naked and alone in saunas are supposed to appreciate a little friendly female company. If my overtures aren't going to work, I'm going to need to shift my plan.

I take a more direct approach. "I heard what happened to you the other day. You must be devastated to have lost so much."

Suspicion brings with it a hint of modesty. The baron shifts so his towel drapes over his lap, and he stares at me through the haze of heat. "Say, here. What is this about?"

"I just wanted to follow up with what you saw, that's all," I soothe. "Two shadow figures, right? Hovering over your safe?"

"I already told the police what happened."

"Of course, of course. But between you and me, I don't know that I'd call Inspector Piper the most open-minded person in the world. I'm not saying she thinks you made *every-thing* up, but . . ."

He sits up straighter, sweat slinging from his brow. "I know what I saw."

I hold up my hands and laugh. "Oh, I believe you. I've seen them, too."

"Wait a minute—I know who you are. You're that paranormal investigator."

"And you're Baron Gendry-Webber," I return. Five minutes on the Internet was enough to tell me why everyone is being so careful to ameliorate this man. The short answer is that he's rich. The long answer is that he's rich because he buys up small, struggling, family-run businesses and grinds them under his heel. He's one of the most hated men in all of the United Kingdom—and considering the current political climate, that's saying a lot. "The other woman who was robbed is named Nadia Gordon. Does that ring a bell?"

He sits upright in a combination of what appears to be fear, interest, and a dangerous tendency toward overheating. I wordlessly hand him the bottle of water I brought in with me. Grateful for this opportunity to hydrate—or to collect his thoughts—the baron guzzles the entire thing.

"I didn't know the old bat was staying here," he says as soon as he's finished. "They got her, too?"

I nod. Like the not-so-good baron here, Nadia Gordon is well-known in upper crust British circles, mostly as a decaying reminder of a class system that puts birth and breeding above ability.

"Well, I'll be." Baron Gendry-Webber releases a long, wet whistle. "Ol' Nadia rarely travels light. What'd they take?"

That's an answer I still don't have, but it doesn't matter. What *does* matter is that both of our theft victims are high-profile and worth a fortune. In other words, the thief—or thieves, as is much more likely—knows what he's doing. These victims weren't chosen at random.

"They took it all," I say, confident that it's close enough to the truth to count. "Scary, isn't it? That someone might have targeted you before you arrived? A man like you must have a lot of enemies."

He swallows convulsively.

"I could help you identify those who might wish to harm you," I offer. "I don't know if you've heard, but I'm well-connected to the spiritual realm. The spirts see things that human eyes often miss."

He's on the hook—I know it. Perhaps it's the heat getting to his head or the mention of Nadia's name or even just a desire for answers, but he wavers close. I'm sure he's about to agree when the door bursts open, bringing with it a blast of cold air.

The baron's yelp of protest covers my own, though I doubt he feels a fraction of the annoyance that I do. Standing on the threshold to the sauna, allowing the warm air to whip around him and build up into a mysterious cloud, is Armand. Not just any Armand, either—he's wearing a black vintage bathing suit that looks like a wrestling onesie.

"There you are," he announces in his most silken voice. "I should have known that you'd be with our dear Madame Eleanor. Has she read your palm yet? Seen your aura? Delved the deep recesses of your psyche?"

I glare at Armand, but he's too busy sweeping into the sauna to read the murder in my eyes. From the moue of displeasure he makes as the door thumps to a close behind him, I can only assume he feels the same way about the heat that I do—that it's the quickest way to flatten his coiffure and send all that eyeliner running.

"Now see here," the baron blusters. All my hard work of the past ten minutes disappears in a flash. "What are you two up to? Who sent you?"

"No one sent us, Baron Gendry-Webber," I soothe. "I'm merely here to offer my assistance, should you require it. I have no idea who this man is."

"Armand Lamont, hypnotist extraordinaire." Armand offers his hand, which the baron reluctantly takes and wrings. "Madame Eleanor and I go way back. Whether ghost or demon or spirit most foul, we cleanse both your mind and your home. Tell me, Baron—who is haunting you?"

Any credence I might have built in the baron's mind is now at an end. I know exactly what he's thinking—that he's once again facing two figures, both of which have a darkness about them, and both of which are acting as though they're going to pin him down and sweat him to death inside this heated box of a room. With a sigh, I step out of the path of the door and watch as he leaps to his feet, wraps a towel around the flapping exposure of his lower half, and takes himself off. Even the blast of fresh air this brings isn't comforting. There goes any and all chance I might have at getting information out of that man. He'll never trust me after this.

"What's the matter with you?" I demand, whirling on Armand the moment the door thuds to a close behind him. "You terrified that poor man."

"Oh, I'm not the one who terrified him. You did that the moment you cornered him in a room with only one exit." Armand tsks his disapproval and sits in the spot vacated by the baron. "Have I taught you nothing? *Gentle*, Eleanor. Always gentle."

"I *was* being gentle," I say through my teeth. "You're the one who burst in here and started yammering on about demons. If I didn't know better, I'd think you were trying to scare him away. Why? Afraid of what he might tell me?"

He laughs, showing me the white line of his teeth. He also closes his eyes and relaxes against the wood-paneled wall as though it had been his intention all along.

"If I wanted that man's riches, I wouldn't resort to robbery." Armand opens one eye, decides I'm not worth looking at, and closes it again. "He lost both his parents at a young age, and his entire life of money and misery has been a feeble attempt to find someone else who will love him like they did. He's the easiest kind of mark there is."

I wish I could discount this, but Armand is right. Theft is one of the riskiest and most difficult ways to get money off a person—mostly because it involves things like the police, as Gillian and her team's presence here indicates. It's much better to worm your way in with charm and promises of the afterlife.

"What about Nadia Gordon?" I ask.

"Please. Her entire collection of jewelry is paste. She's been selling those pieces off and having them replaced with fakes for as long as she's been alive. Whoever robbed her room is in for an unpleasant surprise."

My interest is fully piqued by this time. I wish I could say that it's a purely investigative interest, but I can feel myself slipping. It used to be so easy with Armand, so fun—the pair of us discussing cases, seeking out weaknesses to use to our advantage. If we'd wanted to get money from the baron and Nadia, we could have done it. With finesse and with style and—most important—without harming anyone in the process.

"You think she lied to the police?"

He opens one eye again. "About the value of her things, yes. About the robbery itself?" He shrugs. "Probably not. I think your thief is poorly informed, that's all. Or is it your murderer? I'm having a difficult time keeping track of what you're hunting."

And just like that, the slipping stops. I don't care how good we used to be together. Murder is never a game.

"I'm not hunting anything," I say. "Or anyone. I'm seeking justice."

"Keep telling yourself that, Eleanor. I'm sure it'll stick one of these days."

"I saw a man *die*, Armand. Forgive me for not sharing your amusement."

As he shows little sign of wishing to leave the sauna despite the discomfort, I assume there's more to this visit than interrupting my conversation with Baron Gendry-Webber. "Go ahead," I say. "You might as well get it out."

"Tell me."

"Tell you what? Who's behind all this? Right now, my best guess is you."

He shakes his head so earnestly that I'm taken aback. "How did you do it?" he asks. "The objects in the room and the fire alarm? And why? I'm assuming it ties in to your work on the Hartfords, but I can't seem to puzzle it together. What's your plan for them?"

"I told you already. I don't have one."

He ignores me and heaves a wistful sigh. "Considering how much energy you're putting into this, you must be taking them for everything they have. Please tell me you're taking them for everything they have."

This proves too much for me—the heat and the accusations, the unsteady feeling that I'm in over my head. "When have I ever tried to take everything?" I demand. "For that matter, when have you? What happened to you, Armand? You used to have a moral code—a line you wouldn't cross no matter what. When did you get so . . . desperate?"

His nostrils flare in warning, but I'm starting to feel a little light-headed, so I don't heed it the way I should.

"As for the flying objects, it was probably magic," I continue. "Is that what you want to hear? When my sister died, I gained the ability to communicate with the other side for real. I hear her voice and the voice of another woman who died last year. I see visions of the future. For all I know, I can also pick up random objects and throw them through the air using nothing but my mind. At this point, I'm not ruling anything out."

"Fine. Don't tell me." He jerks himself to his feet and points a warning finger at me. "But if I were you, I'd be a little more careful about who I consider my real friends."

The sensation of dizziness has started to escalate by this time, the sauna spinning faster and my breath coming short and hot. I'm not sure how long I've been in here, but I'm starting to feel I've reached the upper limits.

"What is that supposed to mean?" I demand.

"How about that police inspector you've been following around with big, moony eyes?" Armand releases a short, bitter laugh. "She's using you. She doesn't want to hang out and have drinks after work. She doesn't want to gossip about her relationship with her ex-husband. You're a means to an end, that's all."

I try to get to my feet, but I'm so unsteady that I only make it halfway before I slump in a heap back to the wooden slats.

"What do you know about Gillian Piper?" I ask. And, since it seems a more pressing concern, I add, "Did you turn the temperature up in here? Are you trying to murder me through dehydration? I can tell you right now—you aren't going to get your hands on the Hartford millions if I'm dead."

This time, his laugh is much less sinister. It might just sound that way because he pushes open the door and holds it there, allowing sweet, unheated oxygen to blast its way over me, but I'm not in a position to argue. It feels too good to be breathing again.

"Relax. I'm not here to kill you."

"Then what are you doing?" It's not a very wise question, but I'm drunk on fresh air, reckless with abandon. I'm also able to pull myself into a standing position and move toward the door. "Vivian's not going to hand over her diamonds no matter how much you flirt and croon in her ear. She's old but she's not a fool. She's toying with you."

"I'll tell you my game if you tell me yours," he says.

Therein lies the problem. I'm not playing a game. I'm living my life, trying to do the right thing, spending time with the people I love.

"I'm going to solve the mystery of what's happening around this hotel," I say. "And then I'm going back to my antiquated village to grow old with my cats. I know you don't believe me, but I'm a different person now. That's the sum total of my worldly ambition."

"No one changes that much," he says.

"I did."

If the arch of his brow is anything to go by, he doesn't believe me. That certainty—that malicious sparkle in his eye—

does more to rock my confidence than anything else he's said or done since I found him sitting with Vivian.

A few years ago, I'd have been 100 percent on Armand's side. He and I have always had one thing in common: our ability to read people, to understand them, to know them in ways they can never know themselves. And one thing we both believed is that people rarely change their nature. They change their clothes and their jobs and their spouses, but that core human essence inside—their soul, if you will—always remains the same.

"I'm telling you the truth, Armand," I say, almost pleading. I don't know why I need him to believe me, but I do. "I don't understand what's going on any more than you do. Something happened when you hypnotized me—something outside my control. Something outside yours."

He offers a short, jerky laugh. "Fine," he says. "Let's do it again—right here, right now. Neither of us has had an opportunity to rig the sauna ahead of time. We'll see if you can manifest telekinesis then."

It's in my best interest to take Armand up on the offer. Since I didn't plan to be in the sauna until twenty minutes ago, there's no way for him to have set a trap for me. And I can hardly wander off or start throwing things around; the sauna is self-contained and there's only one access point. It's ideal for an experiment of this kind.

I don't think it's a very good idea, Winnie counsels.

What's the worst that could happen? Birdie counters.

Promise me you won't be alone in a room with him, Ellie, Nicholas's voice from last night echoes.

In the end, I heed my sister's advice and dart out the door. Not—as Nicholas might think—because I'm scared of Armand and what he can do, but because I'm sweating buckets and can't take another minute of these inhumane conditions.

Like Beast, I'm careful how I use my lives.

Chapter 20

❦

"Water." I brush past Nicholas without preamble, pausing just long enough to toss one of his mother's long black evening gowns into his arms. "I need water."

"Hello, Eleanor." His low voice is meant to soothe, but the only thing I need right now is a tall glass of something wet. I make my way to the sink and dip my head underneath the faucet. "If I might point it out, there are several perfectly clean glasses on the sideboard."

"The next time I suggest cornering a man inside a sauna, talk some sense into me, will you?" I counter. My thirst thus slated, I pause long enough to breathe and relax. I'm dressed only in a hotel robe thrown over the top of my swimsuit, my feet bare and my hair a sweaty, scraggly mess, but I feel fantastic. Maybe there's something to sweating out those impurities after all. "And put that on. I want to try something."

Nicholas glances at the gown in his arms with a quirk of a smile. "I thought you'd never ask."

I laugh and push my damp hair out of my face. "Not that kind of something. I need you to pretend to be a ghost."

He heaves a mock sigh. "Of course you do."

"And to scare the doorman."

"Why else would one dress up as one's mother?"

"I'd ask Liam, but he's not tall enough. You and your mother should be about the same size."

At that, he casts the gown aside with a grimace and makes as if to pull me into his arms instead. "It hardly seems worth pointing out, but that isn't the sort of thing a man likes to hear on vacation with an attractive woman."

That bit about being attractive fills my throat with a yearning ache, but I dodge his embrace. My conversation with Armand is too fresh in my memory, as is the looming sensation that this investigation is getting away from me. As much as I'd like to pretend otherwise, this is no romantic getaway for two. This is my past catching up to me. This is my future casting gloomy forebodings.

This is me trying to find someplace between the two where I can comfortably exist.

"What I meant is that you're strong and virile." I jump over the bed and dash to the opposite end of the room to escape him. "A strapping example of manhood."

He doesn't buy it for a second. He also catches up to me much more quickly than I anticipate. With his arms around my waist, he hoists me up and holds me there, proving by his unwavering solidity just how strong and virile he can be.

I give up on trying to escape and allow myself to melt into his embrace. His hands slip under my robe but don't take any liberties, which is how I know he's all in. I've never been able to tell if it's a love of justice or of adventure that compels Nicholas to lend me a helping hand whenever I'm embroiled in a case like this, but if there's one thing I can count on, it's that he'll do everything in his power to assist me.

"I know it's asking a lot, but I'm pretty sure Uli is the ghost maid I've seen skulking around the hotel," I say as he allows me to slide back down to the floor. His hands linger at my sides, holding but not restricting me. "And that he's the one who keeps resurrecting Brunhilde. I'd like to force him to admit it. You don't have to do much—just wander around and scare a few hotel patrons. I'll place myself somewhere close by so I can gauge his reaction."

"Why would a doorman moonlight as a Victorian ghost maid?"

"For fun? So he can run around robbing people's safes in the full light of day? Because he helped murder a man and is trying to cover it up?" I shrug. "I don't know. Why does anyone do anything? I think you should make your appearance tonight, around two or three in the morning. When no one else will be around."

"I like your brother, by the by," he says by way of response. I know him well enough to accept it as an agreement. Now that he's decided to help me, there's no need for further discussion.

"Of course you like Liam," I say, allowing the change of subject. "He runs a one-man show of all my childhood foibles. Don't believe what he tells you. He was always jealous that I had more fun than him."

"He had a lot to say about Armand."

I stiffen. *This* change of subject isn't as welcome. "On the contrary, he barely knows Armand. I didn't make an attempt to introduce them back when we were working together. I know it's hard for you to believe, but we were never close. We were co-workers for a brief space of time, that's all. I never really liked or trusted the guy."

Nicholas nods as though this makes perfect sense, a sad smile touching his lips. "You needed him."

This isn't uttered in a tone of reproof or annoyance—it's stated as a fact. Which, if I'm being fair, it is. The reason I put up with Armand as long as I did wasn't because we were destined to become great friends or great partners, but because I didn't have anyone else. Winnie was comatose; Liam had zero interest in helping maintain her, and I was facing tens of thousands of dollars in medical bills without education, training, or—let's admit it—any idea what I was doing. Armand showed up when I had few other options and took me under his wing. He taught me everything he knows. He helped me when no one else would.

He gave me a chance at a life, however corrupt and shady it might have been.

"I did need him," I agree.

From the brief flash that crosses Nicholas's face, I can tell this bothers him, but I don't know how to fix it. I can't change who I was then and I don't want to change who I am now. As much as it hurts to admit it, those two things are inexorably linked.

"He could tell you things," I say. It suddenly seems imperative that Nicholas hear this from me—the truth, the whole truth, and all the dark undercurrents that uphold it. "Terrible things. About the people we took advantage of, of the ways we did it, of how ruthlessly we took over their lives for money. My past isn't pretty, Nicholas—no, don't say anything. You know parts of it, but you don't know everything. Armand is the only one who does, and he could ruin my life with just a few words dropped in Gillian Piper's ears. He could ruin yours, too. You're tainted by association, and for as long as you're with me, you'll always be in danger. If not from Armand, then from all the other people I've wronged."

My warning doesn't have its intended effect.

"And what about all the people you've righted?" Nicholas queries gently. "When do they get a chance to speak up?"

I can't answer. My throat is too tight, my heart too big for my chest. All I can do is step back, putting distance and air between us. As I do, my gaze lands on the fallen dress—this silly plan of mine to put something good in the world after all the bad I've heaped on it. It's not much, but it's something.

"Two o'clock," I gasp, nodding down at it. "Make it look good and spooky. I'll be hiding nearby."

Nicholas looks as though he has more to say on the previous subject, but he nods and allows the moment to pass. "You can count on me, Eleanor. For this and for everything."

Chapter 21

There aren't nearly as many hiding places in a hotel lobby at two o'clock in the morning as one might hope. In the bright, well-lit company of all this marble, I look out of place and highly visible. It doesn't help that every staff member knows me by name at this point—or that they've been warned to keep an eye on my movements.

In the end, I hang out by the front desk and chat up Laurel instead of hiding. Considering how calmly she accepts me, I assume she's accustomed to patrons spending the dead of night keeping underpaid customer service workers from doing their job.

"You never want to use coconut oil as a makeup remover," I say with a gesture at the smoky eye shadow she has layered on a little too thickly. It goes well with her dark lipstick but is a little much for working behind a desk. "Witch hazel is the way to go. It won't leave any residue behind or clog your pores. I always carry some, if you want to try it."

"You have witch hazel right now?" She runs her eye up and down my person, which is covered in as discreet a costume as I could muster—which is to say a pair of Liam's jeans and one of his white button-up shirts. The jeans are two sizes too big, and I've had to tie the shirt in a knot at my waist to keep it in place, but everything I own screams "skulking in dark corners." I've never been great at blending in. "Like . . . in your pocket?"

I laugh. The only thing in my pocket right now is the gold-and-pearl necklace. "Not literally on my person, no, but up in my room. A good witch never travels without her full kit."

This casual reference to my profession causes a sparkle to light in her eye. She gives up on the pretense of sorting invoices and leans over the desk toward me, her head propped on her hand. "So it's really true? You're a witch in addition to a paranormal investigator? What kind of spells can you do?"

People are always interested in my spells, and I'm always interested in talking about myself, but I'm technically here to do a job. As much as I'd love to sit and chat about the powers of incantation for getting rid of warts—with a side of frankincense and clove for good measure—I need to keep an eye on Uli.

I shift in the direction of the lobby entrance to find that Uli is watching me with equal interest. This doesn't come as a surprise. Considering that he has the habits and routines of every guest in this place memorized, he must know how out-of-the-ordinary my actions are right now.

Which, *good*. I want him thrown off balance, on edge. As soon as he sees that ghost maid, he'll be like putty in my hands.

I'm deriving much more joy at this picture than is seemly when the ping of the elevator doors sounds in the distance. It's late and quiet enough that the gentle sound seems like a starting bell.

The starting bell becomes a downright clamor when I see who's standing on the other side of those doors.

I'm not going to lie—the thought of seeing Nicholas gallivanting about in his mother's gown is one that I've been looking forward to with gleeful anticipation. I left him earlier in the evening with my makeup kit, a few pointers for highlighting his cheekbones, and a promise not to take any photos of the result. What emerges from the elevator is . . . not that.

The Nicholas standing on the threshold is pale and drawn, his normal clothes sitting askew on his broad shoulders, his lips pulled into a grimace that sends a shiver down my spine. Every instinct I have tells me to run to him, to take his face between my hands and demand an explanation. There are too many things that could go wrong: his mother falling ill, a devastating phone call from home, a conversation with Armand that has finally forced him to see me for who I am. . . .

"Oh, dear. Dr. Pierson, are you all right?"

I could kiss Laurel for the speed with which she dashes out from behind the front desk to go to his aid. There's genuine concern in her voice, and she shows no hesitation in leading him toward the nearest chair.

He refuses, of course. Even when he looks as though he's seen—well, a ghost—he's not one to allow himself to be coddled.

"I'm perfectly all right," he assures her—and, with a brief flick of his eyes, *me*. "But I think you ought to call in that police inspector who's staying here."

Although I'm finding it easier to breathe now that I've heard Nicholas speak, that particular sentence sets my heart racing.

"Inspector Piper?" Laurel says. "I'm not sure—"

"I fell asleep," Nicholas says. "I don't know how or why, but when I woke up, it was to find someone breaking into my safe. I'm afraid I've been robbed."

The tale is starting to feel as old as time—and twice as wearisome. I can tell, from the flat line of Inspector Piper's mouth and the nervous twitches of Bertram sitting next to her, that I'm not the only one who feels this way.

The four of us are sitting in a corner of the lobby restaurant, a pot of coffee untouched in front of us as Nicholas gives his report. No one has mentioned how strange it is that I'm sitting in on this interview—or that I was awake and in the lobby when it happened—but I'm not about to point it out. This conversation is one I'm keenly interested in hearing firsthand.

Since I'd like to prove my usefulness, I begin pouring out the coffee and nudging the cups around the table. I also listen. And wait. And listen some more.

As we've all come to expect, the recitation of events exactly coincides with the robberies of Baron Gendry-Webber and Nadia Gordon. Nicholas woke up in the middle of the theft, disoriented from sleep, to the sound of crackling flames and two dark figures hunched over his safe. A man of action, he immediately made a move to tackle his intruders.

That's when things start to worry me.

"There wasn't anyone there," he says, his brow knit and the lines of his face so deep that I have to sit on my hands to keep from reaching for him.

Inspector Piper seems to share my concern. "What do you mean, there wasn't anyone there?"

"I mean I was alone in my room. The safe was unlocked and all my things taken, but no one was with me—not a person, not a ghost, not anyone. Believe me, I checked. The door was locked and my windows shut tight, and there were no monsters either under the bed or in the closet."

"And would you say that you often encounter ghosts and monsters in such a manner?" Gillian asks with a small cough and a glance at me.

Nicholas laughs, though the sound is shaky around the edges. He's not normally one to lose his calm over anything, so I can only assume the encounter hit him hard. "I haven't always believed in the supernatural, no, but a close friend of mine has me growing more and more open to the possibility."

"So you do believe in them."

"I don't *not* believe in them."

"As a doctor—a man of science—you'll sit there and claim that ghosts exist?"

For a moment there, I forgot Nicholas's cover story. He, however, is perfectly composed in his answer. "As a rational human being with over thirty years of experience on this planet, I say that some things—despite our better judgment—defy explanation. And until science can prove otherwise, I think we have to consider all the possibilities."

Bravo, Winnie cries. I'm tempted to set up a rallying cheer myself, but something unsettling occurs to me.

"When you came down, you said that you don't know how or why you fell asleep." It's dangerous to draw attention to myself in this way, but I can't help speaking up. Nicholas is the last man to relax on the job; he once flew a plane with almost no sleep to help me solve a case and sat by my bedside for an entire night after I suffered a head injury. Like almost everything he encounters, sleep is something to be controlled, tamed. "What did you mean by that?"

"Just that," he says. "I didn't even know I was tired. One minute, I was sitting on my bed reading a book, and the next, I was waking up to the two shadows in my room. But if you're thinking I was somehow . . . lulled to sleep, I can tell you right now that I wasn't. I had headphones on."

That bit about being *lulled* is for my ears only. What he means—and what he's really saying—is that he wasn't hypnotized. Armand is talented, yes, but he can only act within the bounds of our physical world.

"What time was it?" I demand. "When you fell asleep?"

"I don't know. Before midnight? I was asleep for a few hours, the closest I can tell."

While I would gladly continue this line of questioning, Gillian has moved on. She pushes a pad of paper and a pen across the table.

"Would you mind listing everything that was taken from your safe?" she asks. "We also ask that you stay out of your room until further notice. Bertram and I will be closing it off until the whole team can get in here to do a thorough sweep."

"Of course. Whatever you need." Nicholas accepts the pen and writes down exactly two things.

Cash, £1,500

Black diamond mourning ring

Both Gillian and I pause as we watch him scrawl out the second line. "A black diamond mourning ring?" she says, her brows knit. "What is that for? Are you in mourning?"

"No."

"Is it an heirloom?"

"Not yet, but I have hopes it will be."

"Because you're planning on killing off someone in your family?"

"Not quite, no." Nicholas allows his gaze to slide over to mine, an apologetic crinkle at the edges of his eyes. I can't imagine what he has to be sorry about until he speaks again. "It's meant to be an engagement ring. I was planning on proposing with it this weekend, so you can imagine how eager I am to get it back."

I have no idea how I manage to keep to my chair. My entire body jerks in a combination of surprise, heart-stopping joy, and devastation. Nicholas bought me a ring? Nicholas bought me a black diamond mourning ring? Nicholas bought me a black diamond mourning ring and was going to ask me to marry him?

And someone had the nerve to steal it?

Bertram, ever diligent, looks up from his note taking with a slightly puzzled air. "Why would you propose to someone with a mourning ring? That doesn't sound very romantic."

"Well, this particular one is cursed," Nicholas says.

"Uh . . ."

"And it has a hidden poison compartment underneath the diamond."

"How is that . . . ?"

"And if you hit the snake's head—I should mention that it twists around the finger in the shape of a serpent—a small dagger pricks out to deliver the poison directly to the bloodstream."

"And what would you say is the value of this ring?" Gillian asks.

"It's priceless, obviously," I say, unable to remain silent any longer. I have no idea where Nicholas found a ring like that, but it sounds *amazing*. "How could you put something like that in your safe when you knew very well there are thieves wandering around the hotel?"

He's not the least bit discomposed by my attack. Shifting his seat so he faces me directly, he says, "I was afraid my, er, intended would snoop around and find it before I was ready to pop the question."

Snoop? I don't snoop. I investigate. I study. "It sounds as though you don't trust your intended very much," I retort.

"I don't" comes his bland reply. "But that's a large part of the charm. One never knows what to expect. Life with my intended will be a lot of things, but boring isn't one of them."

I'm not sure what to make of this. A less flattering proposal has never been offered in the history of romance—if, indeed, this is a proposal at all. Not only does Nicholas no longer have the ring in his possession, but he's making it sound as though I'm less like the love of his life and more like an impending tornado that might come bursting through at any time. I'd be insulted if I wasn't already feeling every instinct to turn into a tornado and burst right *out* of this room. The rational half of my brain knows that marriage is the most realistic outcome of a steady, long-term relationship—that Nicholas, against all odds, seems willing to overlook my past for the sake of our future. The less rational half wants to shake some sense into him, to warn him away before either of us gets well and truly hurt.

I'm not the kind of woman you marry. I'm the bloom of a poisonous flower under the light of a full moon. I'm a creeping, cliff-side mist that draws you into an ethereal trap. I'm—

"Laurel at the front desk will get you moved to a new room immediately." Gillian pushes back her chair and rises to her feet. Her practical, no-nonsense voice has the effect of dispelling my thoughts but not the sentiment underlying them. The tremor I'm unable to subdue in my hands is proof of that. "As soon as we're done going through your room, we'll return any toiletries, clothing, or other personal items. Oh, and Dr. Pierson?"

Nicholas looks up at the sound of his assumed name. "Yes?"

"Don't stray too far from the hotel." She turns to Bertram with a nod. "Let's go take a look at that room."

In that moment, I'm faced with one of the most difficult dilemmas of my life. The proper thing—the *girlfriend-ly* thing— to do would be to stay with Nicholas. From the way he's holding himself, he must still be shaken from his experience with the shadow men, and there's a good chance he'd also like to follow up on that proposal stuff. I should assure him that his sentiments are reciprocated and appreciated. I should take him in my arms and kiss away any lingering fears he might have about the relationship Armand and I once shared.

Then again, I really, *really* want to tag along while Gillian takes a look at his room. I haven't yet had an opportunity to investigate one of the victim's rooms while it's still fresh, and I doubt I'll get another one.

It's not avoidance if I'm on the job, right? Just like it's not cowardice when there's a murderer on the loose.

"I'll pop along with you two, shall I?" I make my decision with much less deliberation than the occasion warrants. Nich-

olas doesn't even flinch. I'm not sure what that says about
him—or about me—but it's almost as though he expects me to
choose the case over him. "Wait up. I want to see if there are
any lingering negative energies from the shadow men."

Gillian casts a look over her shoulder at me. Like Nicholas,
she doesn't show a glimmer of surprise at my request. "Hurry
up, then. We don't have all night."

"You'll be okay without me?" I ask Nicholas, not quite able
to meet his eyes.

"I always am," he replies smoothly.

It's not exactly what I'd been hoping to hear, but I'm hardly
in a position to complain about his lack of sentimentality. After
indulging in a quick, fleeting press of my hand against his, I
bustle to catch up with Gillian and Bertram—and ask the most
important question weighing on my mind.

"Shouldn't you place someone at the doors? And the staff
entrances and exits?" The elevator closes and we start heading
up toward the seventh floor. "It hasn't been that long since the
robbery. You wouldn't want the thieves slipping out while
we're busy searching the room."

"That won't be necessary," Gillian says, her tone curt.

"But if they get away with the ring—"

"That was strange, don't you think?" Gillian ignores me to
direct her question at Bertram. "Mourning jewelry for an engagement, I mean."

"Very strange," Bertram agrees. "One might almost call it
unbelievable."

Despite the haste with which I abandoned Nicholas, I take
great offense at this. "I'm sure it was a very personal and mean-
ingful ring. Dr. Pierson seems like a man who'd put genuine
thought into something like that."

Neither of them bothers to acknowledge me.

"We should run a background check on this Piers Pierson,"
Gillian says.

Bertram is quick to pick up on this. "You don't trust him?"

"At this point, I don't trust anyone." Gillian is careful not to look at me, which I take to mean that *I'm* the one she really doubts. "But, no. He's not currently a suspect."

"Then why—"

"So far, all the victims have been high profile and easily identifiable." The elevator arrives at the seventh floor with a hum and a thump, but neither police officer makes a move to exit. "I've never heard of Dr. Pierson before, but that doesn't necessarily mean anything. See if he's well-known in medical or social circles, if there's any fame or notoriety attached to his name. Chances are, someone knew he was going to be here."

"You don't think it was an accident that he was robbed tonight."

"No." Gillian grimaces. "I think this is all going exactly according to plan."

Although Gillian and Bertram step out of the elevator and begin to head down the hall, I find myself unable to follow. I need a moment to digest Gillian's remarks.

Like her, I already know that Baron Gendry-Webber and Nadia Gordon weren't chosen at random. In fact, if someone had asked me to predict the next victim, it would have been Vivian, who's known to the local public and who's made no attempts to hide her expensive jewels. For the thieves to have selected Piers Pierson, who, up until a few days ago didn't exist, is suspicious in the highest degree.

No one knows who he is. No one knows what kind of valuables he carries. He should have been the safest person in the entire hotel.

"Are you coming or not?" Gillian is already halfway down the hallway and none too pleased to find me lagging. "What's the matter with you? Please tell me it isn't another one of those visions."

It's not a vision, but I'm tempted to pretend it is so I can have a minute to think. Obviously, Liam and I know who Nicholas really is. Same with Vivian. And . . . Marian? She'd be able to detect her old school friend's son at a glance, but I have a hard time imagining her robbing safes and swimming out to sea to push a man to his death.

Don't forget Uli, Birdie says. *He seems to know an awful lot about everyone in this hotel.*

My mouth forms a flat line. In my haste to get away, I'd forgotten about the all-knowing Uli. If anyone would be able to see through Nicholas's Pierson ruse, it's the man who stands at the door, watching the lives of everyone else passing him by.

"I'm not waiting much longer, Ms. Wilde," Gillian warns.

"Sorry." I give myself a mental shake. "You should go ahead without me."

Instead of taking comfort from this, Gillian narrows her eyes in sudden suspicion. "Why? What did you just figure out?"

"Nothing," I lie, and not very convincingly. I'm too amped up with the sudden urge to hunt down the doorman. This is what I get for jumping on the Inspector Piper bandwagon instead of taking my time with Nicholas. If I'd been thinking clearly—if I hadn't been knocked sideways by the prospect of a poisonous engagement ring twining round my finger—Uli would have been my first stop.

Drat Nicholas and his poorly timed declarations of affection. Didn't he know what an announcement like that would do to me?

"I realized how tired I am, that's all. I'm sure you can handle the search without me."

"Madame Eleanor, I wouldn't . . ." Bertram clears his throat before lowering his voice and adding, "It's best if you come along. You don't want to cross her in this mood."

I don't want to cross her at all, but some things must be sacrificed in the name of the greater good.

"If she's tired, then we won't keep her," Gillian says before turning sharply on her heel. "But the next time you want access to one of my crime scenes, you'll find that I'm not so conciliating."

"Are there going to be more crime scenes?" I can't help calling after her.

"If things keep going like this, Ms. Wilde, I'm afraid so."

Chapter 22

"Sorry, hon. You just missed him. He went off shift a few minutes ago."

There's no one in the lobby when I arrive except for Laurel. She's back on the invoices, licking her thumb as she flips each page to tally up the hotel's receipts. She pauses, her finger holding her place, as she fishes underneath the desk.

"He did ask me to give you this, though."

I take the proffered envelope. It has a hotel sticker affixed over the seal, my name scrawled hastily across it. "I wish he'd waited," I say as I look down at it. "If it was important, I would have come right down."

"I don't think he was feeling well. He's been off all night."

"Off?" I echo.

"Sweaty, restless, that sort of thing." She nods down at the envelope. "You going to open that?"

I am, but not while I have an audience. If a sweaty, restless Uli had something urgent to tell me, I'm guessing it has to do with Nicholas and the two shadow men. Nestling the letter carefully in my brassiere, I gesture toward the table where the remains of our coffee are still sitting out. "What happened to the other gentleman? Dr. Pierson?"

"He took off right after you and the police officers did. I put him in the suite next to yours. I hope you don't mind."

I'm unable to prevent a spasmodic twitch from taking over me, but I cover it by pretending to cough. "Next to me? Why? Did he request it?"

"No, but he still seemed a little shaken up. I thought he might appreciate being close to friends." Her expression falls as I stand there, mouth agog. "Uh oh. Aren't he and your brother together? I thought they were together."

"Oh, um. Yes. My brother and Dr. Pierson. Together."

Lauren laughs and pretends to wipe her brow. "Phew. You had me worried for a moment there. I don't normally intrude on people's romantic interludes, but there's something about the doctor I like."

That makes two of us. However, as much as I like Nicholas Hartford III, I'm not ready to meet him face to face. I need a few hours to collect myself, to breathe, maybe even to sleep.

And if I'll sleep a little better knowing he's next door to me? Well, we all have our weaknesses, after all.

"Has Nicholas been in to see you?" I slip stealthily through the door to our hotel room, careful to keep my cats inside and to make as little noise doing it as possible. "Has he told you what happened?"

The fact that Liam is blinking sleepily—and grumpily—at me seems to indicate that he's not yet been made aware of the night's events. Relief floods over me like the crash of an ocean wave, and I suddenly feel the exhaustion of everything that's happened over the past few days.

"Oh, geez. What now?" Liam holds up a hand before I can say anything. "No—don't tell me. I changed my mind. I'm going to sit here in ignorance and bask in the glory of . . . Wait a minute. Are those my pants? And my shirt?"

I release a shaky laugh and lower myself into the nearest chair. "Not so loud, would you? Nicholas is in the next room, and I don't want him overhearing us. He needs rest, poor man. He was robbed."

"Robbed?!" Liam shouts. After a warning glare from me, he lowers his voice to add, "What have you two been doing? And why did you need my clothes to do it?"

Of all the things I've done this evening, my theft of his ratty jeans will forever loom the largest in his mind, so I lose no time in detailing everything else. The plan to dress up as the ghost maid, the robbery, the ring . . . I don't leave anything out.

"What's the note say?" he demands as soon as I've finished. He tactfully—and generously—skips over the part where Nicholas intended to make me his intended.

"I haven't opened it yet," I admit, and rip it open. As I expect, it's been hastily scrawled and contains very little that will help me right now.

Meet me in the sauna. 8:00 a.m. Come alone.

Liam yanks it out of my hand and reads aloud, the line down the center of his forehead deepening with each word. "What does he want? And why do you have to be by yourself?"

"Because he's going to confess to murder and then kill me?" I sigh. "I don't know. Your guess is as good as mine."

"You're not going alone."

"Well, obviously."

"I'm coming with you."

"You can stop playing big brother. I already agreed."

"You should probably bring Nicholas, too." Liam casts a look at the door that leads to the adjoining suite. "He won't like being left out."

Although I know he's correct, and that a man of Nicholas's prowess is exactly what this situation calls for, I shake my head. "You can't say anything, Liam. Promise me you won't open that door. He doesn't need to be involved in this."

"He's a part of it whether you like it or not, Ellie," Liam

says. He's not playing big brother so much now as sympathetic observer. I don't like it any better. "You can't just shut people out because it's convenient at the time."

I'm already feeling guilty and exhausted and worried, but this particular attack feels more personal than the rest. "I don't shut people out for convenience!"

The look my brother casts me contains the wisdom of a hundred years. I have no idea where it comes from, and I'm too scared to ask. "There's an entire human being in this hotel that you worked with for six months, and I'd never even heard of him before this. How many more are there? People? Places? Events? What else are you hiding?"

"You don't tell me everything that's going on in your life," I counter. "And you didn't want to know—the things I did for Winnie, the things I did to survive. You were happy to let me carry the burden for all of us."

"I know," he says, and with such sincerity that it cracks something inside me. His gaze—so much like Winnie's, so much like mine—swallows mine. "And I'll never be able to forgive myself for that. But Nicholas is here, Ellie. He's in the literal next room. I didn't show up when you needed me, it's true, but he *has*."

The cracking feeling inside me doesn't abate. If anything, the rift grows deeper, more pronounced. I have no idea what I can use to fill it—if, indeed, it can ever be filled at all.

"Did you know?" I ask suddenly. "About the ring? About what Nicholas was planning to do with it?"

"No," he says. "Did you?"

It's not as silly a question as it seems. In this day and age, most proposals are expected—anticipated, even. Marriage is something both parties discuss in advance and agree upon. There are so many things to work out first. Whether you'll live in a cottage or a castle, how many cats is too many cats, if one of you is one small step removed from a criminal.

He can't know what he's getting himself into. It's too incredulous, too unreal, too impossible. And that's coming from a woman who talks to the dead.

"I'm going to get it back," I say. It's not an answer, but it's not *not* one either. "Nicholas came all this way to give that ring to me. The least I can do is track it down before Uli disappears with it."

"Or Armand," Liam points out.

"Or Armand," I agree. He's not wrong. My suspicions about Uli are just that: suspicions. For all my sleuthing, I don't have any real answers yet. "Or Marian, if we're being fair. It occurred to me earlier that she's one of the only people who would have known that Nicholas is worth stealing from."

"Marian?" Liam laughs, and just like that, he allows the topic to change from betrothals to betrayals. I'm more grateful for this than I can say. "A nice old lady with enough money to buy this hotel three times over? That's it. You need to get to sleep before you start accusing me."

"It's not out of the realm of possibility," I say, though I listen enough to kick off my shoes and lay back on my bed. My weight sinks with a heaviness I don't expect. My eyelids do the same. "She and Vivian used to steal sweets from their boarding school kitchen—Vivian told me. Maybe she developed a taste for danger. Maybe that's how she made her fortune."

"Sleep, Ellie." He flicks out the lights. "We can talk about it in the morning."

Despite myself, I yawn. There's been too much to this day, and too much left for tomorrow. "Remind me to do some background research on her tomorrow. No one ever thinks to suspect the wealthy matron in pink tweed."

"We'll do that," he promises, and I could almost swear that he pulls the blankets up around my shoulders, tucking me in for the night. I have no way of knowing for sure, because I'm already halfway to sleep by then, lulled by the comfort of having him near.

And, right next door, Nicholas.

* * *

"Mammon seize it!" I jolt up in bed, fully awake and aware of my surroundings. I'm also painfully aware of the events of last night . . . up to and including falling to my mattress without first setting an alarm.

"What time is it?" I glance at the clock on the bedside table. It reads 8:21—twenty minutes past the appointed hour of my meeting—and groan. Leaping to my feet, I toss a pillow at my brother's head. "Liam, wake up. You made this happen. You and your tucking me in all nice and gentle. I should have taken a cold shower instead. I should have set five different alarms. I should—"

"What's going on?" He springs up like a jack-in-the-box, blinking at the full light of day. "Are we on fire again?"

"Of course we're not on fire." I lose no time in shoving my feet into the nearest pair of shoes—plastic flip-flops that do nothing for my sleep-rumpled jeans and oversized shirt—before yanking his blankets back. "We should only be so lucky. We're late for the meeting with Uli."

"We are?" He curses once before rolling out of bed. This might be all his fault, but at least he's quick to understand my alarm. "Hold up a sec. I'm still coming with."

I'm more relieved to have my brother's company than I care to admit. He tosses the complimentary terry cloth robe over his boxer shorts and doesn't even bother with shoes. That's more than enough to convince me that he's just as upset about missing the appointed meeting as I am. He'd never go willingly out into public in such an unkempt state. Even Beast is watching him with wary judgment.

We dart into the hallway to find it empty. Liam pauses just long enough to look at Nicholas's closed door, but I stop him before he can say anything. "Let him sleep. We'll catch him up on the details later."

From the way Liam's mouth clamps shut, I know he's not

happy with this plan—or with me—but we're already running behind. Half an hour isn't long to wait when you're talking about a nice Sunday brunch, but we're dealing with more than belated French toast here.

"I'm sure he'll still be there," I say, more to convince myself than Liam. "He knows how much I have going on."

We don't encounter anyone in the elevator, which is nice, and there aren't any people milling about the landing area outside the spa, either. In fact, as we walk through the doors, it's to find ourselves completely alone.

"They don't even open until nine." Liam points at a sign tacked on the wall. "We have plenty of time. He's probably enjoying himself in there."

I laugh. "In a sauna? For half an hour? I doubt it. I was in there yesterday for half that time, and it felt like I was going to die. Come on—it's this way."

We round the corner to the sauna at a slower pace than we came down the elevator. Assuming Uli is still around here somewhere, I don't want to scare him off. If he was already feeling nervous and shifty, if he knows that I'm onto him . . .

I blame my caution for the fact that I don't notice the chair right away. In fact, Liam is the first to point it out.

"Is that thing supposed to be wedged under there?" He points at the sauna. Sure enough, a wooden chair is propped up against the door, tilted on its back legs at an angle. "That's an odd place for a chair."

I stop in my tracks, an arm upflung to hold Liam back. "Don't move," I warn him. "Go get help."

"I thought we were trying to be stealthy." He laughs but it's a high-pitched sound, unsteady. That sentiment—of sudden, uncertain fear—echoes in the flutter of my heart behind my rib cage. There's no way someone could have put that chair there from the inside.

"Go find Gillian, Liam. Or Bertram. *Now.*"

He doesn't follow my orders. Instead, he takes my hand and holds it, our fingers twined like we're eight years old instead of twenty-eight. "We're opening that door together, Ellie," he says. "I'm not letting you go in there alone."

I shouldn't take him up on the offer, but I do it anyway. I'm starting to get used to this—having a living, breathing sibling by my side—and it fills me with a kind of guilt I've never experienced before.

Sorry, Winnie, I mentally apologize as Liam and I walk with shuffling steps toward that door. *I love you, but sometimes I need an actual person, you know?*

I have no idea if she understands or even hears me. She's nowhere to be found, which is probably for the best. No one—human or ghost—should have to experience what Liam and I do. As we pull out the chair and allow the sauna door to fall open, it's to find Uli waiting patiently for my arrival.

We're too late.

And he's dead.

Chapter 23

〜

Piers Pierson is forced to resuscitate my brother with sal volatile and help him, hobbling, to a massage chair located the next room over.

"What were you thinking, subjecting your brother to a scene like this?" Gillian demands. She's had the sauna room shut off and shut down, the door now barred by a fleet of police officers instead of a chair. While my brother is being given gentle treatment at the hands of my sympathetic—if vexed—beau, I'm being treated like a murderer by proxy. "Shame on you, Ms. Wilde. Have you no sense of decency?"

"To be fair, I didn't know there was going to be a body inside," I say. She's already confiscated my note, warned me that everything I say can be used as evidence, and all but accused me of setting this whole thing up. "How long has he been dead?"

She has me by the elbow and drags me past the open massage room door. From the quick glance I cast inside, I see Nicholas kneeling at my brother's feet, earnestly questioning him as to the events leading up to this disaster. All I've gotten from Nicholas so far is a long, considering glance that even I, in my vast, otherworldly wisdom, have been unable to interpret.

Is it hatred? Disappointment? Or—worst of all—regret?

"I was hoping you could tell me," Gillian says. She doesn't stop dragging me until we reach what must be the acupuncture room. There are all kinds of needles and plastic models of human bodies inside. Just what a girl wants to see after walking in on a half-cooked body before she's had her coffee.

"The note said to meet him at eight. Even assuming he got there a few minutes early, there's no way he'd have died of heat exhaustion already. It's hot in there, but not that hot." A thought occurs to me. "Had anyone messed with the thermostat?"

Gillian's only response to this is a glare, which I take to mean yes. I can't help but feel a little sick. I didn't trust Uli, but no one deserves a fate like that.

"I think I need to sit down," I say.

Her look of disbelief is strong and—frankly—insulting, but she allows me to lower myself onto a stool next to a human head with all the phrenology sections partitioned out. Language, wit, weight . . . of all the pseudo-sciences, I think this one might be the worst. The idea that anyone's life is predetermined by the shape of their skull is at best, insulting, and at worst, dangerous. People change. People grow.

People die, Winnie says.

It's as good a reminder as any that I have work to do. "Are there any video cameras in this part of the hotel?"

Her answer is clipped. "No."

"Does anyone remember talking to Uli before he came in today? Or seeing him?"

"I haven't had a chance to question anyone yet."

"Did you find anything of note in Dr. Pierson's room last night?"

"It was the same as all the other rooms. No sign of forced entry. Everything tidy except the bed." She speaks up before I can ask another question. "It's my turn to ask the questions, Ms. Wilde. What did Uli want to talk to you about?"

It would be very easy to lie. I could pretend I have no idea what was going through the doorman's mind, deny any knowledge of his secret ghost wanderings, or even make up something about a romantic tryst between the two of us. I don't. Uli deserves better than that. He wrote me that note because he had something important to tell me—something related to the gold necklace, to the case. It doesn't take a renowned police inspector to deduce that he was killed for that very same reason.

I shove a hand deep in my pocket and extract the necklace that's been wedged there since last night. It dangles from my finger, glistening in the bright lights of the acupuncture room.

Gillian sucks in a sharp breath.

"My guess is that he had something to tell me about this," I say. "I showed it to him yesterday. He was mightily interested in its origins."

From the narrow-eyed look on Gillian's face, I'm guessing she's also mightily interested in its origins.

"You can have it, if you want." I toss it at her. "Add it to the growing evidence pile."

She doesn't appear to be moved by my generosity. Looming over me like a rugby player about to tackle the opposing team, she catches the necklace and holds it clamped over my head. "Where did you get this?"

"I found it," I say. Before she can ask any follow-up questions—or, you know, attack me—I add, "Is it Nadia Gordon's? From her safe?"

Gillian's mouth forms a flat line as she inspects the necklace in her clenched fist. Each pearl is given her intense scrutiny, each link in the gold chain searched with minute attention. It's not until she rubs one of the pearls against the tip of her front tooth that I realize what she's doing—or what it means.

"This necklace didn't come from Ms. Gordon," she says, watching me.

"Are you saying that because it wasn't included on the list of items she claimed were taken?" I watch her right back. "Or are you saying that because it's the real thing, and everything she had in her safe was a fake?"

Gillian's response is to plant her legs more firmly on the floor. If I had a chance of escaping before—which isn't likely—it's definitely out of the question now. I know as much as she does, and in her eyes, that's way more than I should. I'm toying with the idea of calling out to Nicholas to provide a timely rescue, but I'm saved instead by the appearance of Bertram in the doorway.

"The coroner has arrived. She'd like a word with you before she moves the body." He first notices the way Gillian is staring me down and then fixes on the jewelry she's holding above my head. "Oh, dear. That's not good."

I can't help but laugh a little. Trust Bertram to understate the understatement of the year. He makes a move as if to reach out and touch the necklace but stops himself at the last second. "It looks familiar, but—" He shakes himself off. "Where did it come from?"

Admitting that the necklace appeared in my bathroom is a little too close to home, so I improvise. I want answers, not a life sentence. "It came from inside the hotel. You don't think someone could have . . . dropped it, do you?"

Gillian releases a sound halfway between a snort and a laugh. "No one dropped this, Ms. Wilde—I can promise you that much. Where in the hotel did you find it?"

"I can't tell you that."

"Oh, I think you can. And you will."

"Aren't you going to talk to the coroner? I should probably warn you that the longer Uli's body remains here, the more likely his spirit will linger."

This threat doesn't appear to move her. "You found the vacuum cleaner cases, didn't you? You know where they are."

My eyes flare at the sudden shift in conversation—and at how vehemently she speaks. Truth be told, I haven't thought about those cases in quite some time. They've been so ancillary to all our other problems that I was beginning to think my vision had been a misleading one.

"Bertram, take her to the conference room and keep her there. Arrest her if you have to. Handcuff her to a chair."

I leap up from my chair, my hands up in supplication. This wasn't exactly the outcome I was hoping for. "I'm sure that won't be necessary. There's no need to use force. I'm only here to help."

She shakes the chain. "Then you'll tell me where this really came from?"

"What if I were to say that I've smuggled two cats into this hotel, and one of them is an uncanny creature drawn to a cursed doll who keeps reappearing for no reason and most recently showed up with that necklace tangled in her hair . . . ? Would that be enough to free me?"

Gillian isn't amused. "Nice try. That doll of yours is still in evidence. I examined her less than an hour ago."

"Technically, it's a different one. One who's still intact."

This is the final straw for the good inspector. I can't even blame her for it, since locking me up and swallowing the key is the only real course available to her. It was foolish to hope she'd take my side for this, more foolish still to think she'd open the case files wide and let me help.

"Get her out of my sight, Bertram. *Now.*"

I sigh and hold out my wrists. "I suppose I deserve this. But for the record, I wasn't kidding about the cats. Or the doll."

Gillian's head tilts in interest, but she doesn't say anything. She merely draws a deep breath before turning on her heel and stalking toward the sauna.

"Is all that true?" Bertram asks. "About the necklace being attached to the doll?" He doesn't go so far as to handcuff me, opting instead to nudge me out the door and in the direction of the elevators. Once again, I consider calling out to Nicholas, but truth be told, my chances with the police seem better.

I hold up three fingers. "Zeus's honest truth. It showed up in my bathroom out of the blue."

"And there was nothing else with it?"

"Just the usual clean towels and fresh tissue. But I don't think it was a maid, if that's what you're getting at. It was left overnight, and we had the safety lock on the door."

Bertram makes a harrumphing noise that could mean he believes me—or that he finds me as ridiculous and difficult as Gillian does.

"Are you really going to make me sit in the conference room?" I ask.

"Afraid so."

"Even if I promise not to get in any more trouble?"

"You heard the boss."

I did hear her. I also heard the rest of what she said, up to and including her accusation that I know where the vacuum cleaner cases are. Unless I'm very much mistaken—and I rarely am—that means my original suspicion about those cases was correct. I expected them to be holding millions of dollars in cash or evidence of Leonard's depravity and debauchery. It's starting to look as though the latter is true.

Leonard was a traveling salesman with no ties to anyone or anything, carrying three blue vacuum cleaner cases that are currently missing. He was thrown overboard by two shadow figures who have since gone on to rob multiple people and kill a second. And the one thing that ties them all together—besides me—is that necklace.

"The necklace came from one of the cases," I say aloud, testing my hypothesis. "And it wasn't the only thing in there."

Bertram is startled by my speech but not by what I'm saying—which is all the confirmation I need.

"How long have you guys known? When did you first realize that Leonard was one of the safe breakers?" I think, but don't add, *And that someone killed him for those cases full of loot?*

There's no reason for Bertram to answer me, since he has all the power in this situation, but he does it anyway. "From the very start, Madame Eleanor," he says as he continues leading me away. "From the moment we walked into this hotel."

In my lifetime, I've been through attempted murder, haunted castles, poison by proxy, and international conspiracies, but sitting in a conference room without any access to my cell phone is the thing that's going to kill me. I'm sure of it.

"I won't send any text until you read it and approve it, I swear," I ask Bertram. Beg, really, my hands together in supplication and my most pleading expression on my face. "My brother will worry if he doesn't know where I am."

"Inspector Piper will be done any minute."

As it's already been over two hours without any sign of her finishing up with the coroner, I don't put much stock in this. "At least let the front desk know what's going on. That way, if he calls down to ask where I am, they'll be able to give him an answer."

Bertram considers this for a moment before giving in and reaching for the nearest courtesy phone. "Fine. But I'll do the talking. Not a word out of you, got it?"

"Speak to Laurel," I say.

He holds the phone against his ear. "Why?"

"She likes me."

Bertram's chuff of air showcases his disbelief, but he goes ahead and puts the call through. He tries to lower his voice so I can't overhear what's going on, but all six of my senses are in excellent working order.

"If anyone should ask after Ms. Wilde, please tell them she's under police custody." He pauses. "No—no, not under arrest. Just observation." He casts me a covert glance. "Right now? Not much of anything. Why? Should I be worried? Can she cast spells without my knowing?"

I have to muffle a snort of laughter at that one. If I knew of a spell that would get me out of this room so I can talk to Liam, to Nicholas, to Vivian—to *anyone*—I definitely would have used it already. Now that I know why those vacuum cleaner cases are so important, I'm sitting on a lot of useful information. Especially since I'm pretty sure Uli knew why they were so important, too.

He recognized that necklace the instant he saw it. He knew what it was—what it meant—and lost his life trying to tell me.

"Her lips aren't moving, no." Bertram pauses. "Not a lot of hand movements either. She's winking a lot, though."

I decide I've had enough. "I'm not winking, Bertram. I'm blinking. You remember blinking? A natural, autonomous reaction to keep the mucous membranes moist?"

He must remember because he hangs up the phone and relaxes a little. "She promises to relay your message, should anyone ask."

I thank him for his service but wish I could convince him to unbend a little further. It's not that I object to sitting around while a murder investigation takes place without me but, well, I object to sitting around while a murder investigation takes place without me. I could help Gillian if she'd let me—I know I could. My vision of those blue cases has proven to be relevant, my cat is doing her best to provide us all with answers, and there's a murderous mourning ring somewhere out in the world that has my name written all over it. I'm tied to this case whether she likes it or not.

"If you guys knew all along that Leonard was a thief, why haven't you done more to warn the hotel staff?" I ask. Since a rescue doesn't seem imminent, I might as well do something with my time. Questioning Bertram is a good first step. "If his partners murdered him in cold blood, you should have known there was a real possibility of someone like Uli getting caught in the crosshairs. Or do you think Uli was one of them?"

Bertram coughs nervously. "It's not my place to say."

"And what about warning people not to keep valuables in their safes? Since the thieves have a clear MO and don't show any signs of slowing down, wouldn't it be best to warn people to take more precautions with their belongings?"

His cough turns to a choke. "I'm not in charge of this investigation, Ms. Wilde. I only do what I'm told."

I'm starting to get on a roll here, and I have a few more follow-up questions I'd like to pose, but my rescue appears in that moment. It's not, as I expect, my brother or Nicholas riding in on a metaphorical white horse. It's not even Vivian using her position and wealth to demand my release. To my surprise, it's Gillian herself who swoops in—although she doesn't swoop so much as squawk through the radio at Bertram's hip.

"You can let Ms. Wilde go now." Gillian's voice crackles over the airwaves in what must be the most beautiful sound in the world. "There's no need to keep her any longer."

Bertram's eyes widen, and he looks at me as though checking to make sure I'm not secretly practicing witchcraft behind his back. It's not a wholly unfounded fear—I'm surprised by this sudden shift myself.

"What about the necklace she had in her possession?"

"It's taken care of."

"And the note she received from the dead man—"

"You're not to worry about it."

"But . . . But . . ." Bertram looks as though he's about to cry. "I don't understand. She's—"

"Constable, do you have a problem with the chain of command?"

He practically clicks his heels in response to her voice. "No, ma'am."

"Then do as I ask. Release her. Now."

I try not to be smug as I stand up and make a big show of shaking my limbs out, but I can't help it. I *am* smug. I mean, there's a good chance that Gillian has put Billie or another police officer on a secret watch in hopes that I'll lead her team straight to those vacuum cleaner cases, but I don't hold that against her. It's what I would have done in her position.

"It's nothing personal, Bertram." I extend my hand in a show of solidarity. "If anyone asks, I'll tell them you did an amazing job watching me."

"You will?" He doesn't seem to believe me.

I make the motion of a cross over my chest. "I was terrified every second. Your air of authority, the way you strike fear into the most stalwart of hearts . . ."

He runs a hand over the top of his head. Scraggly bits of his hair stand on end, and he suddenly looks as exhausted as I feel. "There's no need to oversell it." He sighs. "I'm—I'm not really qualified for any of this, you know. I'm just a peon. A grunt. I can't think why Inspector Piper requested me in the first place."

I can't, either, but if there's one thing I've learned over the past week, it's that Gillian Piper is a woman who knows what she's doing.

"You're stronger than you realize, Bertram," I say. Lifting my hand to my temple, I close my eyes and offer him a parting gift of my ethereal wisdom. Now that I'm a free woman, I'm feeling quite charitable. "Your future holds great things. You just need the nerve to reach out and grab them."

Chapter 24

The words of wisdom I gave Bertram haunt me well long after I leave him. Like a ghost I can't exorcise, they flit and dance around me, making it impossible to concentrate on the here and now.

The here is my hotel room. The now is midafternoon. As for who and what and why, I'm no closer to an answer now than I was a week ago.

"Ellie, are you even listening to me?" Liam snaps his fingers. "Hello? Earth to Eleanor."

I shake myself and focus on my brother's face. Thanks to the rapid wanderings of my mind, this is no easy feat. "Sorry," I say, seeing nothing but his dark eyebrows and two holes where his eyes go. "I was just thinking about something."

"About packing up and heading home? That's an excellent idea. Seize the day. Get while the getting's good. Hide your tail between your legs and—"

"Are you absolutely sure that Nicholas is with his mother?" I interrupt. "And will be for the foreseeable future?"

No fool, Liam sees through my question in an instant. "Oh, geez. What are we going to do now?"

I stare at him until he heaves a sigh and answers.

"That's where he said he was going, yes. He said something about strategic retreat and his mother needing someone to carry her shopping bags."

My face heats. There's no use pretending that I don't understand what Nicholas meant by strategic retreat—or that my brother doesn't, either.

"You're going to have to face him eventually," he says. "You can't hide behind murder forever."

He's not wrong. Murder and intrigue and being held in police custody will only keep me safe for a little while. Sometime very soon, I'm going to have to stop running away from reality. And from Nicholas.

"I will," I say, more to myself than Liam. I don't know whether it's Nicholas's annoyance or affection that I'm most afraid of, but there's no denying that the fear is there all the same. *Me*, Eleanor Wilde, ghost hunter and murderer catcher, afraid of a mere mortal man. It's the exact sort of thing that would appeal to Nicholas's twisted sense of humor. "I promise I will. I just need to do this one thing first."

I force all thoughts of Nicholas as far down in my stomach as they'll go and focus on what I told Bertram instead. It was good advice for him, and even better advice for me: *Your future holds great things. You just need the nerve to reach out and grab them.*

"I'm a genius, really," I say. "The only way I'm getting anywhere is if I just suck it up and do it."

"Suck it up and do what?" Liam asks. "Ellie, what are you planning, and why is it making you cackle like the Wicked Witch of the West?"

There's no need for me to explain. Liam is a part of me, a part of all this, and he knows as well as I do that there's only one option left to us.

He groans. "Please tell me you're not about to do what I think you're about to do."

"Oh, I'm doing it," I assure him. "And you're going to help. Find Armand. I think I'm ready to see what this hypnosis thing is really all about."

"Don't wake me up unless I'm in physical danger." I'm seated on a bench along the Brighton promenade, tucked away in relative seclusion from the beach crowds. I can still see plenty of people around us, so I'm not scared of Armand taking advantage of my hypnotic state, but there's no denying that my nerves are high. "Liam, keep hold of that rope and don't let it go no matter what. I don't want to wander into the ocean and drown or anything."

The rope in question is a curtain cord from our hotel room, a lifeline that attaches me to my brother in case I try to make a break for it while I'm under. It might seem like overkill to treat a hypnotic trance like a spelunking adventure, but I'm not taking any chances.

"Don't try to influence me in any way," I continue. "Don't allow anyone to interact with me unless I instigate it. And— this is the most important rule—under no circumstances will you tell anyone what we're up to until it's over and done with."

I can tell that Liam doesn't much care for that last rule, since the *anyone* in question is obviously Nicholas, but Armand allows a grin to spread. He's been itching to get started ever since I knocked on his hotel room door.

"I knew you'd come around," he'd said, biting into a room-service sandwich and looking smug. "When do you want to start?" I hadn't much cared for arrogance, but the eagerness suits my purposes just fine.

"Are you absolutely sure about this, Ellie?" Liam asks now, his words heavy with meaning. He tugs the curtain cord to ensure the sanctity of the knot. "We could wait until this afternoon and ask—"

"Do it." I cut him off before he can mention Vivian, Piers

Pierson, or any member of the police force. "We need to see this thing through to the end—no matter what that end is."

I sit back against the bench and allow my breathing to fall into an even pattern. I don't love the way Armand greedily rubs his hands together or the anxious way my brother checks his phone, but I don't allow the distractions to weigh with me.

When Winnie pipes up, however . . .

I can't reach you when you're under, she says, sounding so much like our mom that it causes me to jump. *I don't know where you go, but it's not anywhere I can follow.*

It's on the tip of my tongue to reassure her, to promise that no harm will come to me while our brother keeps watch, but I don't. I've never once lied to Winnie, and I don't intend to start now.

That's why, for the first time since my sister has started talking to me from beyond the grave, I pretend I don't hear her. I tune out all sounds except the ocean in the distance and the low croon of Armand's voice. I banish thought and fear and reason, and that's when . . .

Chapter 25

I awaken to darkness.

It's not complete darkness, but it's enough that I feel a surge of fear. The worst thing about losing huge chunks of time is that I have no idea how long it's been since I was last myself—how far I might have strayed or what changes might have occurred in my absence.

In this instance, however, it takes only a few seconds for me to recognize my surroundings.

"Really?" My outcry is immediately followed by several people urging me to be quiet. I lower my voice, but there's no way I can stay silent right now. "Are you guys serious? I took us to a movie?"

I'm seated in the middle of a row of red plush theater seats, flanked on either side by Armand and Liam. Liam is still holding my leash, but he's allowed it to grow slack in his grasp. If that wasn't clue enough that this is the tamest of my hypnosis journeys yet, then the fact that he's munching on a giant tub of buttered popcorn would do the trick.

Armand is more alert, his gaze on me rather than the black-

and-white movie flickering on the screen, but he looks a lot less excited about the outcome of this hypnosis than the last one.

"You're back," he says, stating the obvious. "How was it? Where did you go? What did you—?"

"Shh!" The woman seated in front of us turns around and glares. "You're ruining the movie."

The image of Orson Welles looking stern and dapper flashes across the screen. I recognize the movie in an instant as *Citizen Kane*.

"Thank goodness," Liam says as he pops a handful of kernels in his mouth. "It's been almost an hour, and this movie is boring. Couldn't you have taken us to something with explosions?"

"Would you please take your conversation to the lobby?" the woman asks, louder this time. "I want to see how it ends without a running commentary, thanks."

Liam and I immediately apologize and start to make our way to the end of the row. It says a lot about Armand as a human being that he refuses to join us until he leans close to the woman and says, loud enough for the whole theater to hear, "Rosebud is the sled."

"Well, that's an hour of my life I'll never get back," Liam says as we emerge into the bright lights of the movie theater lobby. It's small and quaint, a sort of old-fashioned callback to the theaters of the fifties. Art deco engravings cover the ceiling and noir posters line the walls. It's the sort of place I'd love going to in the normal way of things. At least my hypnotized self has good taste. "Do you remember anything? Walking here? Buying the tickets?"

"Wait—you made *me* buy the tickets? For a movie I couldn't even see?"

"I didn't make you do anything," Liam protests. "You just walked up to the ticket counter and slid a bill across. I've never seen anything like it."

Armand has joined us by this time, blinking as his eyes adjust from the semidarkness of the theater.

"Is this supposed to be a joke?" I demand of him. He had to have done this—planted the idea for us to go to a movie, prodded me along to make some kind of point. I like old movies as much as the next vintage-loving witch, but we've got more pressing concerns. "What are you trying to get at, Armand?"

"Me?" he counters. "I was going to ask the same thing of you. When I hypnotized you that first time, it was . . . surreal. You did things I didn't understand, things I couldn't explain."

"You and me both," I say, but he's not finished yet.

"Your hypnosis by recording was understandably less reactive, since I wasn't there to use my powers in person. It was polluted, diluted. But this—this—" He cuts himself off and pretends to spit onto the swirling red carpet. "A beachfront stroll and an old movie. Bah! If you didn't want to participate, you could have just said so."

"I still don't understand why we couldn't have gone to that modern theater we passed on the way here," Liam says. "What's so special about this particular one?"

Of the two men, Liam's comments are the ones that capture my attention. "We passed another theater on the way here?"

He rolls a shoulder in a half shrug. "Yeah, that big multiplex with the neon marquee that we drove by on the way down. Don't you remember?"

I nod, my memory catching at that particular movie theater. I didn't think much of it at the time—and I still don't think much of it now—but the fact that I singled this one out must mean something. The first time I was under hypnosis, I set the entire hotel into high alert, throwing furniture with my mind and sending crowds of people fleeing. The second time I was under hypnosis, I fell into a revolving door loop next to Uli and said something about asking Inspector Piper a question.

This time, I paid for a midday movie date at an old-school movie theater showing *Citizen Kane*.

"Is it about the sled? Orson Welles? Newspaper magnates?" I ask aloud. Not unreasonably, neither Liam nor Armand answers me. Even if my subconscious mind *had* wanted to highlight one of those particular ideas, there's no way I could have known what movie was playing here. There's something else, something I must be missing—

"There you are!" The lobby doors push open, stopping my musings short. I turn to find a tall, dark figure standing in the doorway, the sunshine breaking all around him and making it difficult to read the features of his face.

Not that I need to see. I know that voice—and even more to the point, I know the man attached to it. He's not, in a word, *happy*.

"I've been searching everywhere for you." Nicholas strides into the lobby, not bothering to hide his feelings. That, more than anything, is cause for alarm. "Did you forget our dinner date? You promised to visit that chip shop with me. I've been looking forward to it all day."

Liam's eyes flare in surprise, but he's my brother for a reason. His recovery is quick.

"Oh, blast!" He palms his forehead in a show of remorse. "I'm so sorry, Piers. It completely slipped my mind. My sister really wanted to see *Citizen Kane*, so we came by for the show."

"Indeed?"

The chilly politeness in his voice is unmistakable.

"It was just a whim," I say, wishing I didn't sound so guilty. I wish I didn't *feel* so guilty, either, but there's little help for it now. I've been caught hypnosis-handed. "Something we decided on at the last minute. We would have invited you to come with us, only . . ."

"Only I would have been in the way. I understand."

He doesn't understand—not really—but there's no way for me to explain myself in front of Armand without giving everything away.

"For future reference, I adore old movies," Nicholas says. He's ostensibly speaking to Liam, but his gaze is fixed on mine. His gray eyes are steely and hard, his voice only slightly less so. "There's something missing in the modern era of digital media, don't you think? It makes me sound old-fashioned, but I've always preferred records to music streaming, projectors to computer files."

That preference is something he and I have always shared. It's difficult to live in a village as small and antiquated as ours and not appreciate a simpler lifestyle. If given a choice, I'd always choose a long, rambling walk through the fields over a nightclub and the flickering, unreliable lights of 35-mm film over—

"Great Goddess Almighty!" I turn to stare at the poster nearest me. It's of a dripping sea creature grasping at a woman in a yellow bikini, but I'm less interested in the image than I am of the meaning behind it. Every single one of these movie posters—and these movies—comes from a world where digital technology never existed. The only way to watch them is on a projector.

Which projects things. Images. Figures. *Shadows.*

I'm practically thrumming with excitement by this time, but I'm not about to divulge my findings while Armand is standing right there. I still don't know how deeply involved he is in all this, but this breakthrough is one that will change everything. This whole time, I've been struggling to reconcile what Liam and I saw on that boat and what Uli saw on that boat, to figure out who—or what—has been breaking into those safes. I've been unable to work out how two shadow men can disappear so quickly that it's almost as though they never existed.

Unless, of course, they never *did* exist.

"What is it?" Nicholas is the first to break through my sudden abstraction. He still doesn't look happy with me, but there's no denying that I've captured his interest. "What do you need?"

"A postcard," I reply. If I'm right—and I'm almost certain I am—then I've just figured out why Uli didn't see what Liam and I saw. *Not* because he was lying, but because there was literally nothing there. For him, at least. If the angle of the hotel overlooking the water, if where we were standing versus where he was holding his post at the door . . . a projected image would only appear to those standing in front of it, and there's a certain aerial shot that will answer everything.

It also just so happens that I know the exact marina where I can get it.

Chapter 26

The first thing I decide to do is separate the group. It's not an easy task, since no one wants to be the one to lure Armand off. Liam feels he has more of a right to this adventure since he's related to me; Nicholas because he refuses to let me out of his sight again. And Armand, sensing something big happening, refuses to be driven off.

There's only one option left.

"Go to your dinner, you two." I smile beatifically on Liam and Nicholas, aware as I do that I'm making both men very unhappy with me. "I've been dying to do some souvenir shopping, so this is a perfect opportunity. Liam always hates it when I spend money on useless knickknacks."

Truth be told, Liam adores useless knickknacks, but he recognizes a ruse when he sees one. "All they do is collect dust," he announces as though he doesn't have an entire collection of *Game of Thrones* figurines sitting in their original boxes back home. "Such a waste. It's not like you have a ton of space to keep them."

"I'm a sucker for kitsch." I smile at Nicholas. "You'll forgive me for taking him to the movies, Dr. Pierson? I'm sure you two have a lot to talk about."

If they didn't have anything to talk about before, they certainly do now. Neither man is pleased at being summarily dismissed, but unless Nicholas is willing to throw his nom de plume to the wind, there's little he can do to fight it.

"I'm sure we'll find a way to fill the time," he says with a tight smile. "If you're looking for good shops, I recommend the ones near the Old Steine."

"Thanks. I'll keep that in mind. Well, Armand? Are you going to keep me company?"

He looks surprised at being included, but he's nothing if not opportunistic. If there's a chance he can use this situation to his advantage, he'll find a way to do it. "Anything you want, Ellie. But I'm not sure I understand your sudden need for post-cards."

He wouldn't, of course. No one currently standing in this movie theater does.

"One must never be dilatory in their correspondence," I say, and leave it at that. At least, I leave it at that until Armand and I make our way out the doors and head in the direction of the marina. He waits only until we're out of range of Liam and Nicholas before pouncing.

"Out with it," he says. "What really happened while you were under? What didn't you want your brother and the man who's been weirdly following him around to know?"

It's not surprising that Armand picked up on how suspicious Nicholas's activities have been. I'm just grateful he hasn't figured out the true state of affairs yet.

"I didn't want to say anything while Liam was there," I lie, thinking quickly. The best thing to do now is to make Armand believe that I have some kind of superpower—that hypnotizing me gives me a direct line to the great beyond. I mean, *something* strange happens while I'm under, but I don't dare define it. "I saw everything. The murder, the thefts, all of it. I know what really happened."

His whole body thrums with excitement. "And the vacuum cleaner cases? You saw them, too? You know where they are?"

I barely manage to avoid giving myself away. Latching on to a cracked sidewalk in front of me, I feign a stumble and grasp onto Armand's arm as a way to cover my discomposure. I could almost curse myself for my clumsiness—the metaphorical kind. It shouldn't come as a shock that Armand knows about the vacuum cleaner cases or that he wants what's in them. If there's money to be gained within a ten-mile radius, he's already sniffed it out, come up with a plan to get it, and mapped out six different exit routes.

"I thought you wanted to take the Hartfords for all they're worth," I say. "Not stolen goods that are linked to a murder."

He doesn't pretend to misunderstand me. "Why can't I do both? There's got to be at least half a million dollars' worth of jewelry in those things. We're in the right place at the right time. It'd be a shame to let them go without a fight."

The fact that Armand has an estimate at hand and ready to go troubles me. It's a strange sensation, to feel this deeply unsettling fear in the midst of the bright holiday setting, but I note a dark cloud on the horizon and take comfort from that. The night Leonard was killed, it was as if the elements knew that something dark and dangerous was about to happen. If things are as I suspect, then the world is about to get dark and dangerous again.

"How do you know what's in those cases?" I demand.

He looks at me as though I have *D-U-N-C-E* written in bold letters across my forehead. "Brighton, Bath, Oxford, Bristol . . . they're all linked. They're all connected."

There haven't been many times in my life when I'm at an

utter loss for what to say. Words—of comfort, of warning, of no particular meaning at all—are my stock in trade, and have been for the majority of my adult life. This is one of those rare moments when my vocabulary fails me.

And Armand, drat him, knows it.

"You don't know, do you?" A Cheshire-like grin moves across his face, his delight palpable. "About the other hotels. About how long this has been going on."

"I do too," I protest.

"I can't believe I didn't realize it before—I must be slipping, too. It's because of all that furniture you threw around with your mind." His grin is still in place, and his pace picks up as we wend our way toward the beachfront. "Let me fill you in. Over the past few months, there have been reports of—"

"I might be a little behind the times, but I'm not an idiot," I snap. And it's true, too. Eleanor Wilde from five minutes ago might have been operating in the dark, but the Eleanor Wilde of right now has pieced a few things together. "Over the past few months, jewelry has been stolen from upscale hotels across England—always by two shadow figures hunched over a safe, and always while the victim is asleep. In addition to the MO, the thing that links the cases is a certain wandering vacuum cleaner salesman who's stayed at each hotel under a different name."

Most of what I've just said is a guess, but by the time I'm done, I know I'm right. Armand's look of self-satisfaction tells all. So does common sense. In addition to admitting that the gold-and-pearl necklace came from one of the vacuum cleaner cases, Bertram confessed on his first day that the great Gillian Piper is only brought on for the big jobs—and that she specifically requested this one. A nationwide spree of thefts, most of which are targeting the rich and famous, would definitely fall under the category of "big."

"Either Leonard got too greedy and wanted to keep all the jewelry for himself, or there was a falling out between him and his partner, because he was murdered," I say, gaining speed as well as understanding. Greed might not make for the most glamorous motivation for killing another human being, but that doesn't make it any less common. "Except the cases are missing."

All three of them, lined up against the wall, heavy enough to leave impressions in the carpet, and important enough to appear in my vision.

"That's why the partner hasn't moved on to a new location even though the hotel is crawling with police," I continue. And why Uli was killed. If he knew what was in those cases, if he knew where they were . . . "Whoever it is can't—or won't—move on until he finds them. Half a million dollars isn't easy to walk away from."

"Partners," Armand corrects me. "There are two, remember?"

It takes me a moment to realize what he's saying. That, more than anything else, convinces me of Armand's innocence—at least in this regard. It's simple math. Two shadows, two bad guys. He doesn't know about the projectors.

I don't bother enlightening him. Part of it is my reluctance to tell him *anything*, since he's made it clear that his goal is to get his hands on those cases of jewelry before the police do. However, I'd be lying if the sight of the marina in the distance didn't also play a role. We've been so busy talking that I failed to realize how far we walked.

"They have postcards in there." I point at the marina. "I saw them when I was questioning the owner the other day."

Armand isn't fooled. "What do you really want the postcards for?"

"They're for Nicholas." I march in that direction without explaining further. Armand trots to keep up, his footsteps dogging my own. I ignore him as I pull open the cheerfully jangling door. I continue ignoring him as I approach the man at the counter, who looks just as bored and bereft as the last time. I even ignore him as I spin the postcard rack, searching in vain for the aerial shot of the hotel.

"You're back!" the man cries, sensing an opportunity. I can hardly blame him for it. Even though the beach has been more crowded the past few days, no one has been brave enough to rent one of his death boats. "A clipper? A slipper? A—"

"No yawls for me, thanks." I tap the empty slot on the postcard rack. "What happened to the ones that were here?"

He blinks and scrubs a hand over his grizzled jaw. "Those old ones from the nineties? I threw them out. I didn't realize how out of date they were until you bought one."

"They're gone? All of them? For good?"

"Out with last night's rubbish. They'll be on their way to the landfill by now."

I could almost curse my bad luck. If only I'd allowed myself to be hypnotized the first time Armand offered, if I'd refused to give in to Nicholas's fears . . .

"And you don't have any more? In the back? I really liked the aerial shot one."

"Sorry, miss. I wouldn't even know where to order that particular postcard anymore. You likely have the last one on earth." He rolls his shoulder. "Well, the person you sent it to has the last one, anyhow. Mayhap they can send it back to you."

Some of my disappointment ebbs away. This isn't as terrible an idea as it sounds. I sent that one to Peter, and there's no way he took the initiative to throw it in the garbage yet. He isn't nearly as tidy a human being as one would expect a police inspector to be. He flicks cigarette ashes and gum wrappers all over his crime scenes.

I rap my knuckles on the counter. "You're absolutely right," I say. "I'll call my friend right now. You've been a big help."

"What about your companion?" the man asks, ever hopeful. "Does he want to rent a boat?"

Armand shakes his head in a resolute no. "I'm not going anywhere near the water while I'm in this woman's company." He flashes his teeth in a smile that doesn't quite reach his eyes. "She's already killed me once. There's no way I'm making it easy on her a second time."

Chapter 27

"Peter! My dearest friend. My darlingest foe. My second favorite police inspector in all the world."

I'm sitting alone on the beach, my bare feet shoved into the sand, watching as the storm rolls in over the waves. My toes are the only warm part of my body, since the sand retains some of the heat of the sun. Everything else is wind-whipped and chilled from the ocean breeze, but I don't mind. At least I can have my phone call in relative isolation. As was the case the night of the murder, no one wants to be caught out in yet another freak storm.

"Why am I only your second favorite police inspector?" Peter demands. His voice is gravelly and coarse, either because I've awoken him from sleep or because he's started smoking again. Neither thing is likely to put him in a good mood. "What has Gillian been telling you about me? They're lies, all of it. Don't trust a word out of her mouth."

"Oh, good. You got my postcard."

"Of course I got your postcard." He pauses. "Are you really embroiled in a murder investigation down there? It's been a week, Eleanor. How can you run into that kind of trouble in such a short space of time?"

Peter obviously underestimates my capacity for intrigue. "This one wasn't my fault. I was a witness, that's all. Naturally, the police wanted to speak with me regarding what I saw. I could hardly let things stand after that. I like your ex-wife, by the way."

"Of course you do."

I laugh at how grumpy he sounds but lose no time in getting to the point. This is no mere social call. "Do you still have the postcard in your possession?" I ask.

"Yes. Why? Does it have a secret code on it or something?"

"No, but that's a really smart idea. Next time I'll be sure and include one. Can you do me a favor?"

"That depends on the favor."

His voice is still reticent, but there's a hint of interest in there, too. "Take a quick picture of the front and send it to me, would you? I need to measure something."

"What kind of something?"

"I'll tell you if it checks out," I promise, and wait as he goes through the process. I can hear him grumbling and fumbling the entire time—he's not the most technologically savvy man, opting instead for old-school methods of detective work—but the fact that he's trying is a plus.

"There. Did it go through?"

I wait a moment until the incoming text alert comes in. It doesn't take me long to find what I'm looking for. The image might be grainy and old—and Peter's photo-taking skills leave something to be desired—but there's no mistaking it. The angles of the hotel, the front door, and the beachfront check out. Assuming our murderer/thief was projecting that image from one of the rooms on the farthest end of the hotel, it would have perfectly cast onto the boat where Leonard died. And Uli, standing guard at the doors, wouldn't have seen a thing.

Which means my two shadow men are just that—shadows. Images, projections, a hazy play of light and dark.

It's genius, really. I only wish I'd figured it out sooner—or, to be honest, at all. It wasn't me who put two and two together, but whatever entity is speaking to me from the deep recesses of hypnosis.

"Hello? Eleanor? Are you still there?" Peter's tinny voice sounds from the speaker of my phone.

"Sorry!" I'm breathless as I resume the call, but more from excitement than fear. "Thanks. That was exactly what I needed. Hold on to that postcard, would you? Gillian may need it for evidence."

"What kind of evidence? Eleanor, what aren't you telling me? What exactly are you and Gillian doing down there?"

I tug my feet from the sand and wriggle my toes to get them clean again. "Solving crimes together, of course." I shove my feet into my sandals and fumble to clasp them while holding the phone to my ear. "We're a buddy cop comedy, just like you and I used to be. I love everything about her, by the way. Did she used to be a rugby player or something?"

"Rugby?" he echoes.

"Rugby, rugger, whatever you guys call it. She's definitely built for it. I saw her leap over a potted plant like it was nothing. For a woman of her stature, it was quite impressive."

"What are you talking about? Gillian? *My* Gillian?"

For the first time since I initiated this conversation, I feel less than certain of my ground. "Inspector Gillian Piper of the Metropolitan Police Service? That is the woman you were once trothed to, yes?"

"Of course it is. But she's never touched a rugby ball in her life. Or leaped over anything bigger than a bread box. She wouldn't want to risk breaking a nail."

At this, my uncertainty takes on new proportions. The Gillian Piper I've been working with all this time barely has fingernails.

I mean, she *possesses* them, obviously, but they're worn down with work and anxiety, jagged and shorn in a way that denotes long-term neglect. If she's ever gone anywhere near a manicure, I'll eat the sand between my toes.

"Peter, please tell me your ex-wife is a statuesque woman with mousy brown hair, thighs that regularly crush watermelons, and eyes so cold they could freeze the Sahara."

"Uh . . ."

"Peter, please tell me that your ex-wife is brusque to the point of rudeness and that she terrifies every subordinate who crosses her path."

"I'm not sure who you're talking about, but that's not my Gillian. Her eyes are brown, and she's never crushed a watermelon in her life. With her legs or any other part of her anatomy. I doubt she could. She's not much bigger than you are."

It's on the tip of my tongue to inform Peter that size can be misleading, and that should the urge strike me, I could demolish scores of watermelons, but I don't. My head is too busy whirling with the implications of what he's saying. At no point during this investigation have I actually seen Gillian Piper's credentials. Why would I? Her air of command, her knowledge of my relationship with Peter, even the way all the other police officers defer to her . . . there's been no reason for me to question her authority. She's been everything I expect of a police inspector and more, and I've been walking around with so many stars in my eyes that my vision is blurred.

But the truth is, no one here has actually met her before. Both Vivian and Nicholas confessed to knowing her only by reputation, and even Bertram himself admitted that he'd never worked with her because she only appears for the big cases. What are the chances that all the other cops milling about around here would say the same?

I can hardly believe it, but there's no other explanation. With the right amount of confidence—a thing *my* Gillian has in abundance—it would be easy to waltz into a police investigation and claim ownership over it. And so many things about her have been just a little off—not enough to question at the time, but enough to linger in my memory: the glove she switched from hand to hand, as if she couldn't remember which one she was supposed to be using; how quickly she let me inside Leonard's room after I threatened to call Peter on her behalf; the paperwork trail she avoided by telling Bertram to keep me off the books.

"Eleanor?" Peter sounds as agitated as I feel. "Eleanor, are you still there?"

"I'm here," I say. The words feel detached and distant, as if issuing from someone else. "Peter, if the Gillian Piper I've been working with this whole time isn't your ex-wife, then who is she?"

"Forget that." The sound of something loud and metallic clatters over the phone. "If the Gillian Piper you've been working with this whole time isn't my ex-wife, then *where* is she?"

That's an equally valid question, but not the one that's most pressing on my mind. What's really bothering me—and what's making my heart thump—is the knowledge that half a million dollars are currently missing. And the one woman who's been trying hardest to uncover them isn't who I thought she was.

Everything clicks into place at the same time.

Not-Gillian knew about those three vacuum cleaner cases in Leonard's room before I did . . . because she's been looking for them from the start.

Not-Gillian believed me about the two shadow men on the boat . . . because she's the one who projected them into the ocean.

In other words, Not-Gillian is a murderer and a thief. And I, like an infatuated fool, have been helping her since the moment we met.

"I have to go." I shake off the last of the sand and turn back toward the hotel. I'm not a hundred percent sure what I plan to do, but I'm not about to let myself be used like this without a fight.

"Wait, Eleanor. If Gillian is missing—"

"She is, but I can't worry about that right now. I need to talk to Nicholas. I need to see Liam. I need . . ."

I'm not sure exactly what I need, but it includes Not-Gillian, a pair of handcuffs, and three missing vacuum cleaner cases full of loot. In no particular order.

"Don't do anything until I get there."

That gives me pause. "Wait—you're coming? To Brighton?"

"I'm already halfway out the door." The continued clatter of metal in the background bears witness to this claim. "Don't let that impostor know you're onto her. If she's done anything to hurt Gillian, I swear on everything—"

I have no way of knowing what he swears because the phone cuts out before he's halfway through. Peter's concern for his ex-wife is sweet, and under any other circumstances, I'd have donned a pair of angel wings and played Cupid. Not this time, however. My steps are dogged and my intention resolved.

Romance is all well and good in its place, but there comes a time when proposals of marriage and ex-husbands coming valiantly to the rescue have no place.

Two men have been murdered, and I know who did it. Love will have to wait.

Chapter 28

As fortune would have it, I run into Gillian as I'm hightailing back to the hotel.

And by *run into*, I mean literally. In an attempt to avoid her, I duck in through the side door—the one where all the cigarette butts are piled—without looking where I'm going. One second, I'm pushing my way inside, and the next, WHAM!

Gillian grabs me by both arms to steady me, her grip strong enough to snap a pair of tree trunks. She doesn't release me right away. Instead, she shoves those icy blue eyes close to mine and stares as though she can see straight through to my soul. "What's the matter with you?" she demands. "Where are you headed in such a hurry?"

Not for nothing have I spent a lifetime lying to people for personal gain. Although I'd like nothing more than to kick this woman in the shins and demand answers, I laugh and put a hand to my hair as if to straighten it.

"Do I look a fright?" I ask as I tuck a wayward lock behind one ear. "It's getting awfully windy out there—it's almost as dark as the first night I arrived. The weather here is something else, isn't it?"

Her eyes narrow but she doesn't answer.

"It's almost as though it's connected," I persist. "As if it knows what's coming next."

She doesn't mistake my meaning. "Why? What's coming next? What did you discover?"

There are enough people around that I could reasonably confront her with the truth. *I know you aren't Gillian Piper. I know you're only here to find the vacuum cleaner cases. I know there's a good chance you were involved in the deaths of Leonard and Uli.* Then again, if it comes down to my word against that of a woman who's been accepted and hailed as the head of this investigation, what are the chances I'd get out of this alive? Until I have a chance to contact the *real* authorities, I'm going to have to tread carefully. Someone who's murdered at least once in the name of greed won't be afraid to do it again.

Although the smart thing to do in this situation would be to adopt the same carefree, interfering psychic façade I've worn from the start, I can't help but respond in kind. "Mother Nature isn't pleased at the way things are going," I say. "She won't rest until the perpetrator is caught. And neither, Inspector Piper, will I."

It would have been so cool if lightning struck at that exact moment, or if a rumble of thunder rocked the darkening skies, but a low growl from deep in Gillian's throat is the closest I get.

That low growl says everything. She's not pleased at my reticence and, if I'm not mistaken, is rapidly losing her patience. It's no wonder—the longer she hangs around, searching for the missing cases under the pretense of running an investigation, the greater the likelihood that someone will find her out. Especially if people keep dying. It's only a matter of time before one of the police officers milling about around here realizes that their star investigator isn't who she claims.

"If you know something, Madame Eleanor, you need to share it with the authorities," Not-Gillian warns. She finally releases me, the pressure points of her fingers flooding with sudden sensation. "I've been lenient with you so far, but there's an end to my patience."

"You *have* been lenient with me," I agree. "Why is that, I wonder? It's almost as though you're afraid of what might happen if your superiors find out that I'm helping you—of what it might uncover."

She jumps back with such speed and alarm that it confirms everything I already suspect. This woman is no more Gillian Piper than I am. Since I've already said too much, I lose no time in taking my departure. "Unless I'm under arrest, I'm going to head up to my room now," I say. It's a risky move, since she could theoretically arrest me and shove me in a trunk somewhere, but she only watches me go with cold, angry eyes.

"I don't know what you're up to, but I wouldn't try it if I were you," she warns.

Since I'm safely out of tackle range by this time, I don't hesitate in answering in kind. "Then it's a good thing you're not me, isn't it? You're Inspector Gillian Piper."

"Yes, hello? Is this the police? I'd like to report an impostor."

The click of the door interrupts me before I can make my claim. I glance quickly up, but it's only Liam and Nicholas coming to question and berate me. Holding up a finger to silence them, I continue my call.

"The woman you have leading the investigation down here in Brighton—the murder and the thefts? She's not actually Gillian Piper. She's been replaced by the real culprit. Yes, I'm serious. No, this is not a prank."

My cats yawn and stretch as they greet the newcomers. Nicholas takes a moment to give them their customary pats, but Liam loses no time in pouncing on me instead.

"What are you doing? Have you lost your mind? Hang up the phone!"

I ignore him and roll out of the way. "What do you mean by

proof? Send someone down here who knows her personally, and you'll have your answer. She's literally a different person than who she claims to be. It'll take two seconds to verify."

The woman on the other end of the line isn't amused. It took me half an hour to get through to someone with the actual authority to do something, and she's convinced I'm one witch short of a coven.

"Then send a picture of her to the hotel. Or to Officer Bertram Davies. I'm telling you, the woman you have working here is not Gillian Piper. Something terrible is going on, and until you send someone—" The phone cuts off as the woman hangs up on me. I stare at the receiver for a moment, blinking at it as if the woman might magically return to the call.

She doesn't.

"Oh, dear." Nicholas takes the receiver from me and puts it back on the cradle. "That didn't sound productive."

"She didn't believe me. She called me hysterical." I laugh in a manner that can only be described as, well, hysterical. "Can you believe it? *Me?*"

Nicholas wisely keeps his own counsel, but Liam shows no such tact. "Uh, Ellie? Have you looked in a mirror lately? Because whatever is going on with your hair—"

"It's windy, okay? And I didn't have time to fix it. I'm busy trying to stop a murderer—more specifically, the woman masquerading as Inspector Gillian Piper." At my brother's look of surprise, I give a triumphant laugh. "That was my exact reaction. Who's the hysterical one now?"

Nicholas clears his throat and seats himself calmly at the foot of my bed, Freddie settling contentedly in his lap. "I take it your souvenir shopping was a success?"

Even though it's only been a little over an hour since I last saw these two, there's a lot of new information to share. My realization about the projector images, the photo of the postcard on my phone, my conversation with Peter Piper . . . a lot has happened, and it should be a moment of triumph. I did it. I solved the case. I figured out how and why those shadow figures keep popping up only to disappear again, who's behind it all, and why Gillian resorted to murder in the first place. It's all so obvious now, and I don't hesitate to let these two know.

"Yes, but even if there was a projector casting those shadows onto the boat, how did Not-Gillian do the actual killing?" Nicholas asks. "If there wasn't anyone physically on the boat to do the pushing, then Leonard must have jumped."

I open my mouth only to immediately close it again. Nicholas has made a valid—and unfortunate—point.

"And if it's just shadows being projected into the room while the safes are robbed, then how is she taking the goods?" Liam's contribution is no less unfortunate. Or less valid. "How does she get in and out of the room without being seen?"

Nicholas decides to pound one more nail in the coffin of my theory. "And don't forget that you were with her when most of the thefts occurred—including mine. She could hardly have been in two places at once."

"She has an accomplice, obviously," I say, even though there's nothing obvious about it. "A hypnotist would serve nicely in the role, don't you think?"

Nicholas shakes his head. He's still stroking Freddie in a negligent, detached way, as if each movement of his hand over her fur is bringing him closer to an idea. "I don't think that's it," he says, and so calmly that I'm forced to agree with him. "There was no one in my room when I was robbed—I'd bet my life on it. I woke up to see the two shadow figures hunched near the safe. I got up to confront them, but they disappeared before I managed to make my way across the room. Only then did I take stock of what was in there. The theft could have occurred at any time before that. Hours, even."

"What bothers me," Liam says, speaking much more slowly than he's accustomed to, "is *why* she robbed you. How did she know you'd be carrying an expensive old piece of death jewelry?"

"It's not death jewelry," I protest. I may not have actually seen the ring yet, but I feel a strong sense of ownership over it. "It's mourning jewelry."

"How is that different?"

"Because you don't put it on a corpse, stupid. It's meant to be worn. *Cherished*."

"It's depressing, if you ask me."

"Good thing no one asked you."

Nicholas speaks up before we can descend into a full squabble. "Your brother has a point. The other two victims—or, if Armand is to be believed, the several dozen victims throughout England—were wealthy and well-known. I'm a made-up personage. There's no reason to have sought me out . . . unless, of course, my cover isn't as good as I'd hoped."

"Not-Gillian would know. Not-Gillian has known everything from the start. She knows all about me and my relationship with Peter. She knows I have visions that can help her track down the missing vacuum cleaner cases." I shake my head in a combination of both consternation and wonder. "I wasn't wrong to idolize her as much as I do. She's brilliant."

Liam is appalled. "She's a *murderer*, Ellie."

A flush of heat rushes to my cheeks. "I didn't say I wanted to elect her prime minister. I only meant that she's smart and she's done her homework. She could have easily identified Nicholas and put her plans into action."

Nicholas nods as though this makes perfect sense. Which, in my defense, it does. "Then all we have to do is wait. You said Peter is on his way down? The police might not believe *you* when you say she's an impostor, but he can confirm it. And he has enough clout to do something about it."

It's a decent plan. With any luck, Peter will arrive within the hour, furious and righteous and on our side. All we have to do is sit tight and hide away until his arrival, avoiding any more trouble or shadow apparitions on the wall. Waiting, however, has never been my strong suit, and there's something about the way Nicholas is looking at me that's making me nervous.

He glances at his watch as though time has no meaning, but when his gaze catches mine, there are several layers of meaning supporting it. "While we wait, I'd like to hear a little more about this plan you two enacted to hypnotize Eleanor behind my back," he says.

I recognize this for the trap it is and shoot Liam a warning glance, but he's always been useless in moments like these. In a sports match, he has the reflexes of a tiger. In a battle of wills, he withers and falls.

"It was Ellie's idea, I swear!" he cries, his hands coming up. "I tried to talk her out of it, but she insisted. She wanted to do it while you were preoccupied."

"That appears to be a common theme for this particular case." Nicholas smiles slightly, but I'm not fooled by it. "First the thief, and then you. I had no idea I was such an ogre."

"You're not an ogre."

"A killjoy, then. The headmaster at a school that serves liver and onions for lunch every day."

"Nicholas, that's not what I meant, and you know it. I had to try one more time. I had to see if I could understand what was happening to me, see what my subconscious mind knew that I didn't. It had already cleared an entire building with a fire alarm and then sent me through the revolving doors with a muttered message about asking Inspector Piper—"

I cut myself short, watching in a mirror behind Liam's head as my own eyes grow wide.

"What?" Nicholas leans forward, dislodging the cat in his lap. "What is it?"

With a snap of my fingers, I spring to my feet and begin pacing the length of the hotel room. There's not much space, and I have to step over Nicholas's long legs with each turn, but the repetition clears my mind.

"I wasn't telling myself to ask Inspector *Gillian* Piper something," I say, remembering Uli's genuine concern for my well-being as I went round and round those doors. "I was telling myself to ask Inspector *Peter* Piper. I must have known. Even then, I must have known. Well—either I knew or whatever is trying to talk to me through the darkness knew. I'm not prepared to say which."

"Eleanor . . ."

I jerk myself back to focus, pulled by the concern in Nicholas's voice. "I know it sounds like I'm babbling, but everything is finally starting to make sense. While under hypnosis today, I took Armand and Liam to that movie theater because it has projectors and because projectors are responsible for the shadow figures. It was a message, a reminder."

I'm gaining traction now, and it shows. My pace starts picking up. "The same thing happened before. While under hypnosis by virtue of your mother's recording, I talked to Uli about needing to ask Inspector Piper about something. Because I needed to ask Peter about his wife. Because I—or the dark-whatever-thing—knew she wasn't legitimate."

"What are you saying, Ellie?" Liam asks.

"I'm saying that as interesting as those two particular events are, they've got nothing on the first time I was under hypnosis, when I screamed and threw furniture and made the fire alarm go off."

The tight knit of Nicholas's eyebrows indicates that he's following the line of my argument but isn't particularly pleased at the reminder. I don't allow myself to be sidetracked by it.

"At the time, it seemed like I just sort of lost it or that something terrible had happened to me, but I was never in any real danger. All I did as soon as I woke up was go upstairs to check on my cats—and, in the process, had my first ghost maid sighting. Because I needed to see her. I needed to know about her."

"That seems like an awfully dramatic way to go about it," Liam points out.

I can't disagree, but if all of this is my subconscious mind at work, it makes sense that I'd be dramatic. I love a good show.

Don't we all, dear Ella, Birdie agrees. *Don't we all.*

"That's all well and good," Nicholas says carefully, "but I'm not sure I follow. How does it help us to know about the ghost maid? If all of this is leading up to you wanting to be hypnotized a *fourth* time . . ."

I shake my head. As enlightening as it's been to give myself over to the darkness, I'm not sure I'd like to keep doing it forever. There's something unsettling about going to a place where Winnie can't follow. I need her.

Nicholas sighs. "This is about me dressing up as the ghost maid again, isn't it?"

The need to pace the room is no longer quite as urgent, so I pause and lean down to kiss Nicholas's cheek. "You're sweet to offer, but no. There's no need. With Uli dead . . ." I trail off and let a sudden pang of sadness overtake me. It's not just a selfish sadness, either. While this next part would be much easier if Uli were alive to provide us with answers, I'm also genuinely upset at having failed him.

If I'd just figured all this out yesterday, if I hadn't been so dazzled by Not-Gillian's abilities . . .

"With Uli dead, what?" Liam asks. "What do we need to do?"

"We need to find the ghost maid."

"But I thought you said Uli was the ghost maid."

"He was," I say, and turn my head to look at my Beast. She's sitting stately and unruffled, her gaze fixed on something none of us can see. "And somewhere in this hotel, there's proof of it. Unfortunately, only one of us knows where that is."

Liam groans. "Are you about to tell me that the *one of us* is a cat?"

"I don't need to tell you. It's what Beast has been trying to say this whole time."

And there it is, the final piece of the puzzle. I put the collar back on Beast a few days ago, the bloodstain mostly wiped out, but traces of it remain. I point at those fading splotches now. Once upon a time, Beast came in covered in blood and without a scratch on her, carrying Brunhilde. Once upon a time, Beast came back with another Brunhilde—a different one, a fresh one—tangled up with a necklace that didn't come from this hotel.

Brunhilde has been down a garbage chute and to the bottom of the ocean. She's currently locked up in evidence and also in my bathroom. She's everywhere.

And I finally know why.

"Somewhere in this hotel, I'm guessing there's a box of identical creepy dolls, a bloodied ghost maid costume, and three vacuum cleaner cases full of jewelry," I say. A treasure trove of everything Uli was trying to hide—his ghost maid costume and his doll pranks, the jewelry that everyone in this hotel is frantic to find. I don't know if Uli was part of the thefts or if he merely stumbled across the vacuum cleaner cases during his ghostly wanderings, but there's no denying his involvement. He recognized that gold-and-pearl necklace the moment I showed it to him—and he was killed before he could tell me why.

Because he was the only one in the hotel who knew where it had really come from.

"And you think a cat is going to lead us there?" Liam demands.

I reach down and scoop Beast up before she can take it into her head to flee. She's none too pleased, but she knows a lost battle when it's holding her in its arms.

"I think a cat is very well going to try."

"At what point do we accept that following a cat around a hotel is an exercise in futility?"

All three of us stop and stare as Beast turns back the way she came and parks herself at our feet. Thus far, she's taken us up to the tenth-floor snack machine, investigated a dark corner festering with dust bunnies, and cleaned every last one of her whiskers underneath the emergency stairwell.

Needless to say, we have yet to find Uli's secret stash.

"She's making sure we're wholly invested before she leads us to the treasure," I say. Even I know how ridiculous this sounds, but I can't back down now. Not when we're so close. "She's been there at least two times already. It's only a matter of time before she goes again. Cats are creatures of habit."

Nicholas clears his throat. He's our self-appointed lookout, by which I mean he's trailing after us, casually keeping an eye out for Not-Gillian or anyone else who might be interested in our findings. Like Liam, he's undertaken this expedition more out of loyalty to me than a belief that we'll find anything. "I wonder if our purposes would be better served by simply scouring the hotel from top to bottom? Breaking and entering must be easier than this."

I point a warning finger at him. "You're the one who gets angry if we don't include you."

"I wasn't angry."

"Annoyed, then."

"No."

"Insulted?"

"Getting warmer."

I can't help but relax a little. Although there's still a tangible amount of tension between the two of us, the beginnings of a smile lurk in Nicholas's eyes. I'm tempted to follow up on it—perhaps, even, to throw all this cat-following nonsense to the wind—but Liam speaks up before I can act.

"Wait—I think she might be doing something. Finally."

I turn to find Beast on alert, her ears pricked up and her tail two times its normal size. Something has caught her attention, and since we're standing in a fifth-floor stairwell that's empty of people and objects, I can only assume that something is of supernatural origins.

"This is it." I whisper so as not to disturb her. "Brunhilde is calling to her."

Liam snorts, but my cat immediately swishes her tail and darts down the stairs. She's fast, too—so fast we almost lose sight of her. Fortunately, this is one more instance where Liam's gym-teacher reflexes are useful. In a move that would do an action hero proud, he leaps over the banister, bypassing an entire flight of stairs to keep pace.

"He comes in handy, doesn't he?" Nicholas murmurs. He makes a move as if to do a little banister-leaping of his own, but I put a hand out to stop him. I'm not sure what I want to say to him, but several options leap to mind. Any of them would work—*I'm sorry, I love you, what on* earth *makes you think we could be married*—but the door behind us bursts open before I can choose. It's not, as I initially fear, Not-Gillian come to murder us.

It's the next worst thing.

"Thank the mesmeric gods. There you are." Armand stands on the threshold, looking more disheveled than I've ever seen him—and that's including the time I dressed him in half-charred clothes and threw him out in the rain. One of Armand's signature qualities is that he always looks like he's about to attend a posh funeral. "I don't know how much time we have. Come with me."

It's not in my nature to take Armand at his word, and I'm not about to start now. "What's this about?" I ask, but not before peeking over the railing to ensure that Liam and Beast are out of sight. To my relief, I don't see either of them. Wherever Beast was going, she was headed there in a hurry. "Is this a trap?"

"No trap." Armand pants heavily and turns his attention to

Nicholas. "It's your mother. There's something wrong with her. She's not—"

"You know?" I cry before I realize how misplaced my priorities are. Armand's knowledge of Piers Pierson's real identity—while alarming and possibly game changing—isn't the most important bit of information being shared right now. I correct myself almost immediately by grabbing Armand's arm and twisting. Hard. "Where is she, and what have you done with her? So help me, Armand, if you've done anything to hurt her . . ."

"I didn't hurt her!" Armand turns a supplicating eye on Nicholas. "I'm telling the truth. I went up to her room to invite her to dinner, but I found her in the hallway, and she's barely conscious. I don't think she's had too much to drink, but with the way she kicks those cocktails back—"

Nicholas nods once. He's in much better control of his reactions than I am because he follows this up with one curt command: "Take me to her." Anything else he feels in this moment—for me or for Armand—takes a backseat.

Leaving Liam to his fate and a fervent hope that he's able to keep pace with Beast, we follow Armand back the way he came. Vivian is exactly where he left her, which is a relief, but she's seated on the floor with her legs extended in front of her. It's a girlish pose, rendered all the more youthful by the fact that she's once again wearing her yellow-skirted swimsuit, albeit with a white crocheted cover-up over the top.

"Hello, darling," she says as Nicholas appears in front of her. She blinks a few times as if finding it difficult to bring him into focus. "Please tell me you aren't here to make me get up. I'm so comfortable."

"Of course not," he soothes. Squatting down to her level, he takes both her hands between his and chafes them. "What's happened to upset you?"

"I'm not upset." Just now noticing that Armand and I have also come to her rescue, she adds, "Eleanor, love. I'm sorry to say it, but that friend of yours is starting to get on my nerves."

That makes two of us.

"I'm afraid he also knows who Nicholas really is. The cat, as they say, has escaped the bag."

With any luck, *the cat* is currently tracking down a trio of missing vacuum cleaner cases, but I'm not about to attempt an explanation. "How much have you had to drink?" I ask instead.

"Just the tea that was brought to my room," she says. Her brow wrinkles as though she's deep in thought. "I don't recall ordering it, but they never leave me alone, these waiters. Every time I turn around, they're offering me something new. Nicholas, how much money did you give these people?"

"Not enough, apparently," he says.

"What tea?" I ask. I crouch down next to Nicholas and examine Vivian closely. She looks much the same as she usually does, but her eyes are unfocused and I could swear that her pupils have dilated. "Vivian, is the tea you drank still in your room?"

"What?" She blinks at me without answering my question. "I think I'll lie down and have a little rest, if that's all right with you. Nicholas, love, could you fetch me a pillow?"

"I'll get it," Armand offers. He makes a move as if to enter Vivian's room, but I fling a hand up to hold him back.

"Don't you dare. You're not going anywhere near that room."

Nicholas is busy trying to find a comfortable slumping position for his mother, but he pauses long enough to look at me. "What is it, Eleanor?" he asks quietly. "What have you figured out?"

I'd rather hold this conversation somewhere Armand can't overhear, but it's too important to put off. "The night you were robbed—did you drink anything before you fell asleep? Something from room service, something that left your sight for any period of time?"

Behind me, Armand sucks in a sharp breath.

"Coffee," Nicholas says, his gaze holding mine. The gray of his eyes sharpens to steel as he realizes what I'm getting at. "I ordered a coffee to help me stay awake."

"And was the room service tray in your room when you woke up?"

Armand claps his hands before Nicholas can answer, but I don't need to hear my theory confirmed. The expression on Nicholas's face says it all.

"See?" Armand says, almost gleeful. "I'm not the one you should be blaming. Those people weren't hypnotized—they were poisoned."

"Don't let Armand out of your sight," I tell Nicholas.

"What are you talking about?" Armand demands. He takes a step back, his hands up as if to ward me off. "You just proved that this has nothing to do with me. Why would I resort to poison when hypnosis is so much easier and doesn't leave a trace?"

"Because there's only one concoction I can think of that lulls a person to sleep for just a few hours." I grab Vivian's key card and wave it over the lock on her door. "Only one concoction that makes it possible to lure someone out into—let's say—a lightning storm before unconsciousness sets in."

All the blood drains from Armand's face. "Ellie, I didn't—I wouldn't—"

"I'll be right back," I say, and dash into Vivian's room. It looks just as spacious and glamorous as before, although a few crumpled dresses lay scattered across the couch. I make a bee-line for the room service tray and the half-empty teapot. Careful not to leave any fingerprints behind, I lift the lid and sniff.

I'm no tea connoisseur, but I do know my way around herbal remedies. I couldn't swear that the tea contains my personal mixture of valerian root, St. John's wort, and magnolia bark, but at least one of those ingredients is in there. As Liam would be the first to point out, it smells—and likely tastes—like the inside of an earthworm.

"Everything is finally making sense," I murmur. A tincture like this would be ideal in leaving no trace, in lulling its victims into a nap that could be brought to an end by a light, soothing sound like the crackling of flames.

Or a film projector running on the balcony.

My heart gives a thud and then turns over. It's genius, really—alibi-proof and ideal for a busy police inspector who needs to crack a safe and then make sure she's somewhere else when the victim wakes up and puts a time stamp on the theft. If this robbery had gone as planned—if Armand hadn't shown up when he did—then Vivian would have fallen asleep right here on her bed. Not-Gillian would have come in, robbed the safe, set up a projector on the balcony, and timed it to go off a few hours from now. As soon as the sound woke Vivian up, she'd see the shadow figures and assume the worst. And because the first thing she'd do is alert the authorities, Not-Gillian could make sure that no one thought to look for the projector until she'd had time to remove it.

I walk out into the hallway with steps that are both light and heavy, like walking through a storm cloud.

"Nicholas, did you think to check your balcony after you were robbed?"

He's alert and ready for me, one hand on his mother's shoulder, the other suspended in midair. I don't know how that's keeping Armand from fleeing, but it is.

"No." He pauses and thinks for a moment before repeating with heavier emphasis, "*No*. I checked to make sure the window was secure, and it was, but I didn't literally step outside. Why? What's on my mother's balcony? Is Not-Gillian out there right now?"

"Not Gillian?" Armand echoes, a bemused expression pulling at his lips. "Why would—"

I cut him off with a glare. "Were you the one who gave her the recipe for the sleeping draught? Are you in this together?

No, Nicholas, sit back down. She's not out there. I just have a theory."

He doesn't say anything, patient—as Armand never was and never will be—for me to unfold the tale in my own time.

"Am I in what together?" Armand asks. He takes a step toward me, but an honest-to-goodness growl escapes from Nicholas. Armand reacts to it like a dog hearing a word from its master. "Eleanor, I've told you a dozen times that none of this has anything to do with me. I don't poison people for the sake of convenience. We have a code, remember?"

I do remember, actually. But to have my words flung back at me like that—when I once literally poisoned him for the sake of convenience—is a bit much under the current circumstances. I falter a little, bracing my hand on the door frame as I steady my thoughts and my nerves.

"I think I'd like you to go away now," Vivian announces. Her words are starting to slur, her whole body drooping into the carpet. "I'm quite tired."

"You can't let her sleep here," I say before Nicholas tries to introduce the idea. The bed a few feet away might be the most logical choice, but it's not the safest. "It's too risky. Not-Gillian is going to be here any minute to finish the job she started."

His lips form a flat line. "I'd like to see her try."

"She carries a police wand and a stun gun. If she's caught in the act, trying isn't all she'll do. None of your mother's jewelry is in that safe, is it?"

"No, I had it moved to the jeweler after my things were taken. It seemed the most logical choice."

I nod, relieved to find that one of us, at least, is leaving this place with all of our belongings. "Then go," I urge him. "I don't know how much time we have before she shows up."

Common sense prevails, and Nicholas heaves a sigh. He also heaves his mother into a standing position. As was the case when I "murdered" Armand, she's able to walk on her own two feet, albeit shakily and without much awareness of what she's doing.

"I'll take her to your suite," Nicholas says.

"That's a good idea."

"But only on the condition that you promise not to be anywhere near this room when Not-Gillian arrives. If it's unsafe for my mother, then it's unsafe for you." His gaze meets mine. "I mean it this time, Ellie. I know I don't have any right to dictate your actions, and you and Beast have your own way of making it through these things alive, but I can't—I don't—"

As he cuts himself off, the concern in his voice is so deep and so real that I'm unable to release my steadying grip on the door frame. Having this conversation in front of a three-quarters sleeping Vivian and an unabashedly staring Armand is hardly ideal, but what about our relationship is? Since the day I rode my metaphorical broomstick into Nicholas's life, it's been nothing but mischief and mayhem as far as the eye can see.

But he's still here. And with *such* a look in his eye . . .

"If anything were to happen to you, I don't know if I'd be able to survive it." His voice cracks. "For the Lord's sake—and for mine—please be careful."

I don't know how long we stand there staring at one another, so much more than a plea and a promise being exchanged between us, but it must be a while. Armand is the first to break the silence, which he does with a cough and a sad, mocking laugh. "I don't know why you two thought you could pull off that whole Piers Pierson nonsense. I knew who he was the moment you stood in a room together. Any fool could see it."

There's so much more I need to say, but this is hardly the time or the place to do it. Especially since Armand chooses that moment to sigh in a way that can only be described as lovelorn. It's all nonsense, of course, and I don't need that smug look from Nicholas to remind me that he's the one who first floated the idea that Armand is after googly-eyed hearts and romance instead of cash, but that's okay. I've finally figured out what Armand wants.

This isn't about love. It isn't about money, either. He misses the game, the intrigue, and, most of all, the *companionship*.

In other words, he's lonely. As much as I'd like to hate him for it, I can't. I too have known that despair and isolation, and I too once walked that path alone. It's only now—surrounded by my family and friends, side by side with the man I love—that I realize how empty Armand's life must be. How sad.

"What are you two going to do?" Nicholas asks as he whirls Vivian in the direction of the elevator and gently nudges her that way.

"I don't know yet," I say. "But when Madame Eleanor Wilde and Armand Lamont are on the case, the one thing you can count on is a good show."

Understanding this, Armand swells to two times his size. "You mean it? You don't think I'm a murderer anymore?"

"You're a liar and a con man and one of the most despicable human beings I've ever had the misfortune to meet," I say. "But no, I don't think you're a murderer. In fact, I think you might be exactly what this situation calls for."

Chapter 29

Liam doesn't pick up his phone when I call, which I take to mean that he's hot in pursuit of Beast and the vacuum cleaner cases—not that he's been clobbered over the head and is slowly bleeding out somewhere. I'm not normally an optimist, but I can't dwell too much on all the darker possibilities right now.

Mostly because I'm trying to manifest them.

"Why do I feel like this is going to end up with me dead and out in the middle of a storm again?" Armand kicks the blue vacuum cleaner case that he charmed out of one of the maids and casts a look out the nearest window. Sure enough, the weather has fulfilled all my prophecies. It's almost as dark as it was that first evening, the wind blowing so hard that tree limbs and wayward beach paraphernalia fill the air. From our vantage point in the second-story bar that overlooks the lobby, we can see the last of the stragglers running in from the storm. "Fair warning—I'm not drinking anything that doesn't come out of a sealed container."

"Relax," I say, even though my own adrenaline is so ratcheted up that I can't hold still. "That was one time, and you deserved it. Admit it, Armand. You went too far."

He kicks the vacuum cleaner again and sighs. "I still don't understand why you couldn't just let me help you take the Hartfords down instead. You have no idea what you're getting into. Married money is hard earned."

"Then it's a good thing I'm not marrying him for that reason," I retort. At this point, I'm technically not marrying him at all, but I'm not about to quibble over the details. For one, I don't know that Armand will ever understand what it means to love someone more than himself. For another, it's high time we put this plan into action.

"Your job should be easy enough," I say. "Just walk past the conference room with that sucker dragging behind you. Don't draw attention to yourself, and don't act as though you're up to anything nefarious. We just want to see what she does."

The she in question is obviously Not-Gillian. I haven't seen her or her entourage of blue-uniformed police officers anywhere, so I'm hoping they're once again holed up in the conference room. Uli would have known how to find them, but she ensured that he wouldn't be alive to offer me any more information or support.

"What if she arrests me?"

"Then let her arrest you. It's not illegal to walk around with a hotel vacuum cleaner." I pause and run an experienced eye over him. "Unless you have someone else's valuables in your pockets right now?"

He pretends to be insulted, but he's loving this, I know. Now that I've let him in on the game, he's almost back to his old self again. "Eleanor, I would never."

I waggle my fingers at him. "Just hand it over, and I'll keep it safe until you're done."

"Marian gave me this ring," he says as he slips a hand into his pocket and extracts a gold band that looks as though it might be a man's wedding ring. "As a gift. It was her husband's before he died."

"You took her dead husband's ring? What's the matter with you?"

He laughs and tosses it to me. "Oh, don't get all high and mighty. He was a scoundrel, from all she's been telling Vivian. Apparently, she came here to dump his ashes in the toilet of the hotel room where he first cheated on her. She said she'd much rather it fall in the hands of a smarmy hypnotist than sit in her jewelry box forever."

I can't help but laugh as my fist closes around the ring.

"I know you think I'm a terrible person, but no one gives me anything they genuinely value. No amount of hypnosis or mind-reading in the world can do that." He pauses. "*You* know what I mean. It's why you're trying so hard to get that mourning ring back before Not-Gillian runs off with it. It means something to you."

I point a warning finger at him. I may have accepted him as an accomplice, but we're not friends enough for me to discuss my relationship with him. "Just go lure our fake police inspector out, would you? Then we'll talk about what you are and aren't allowed to accept from wealthy, unhappy widows."

He grins and nods, aware—as I am—that I'm not going to fight him over Marian's ring. If it pleases her to hand it over to a louse like Armand, then who am I to stand in her way?

The plan is for me to remain up here to watch the comings and goings of everyone in the lobby while Armand thumps around with the vacuum cleaner case—which, I'm sure you've guessed by now—contains nothing but a vacuum cleaner. I order a seltzer water from a passing waiter and settle myself in to wait.

Because the vacuum cleaner case is so heavy, it takes Armand some time to make his way downstairs and down the correct hallway. I'm leaning a little too far over the railing, trying to see if anything is happening, when a voice hails me from behind.

"Hello, Ms. Wilde. I've been everywhere looking for you." Bertram is standing a few respectful feet back when I turn around, a tentative smile on his face. I've been so focused on tracking—and stopping—Not-Gillian that his presence takes me momentarily aback.

"Bertram!" I cough and attempt to keep my drink from spilling. "I mean, Officer Davies. Of course. Some storm we're having, isn't it?"

He casts a wry grimace at the airborne towel whipping past the window and nods. "I'll be glad enough to leave this place behind. I don't know why anyone holidays on the coast. Nothing is more unpredictable than conditions like these."

He's right about that in more ways than one. This whole holiday has been unpredictable.

Only—"What do you mean, leave this place behind?" I ask. It's only then that I notice the leather bag over his shoulder and the official-looking file folder under one arm. "Bertram, you guys aren't leaving? *Now?*"

He gives a salute-like nod. "Boss's orders, I'm afraid."

"In the middle of a murder investigation?" I can hardly believe it. "*Two* of them?"

"It doesn't make any sense to me, either, but it's not my call to make. Most likely they'll reassign it to a new team or kick it up to MI-6. You know how bureaucrats are."

I'm fairly certain bureaucrats don't abandon a ring of theft and murder while it's actively going on, but Bertram seems to take Not-Gillian's word as law.

"I didn't want to go without saying good-bye," he adds with a nervous brush of his hand over his thinning hair. "It's not often I get an opportunity to work alongside a psychic. I won't forget it anytime soon."

My response to this is to lean even farther over the railing, straining to catch some sight of either Armand or Not-Gillian.

Neither of them is within my line of vision, and I have the sudden, sinking fear that I'll never see Not-Gillian—or her stolen goods—again.

"Oh! And I ran into your brother earlier. He wanted me to relay a message."

That's the only thing that could possibly pull my attention away from the lobby. "Thank the Good Goddess." I turn back to face him. "He was conscious and intact?"

"Um . . . yes?" Bertram reaches into his pocket and pulls out a note. Reading from it, he says, "*Tell Eleanor that Beast came through and that the Brunhildes and I will meet her up in Vivian's room.* You can see why I had to write that down. Who is Brunhilde? Or Beast, for that matter?"

Any relief I feel at Liam making it through this escapade alive is gone in a flash. If Not-Gillian went through with her strike on Vivian's room after all—if she's aiming for one last score before she leaves—then Liam is in the path of danger. And since it sounds as though he has the loot with him, she's going to get away with it all.

I cast one more frantic look over the lobby, but there's no one who can come to my aid. Although I'd have preferred to wait for Peter Piper to arrive before I attempt any conformation, it's now or never.

"Bertram, you can't, under any circumstances, let Gillian leave."

He blinks, the piece of paper with Liam's message fluttering to the floor. "What do you mean? She's the one who made the order, not me. I'm only—"

"A peon, a grunt," I finish for him. "I know. But if there's ever been a time for you to assert your authority, this is it. Call her superior. Call her superior's superior. Call every friend you've ever made on the force and recruit their help."

I finally get Bertram's attention, because his lower lip falls open. He looks like a fish dragged from the depths of the ocean, but I barrel on anyway.

"She's not really Gillian Piper," I say. "She's an impostor. A fake."

He releases a shaky laugh. "Don't be silly. Of course she's Gillian Piper."

"Have you personally seen her badge? Has anyone currently working on the case met her in person before?"

"Well, no, not that I know of, but—"

"Gillian Piper has brown eyes and is the same size as me. I'm telling you, Bertram—she's a fake, and she's been using all of you to help cover up the fact that she's the one who murdered Leonard Mayhew and robbed those safes." I can see the realization starting to dawn in his piscine expression and keep going. "She's been hitting hotels all over England under who-knows-what name and who-knows-what guise. She and Leonard both."

"But—"

I have neither the time nor the energy for his protestations. "But something went wrong, and she had Leonard killed. I'm not sure how yet, but I think it has to do with the sleeping draught she's been using for the robberies. If she got him outside in the daytime and gave him the drink at the marina, if she put him on that boat while he was asleep and shoved him out to sea, it fits. He'd have woken up, drugged and dazed, to find himself in the middle of an ocean storm. In the dark, falling overboard looks a lot like a struggle with two shadow men."

There's so much more I could tell him—about the projector and the gold-and-pearl necklace, about how Uli stumbled on the truth and was killed for it—but there's no need. Bertram believes me.

"She's not really Gillian Piper," he repeats, slowly and with heavy emphasis. "She's someone else."

"Her ex-husband will be here any minute to confirm it."

"And you know," he says. "You know how she did it. You know everything."

"Even better," I say. Of all the police officers I know, Bertram isn't the one I'd have chosen to help me rescue my brother, but I can only work with what I'm given. "If you come with me, I'll show you proof."

Chapter 30

❧

I'm not sure if it's breaking my promise to Nicholas if I return to Vivian's room now that I have a police officer with me, but I offer him up a mental apology anyway. To further soothe my conscience, I catch sight of Liam struggling down the hallway with a bulging pillowcase over his shoulder and heave a sigh of relief. Beast is nowhere to be seen, but my brother appears to be in full fighting form.

"Oh, Ellie. There you are!" As soon as Liam sees me, he drops the pillowcase to the floor. It jangles and clatters in a way that can only belong to mass quantities of jewels and/or porcelain dolls. "I knocked and knocked, but no one is here. Where did everyone go?"

"Somewhere safe," I say. "Not-Gillian has Vivian earmarked as her next victim. For all we know, she's in there right now, robbing the safe and clearing away the evidence."

Liam casts a wide-eyed look at the door and gulps. "Inside? Right now?"

"Bertram will protect us," I say, only partially ironic. So far, he hasn't said anything, content to stand behind me and watch events unfold. "Nicholas took his mom back to our suite, so we should head that way. I'm assuming you found everything?"

Liam holds up his hand to show me his palm. A streak of blood coats it. "Everything and then some. That blood on Beast's collar? It was a special effect, the kind you buy at Halloween to make yourself a vampire. There were several bottles of it next to the ghost costume."

"Where did Beast take you?" I ask as I help him hoist the bag and head toward the elevators. It's *heavy*, so my brother is forced to carry the bulk of it. "It must have been somewhere in the hotel, right?"

Liam casts a wary eye over Bertram, so I nod once to show my approval. "I told him the truth about Gillian. He's on our side."

"It was some weird basement storeroom behind a false wall. I have no idea how your stupid cat found it, but she led me straight there." He shakes his head. "It was just as you predicted, Ellie. A box of identical Brunhildes, the ghost maid costume, and all three vacuum cleaner cases. There was so much jewelry in there, it was spilling out the edges. This is only half of it. I couldn't carry any more."

"Where did you say the basement storeroom is?" Bertram asks suddenly. We've made it all the way to the end of the hallway by now, but since my and Liam's hands are full, we haven't pushed the elevator button yet.

"Near the north wall, I think. It's almost like a false room, the kind that—" Liam drops the bag with a start. As I'm left holding what must be about eighty pounds all on my own, I fall to the ground with it. It takes me a second to gain my bearings, a second more to realize that Liam has both his hands up and has grown deathly pale.

As soon as I catch sight of Bertram standing a few paces away with a gun pointed at us, I put my own hands up. It's not the most comfortable position, lying on my stomach with my arms in the air, but I don't dare move. Police officers in the UK don't carry guns unless they have special reasons. I highly doubt the Glock pointed at us is regulation.

"Oh, for archfiend's sake!" I cry, equally annoyed and afraid. "Are you in on it with her? Is that what's happening? Are you a fake Bertram Davies?"

Bertram has the audacity to laugh. "I'm the real deal, I'm afraid, and I work alone." His laugh turns bitter. "At least, I work alone now. Only because that scummy partner of mine cut a deal with the police. I knew he was going to turn on me—turn over everything. He brought this on himself."

He must realize that standing right outside the elevators in a hotel hallway isn't the smartest place for this conversation because he waves the gun at Liam. "Pick that bag up. Since you so obligingly cleared the old lady out, we'll do this in her room."

One of the first survival skills I learned as a young woman embarking on a life of fake mediumship is that you should never follow a murderer into a secluded place. Our chances of survival are much higher out here where there's the potential for witnesses than inside a room where we might not be found for hours.

"Don't do it, Liam," I say. "Stay where you are. If he wants that bag, he can carry it himself."

Bertram's voice rises an entire octave. "I'll shoot you—I'll shoot you right here and now. I killed Leonard already."

"I'm aware of that, thanks. But you should have just stuck with the plan to make it look like suicide. When did you decide to throw away the note about his mother?"

He gives a small jolt. "You weren't supposed to see that. No one was."

If he didn't think the impression of a pen on a pad of paper would be the first thing the police looked for, then he's a worse investigator than I initially gave him credit for—which isn't a lot.

"I killed the doorman, too." He tries the intimidation route again, this time waving the gun for good measure. "The one who stole my vacuum cleaner cases, the one you tipped me off to with all your sneaking and whispering. He wouldn't talk, you know. No matter how hot I made it in that sauna, no matter how much he banged to be let out. I won't hesitate to do it again."

Although I've held it together so far, this confession leaves me shaken. It's one thing to bravely face down an angry murderer with a gun; it's another to face down an admitted torturer.

"Please, Ellie," Liam begs. "I know you think it's fun to talk to Winnie from beyond the grave and all, but I don't want to die. I don't want to be a ghost forced to watch you live your life instead of having one of my own."

It's a fair request, and for his sake, I relent. Well, for his sake and because it suddenly occurs to me that something strange is going on—and I don't just mean that I'm lying next to a bag of fake cursed dolls and stolen jewelry and a nervous, whingy police officer who's threatening to kill me in cold blood.

While I'm willing to accept that I pinpointed the wrong police officer as the murderer, the fact remains that Inspector Gillian Piper isn't, in fact, Inspector Gillian Piper. If she's not hiding under a nom de plume because she's secretly stealing jewelry and murdering people, then she must have another reason for it.

That's when it clicks—all of it, every last detail, the knowledge of the universe suddenly crashing down on me.

"Okay," I say, rising slowly to my feet. "We'll go to the room with you."

Bertram is smart enough to detect a trap but not so smart he can figure out what it is. "Why? What are you going to do?"

I laugh. "You're the one with the gun, the badge, and all the power in this situation. I'm going to do what any reasonable woman in this situation would. Comply."

*   *   *

Liam is none too pleased to find me sitting calmly at the desk in Vivian's room, tapping a pen up and down on the table. As I expected, Bertram not only had a master key to get us in here, but the first thing he did upon entry was open the safe.

"Did you know that almost every hotel in the United Kingdom uses the same model of safe?" he asks as he swipes some kind of mechanical device over the safe door and swings it open. He notices that there's nothing in there but a bar of complimentary hotel soap and a bottle of shampoo. "So the old bag moved her stuff out, did she? No matter. Now that I have the rest of the jewelry, she can keep it."

"If it's not too much of a problem, could you also return the mourning ring you took from Nicholas Hartford the Third?" I ask. "You can keep the money, but I'd really like to get that back."

"Ellie, have you lost your mind? He's going to kill us, and all you care about is a stupid ring?"

Since Liam is the one with the gun currently pointed at his head, I can understand his nerves. However, I have every expectation of being rescued in the next few minutes, provided I can keep Bertram in the room and talking until it happens.

"How did you know who Piers Pierson really is, by the way?" I ask Bertram. "Was it the name? I feel like it was the name."

He laughs and goes so far as to lower his gun a few inches. "No, it wasn't the name. It was the way he looked at you. *And* the way he looked at that hypnotist friend of yours."

That gives me some comfort, at least. It's nice to know it was Nicholas's discretion that was lacking, not mine.

"What are you going to do now?" I ask. "The other half of the jewelry is still in the basement, and you can hardly fire that gun without drawing the attention of the whole floor. If you want enough time to get your loot and get out of here, you're going to have to let us go."

"There's more than one way to shut a person up," he says, and promptly slams the butt of his gun into the side of Liam's head. My brother has a thick skull, but he's no match for blunt force trauma. He cries out once before crumpling into a heap on the floor.

Since unconsciousness is preferable to death, I'm relieved at Bertram's solution . . . until he yanks the nearest curtain cord and approaches me with it. The irony of being strangled by the very lifeline that Liam used to prevent my hypnotic wanderings isn't lost on me.

Although Bertram isn't a physically imposing man, I don't like my chances of surviving this encounter. "Drat that woman," I say in one last effort to buy myself time. "I didn't think it would take her this long."

As I hope, he halts in midstep. "What woman?"

"Laurel." I nod down at the telephone sitting on the desk. As soon as I sat down and started playing with the pen, I knocked the receiver from the cradle and hit the front desk button. She should have heard at least part of this conversation. "Or, as is probably more accurate, Gillian Piper. The *real* Gillian Piper."

Bertram's whole body jerks in surprise. I'm half afraid the gun in his hand will go off, the bullet ricocheting into my body as a result, but it doesn't. Instead, the door to the room is kicked open with the kind of force that can only come from a woman who spent her university years playing rugby.

I don't know who she is, and I don't know her name, but I know she's in on this. And her partner, a slight, brown-eyed front desk clerk, is right behind her.

"Move!" Gillian calls to me as she follows in Not-Gillian's wake. Without hesitation, I do as she says—and a good thing, too, because Bertram makes a dive to grab me and hold me as a hostage. I'm too quick for him, and so is Not-Gillian, who has him tackled and pinned to the ground while I'm still somersaulting in the opposite direction.

I end up right next to Liam. His eyelids flutter and he struggles to say something, but I quiet him with a hand on his shoulder. "It's okay, Liam. The cavalry has arrived. We're safe now."

Physically, this is true. Now that Bertram is being wrestled into submission and slapped with a pair of handcuffs, the chances of either of us dying are low. However, one look at Gillian's pursed burgundy lips, and I'm not so sure about our emotional well-being. That's not a woman who's delighted to have had a case solved for her.

"You can't quit smoking either," I say, since I'm not sure how else you're supposed to break the ice in a situation like this one. "That pile of cigarette butts should have been my first clue. Does Peter know you chain-smoke in dingy alleyways when you're stressed?"

Laurel—Gillian—turns toward me. "I'd like to know what my ex-husband has to do with anything, Ms. Wilde. I came here to catch Bertram Davies in the act of robbery, not rehash every aspect of my failed marriage with a psychic."

I wince and point over her shoulder. "Then I'm guessing now isn't a good time to point out that he's finally here."

She whirls to find Inspector Peter Piper standing in the open hallway. He's not the only one to have gathered during this time—the commotion of Liam being struck over the head and two police detectives kicking down a door has drawn quite a crowd.

"Hullo, Gillian," Peter says. Of all of us, he's the most in control of himself. I can only assume that's due to our past associations. Nothing about finding me embroiled in the middle of a mess is new or surprising to him. "I came as soon as I could."

"What on earth for?" she demands, arms akimbo and glaring ferociously at her ex-husband. "I don't need your help catching criminals, Peter, and I never have."

"No," he agrees with a blink and a slow drawl. "But I'm guessing you'll need a hand—or twelve—with Madame Eleanor Wilde."

Chapter 31

"I'm just saying—a thousand pounds for every week you spent chasing Bertram seems like a fair deal to me." I hold out my hand across the conference table, my palm up and still empty. "Who knows how much longer you'd have been trying to catch him? I probably saved taxpayers ten times that much."

No one seated on the other side of the table is moved by my logic. Gillian, Not-Gillian—whose name, as it turns out, is Fran—and Peter all share a look that's meant to make me feel as though I'm the nuisance here.

Which, please. Not only did I find the three missing vacuum cleaner cases, which they needed in order to prosecute Bertram, but I got him to confess to both murders *and* attempt two more. A cash payout seems fair to me.

"At the very least, you could give me Nicholas's mourning ring," I say. As this is my real aim—and everyone at this table knows it—I don't hesitate in stating my claim. "You have more than enough evidence already. There's no need to lock it up in red tape for the next few months."

"Let's get one thing straight," Gillian says, but she nods to

Fran in a way that seems an awful lot like capitulation. "Although we appreciate your assistance, we never actually *needed* you. The case was closing tight long before you got here."

"Only because Leonard Mayhew turned himself in for a plea bargain," I point out. "Except he was killed before you could get him into custody and take his official statement. Then, when the vacuum cleaner cases where he was hiding all the jewelry from Bertram went missing—"

"When Uli stole them."

"You mean, when Uli stumbled upon them during his ghostly wanderings and thought they might be worth keeping an eye on," I correct her. "You didn't have any choice but to accept help from a famous psychic who happened to be sharing the hotel. That's not a tight case. That's good luck."

"*Good* luck?" Fran snorts. She's no less gruff or skeptical now that she's a different person, and I'm no less in love with her. More, probably, now that I've seen her tackle a man in one flying leap. "You've been nothing but a thorn in my side since you walked through those doors."

"You're welcome."

She snorts, but I could almost swear that the ice in her eyes thaws. "It was only a matter of time. We knew Bertram was responsible for those thefts and Leonard's death, but we didn't know how he was doing it. He always had an air-tight alibi, always managed to be in two places at one time. Without proof, he was untouchable."

Projector shadows—like I said, *genius*. I'm guessing it will turn out to be Leonard's idea rather than Bertram's. Bertram isn't capable of that kind of thinking on his own.

"We knew he'd slip up eventually," Fran adds. "And because he was preoccupied with thinking that I was Inspector Piper, he failed to realize the real Gillian was one step behind him the whole time—and that everyone on the case except him was in on it."

"And me," I say. "No one told me what was going on, yet I'm still the one who saved the day. Which brings me back to the small matter of a certain ring . . ."

"This is highly unorthodox," Gillian warns.

"It could mean our jobs," Fran says.

"Believe me when I say you're getting off easy," Peter puts in. "*You* can just give her a ring and get her out of your hair forever. I still have to live in the same village as her."

Fran cracks a laugh, but Gillian isn't so easily amused. "You told me she was observant, Peter, not that she has actual psychic powers."

"That's because she doesn't have actual psychic powers. Gilly—you know she's not real, right? Please tell me you didn't fall for her nonsense." Peter turns to his ex-wife with a grin. It's the first time I've ever seen his grizzled exterior crack into a smile like that—flirtatious and lighthearted and *happy*—and it hits me hard. If that's what Armand meant when he said he could detect Nicholas's identity with just one look, then I'm a goner. "Of all the women I thought would see through her façade . . ."

"It's not nonsense to set a fire alarm off from a distance of several hundred feet, and how many times have I told you not to call me Gilly?"

"She probably rigged it hours in advance. Since when did you become a mystic?"

"Being open-minded isn't mystical. It's practical. God forbid someone open themselves up to the possibility of something new for a change."

"What Madame Eleanor does isn't new. It's the oldest profession in the world."

"Hey!" I feel the need to issue a protest.

"All right, the *second* oldest profession," he capitulates before launching right back into his argument.

Fran and I might as well not be in the room for all the attention they pay us after that, but it ends up working in my favor. Fishing into her pocket, Fran extracts the most beautiful piece of jewelry I've ever seen in my life. It's everything Nicholas promised and more—a dark, twisted, serpentine masterpiece with a catch to deliver a sharp prick whenever the urge should strike.

I suck in a breath, almost afraid to touch it for its perfection.

"It doesn't look like much to me," Fran muses, twirling it on her finger. "Are you sure you want to marry a guy who thinks it's romantic to—OUCH!"

I laugh as she pulls the ring off her finger and flings it at me.

"It bit me. Your ring bit me!"

"Hopefully, the reservoir hasn't been filled with poison anytime recently, or you're going to want to call an ambulance," I say. I palm the ring, careful to ensure the clasp is closed first. "And for the record, it's not my ring."

"Well, I don't want it back, so it's yours now," Fran grumbles. She eyes the wound on her finger as if deliberating the need to suck any potential poison out. "And for what it's worth, it's been a real pleasure, Ms. Wilde. You did good work today. I don't know how you figured out the half of it."

"Technically, I didn't," I admit with a silent prayer of thanks to Winnie, Birdie, and whatever dark forces watch over Armand. "When you have all the power of the universe at your back, solving murder is only a matter of sticking to it."

Chapter 32

Everyone seems to want a piece of Madame Eleanor Wilde, but I tell each and every one of them to bugger off. Armand wants to know why I didn't wait for him to return before getting to all the good parts of the investigation, Liam is demanding all kinds of medication and soothing beverages to help heal his aching head, and Vivian wants to know if we're ready to head home yet.

Even Beast and Freddie seem to want me, the pair of them blinking expectedly up at me when I enter my suite to change my clothes and tidy my hair.

"Not now, loves," I say as I gently nudge my way past them. I left Liam recuperating up in Vivian's room, but I have no idea how long that will last. "I'm in a bit of a rush. I don't have much time before—"

The adjoining door swings open before I can finish. Even though I already know who to expect, the sight of Nicholas takes my breath away. Unlike me, he hasn't recently been in a fight to the death with a greedy police officer or sat across from a metaphorical firing squad of all his personal heroes. He's groomed to within an inch of his life, his tailored slacks fresh from the ironing board and his shirt so white I suspect it must be new. Even his hair is swooped across his forehead just the way I like it.

"You look like you just went down the garbage chute with Brunhilde," he says, taking me in without a blink. He leans against the door frame as though we're chatting about dinner plans instead of a recent attempt on my life. "How'd it go?"

I grimace. "About as well as you'd expect. Liam filled you in on most of it?"

He nods.

"Then there's not much to add," I say. "Bertram has already been escorted to the station. They're bagging up the evidence and taking statements. Our services are no longer required—or, indeed—accepted. It's over."

He doesn't say anything, content to stand there and watch me. Even though neither of us speaks, we're thinking the same thing: it's time. Despite everything that's happened today and all the terrible events of the past week, this is our real moment of reckoning.

"Eleanor, I—" he begins, but I cut him off.

"No, let me," I say, and promptly fall to one knee. At first, he's unsure what's happening—if I've tripped or succumbed to a maidenly swoon—but I pull out the mourning ring and hold it aloft. He starts and then stares and then laughs.

It's the best sound in the world.

"Er, this isn't quite how I expected this to go," he says, but I immediately shush him.

"Don't interrupt me," I say. "It's rude to stop a girl in the middle of a proposal."

His lips quirk in a smile. "Then by all means. Let's hear it."

"I didn't have a lot of time to prepare, so this is just the rough cut, but here goes." I draw a deep breath, my lungs and my heart full to bursting. "You are, without a doubt, the most

unusual man I've ever met. I don't know what you see in me—
if I make you laugh or I keep things interesting or you just have
a really strange affection for the macabre—but I appreciate it
more than you will ever know. There aren't many people in the
world who are willing to accept me for who I am. There are
even fewer who love me for it."

"Yes, Eleanor. I will—"

"I haven't asked you anything yet!" I jump to my feet and
wave the ring at him. He's wary enough of the poison catch not
to whisk me into his arms. *Yet.* "I may not understand what's
going on inside your head or your heart, but I do know that
you walking into my life was the best thing that's ever happened to me. You're strong and capable and kind. You're nice
to your mother when she doesn't deserve it. You're nice to me
when I don't deserve it. You were even nice to Armand despite
thinking he has romantic designs on me."

"He *does* have romantic designs on you."

"And that's why I'm asking you to marry me. No one else in
the world would think to be jealous of a man in a purple velvet
jacket." I laugh and lift a hand to the side of his face. He turns
into it, his lips pressing a soft kiss in the center of my palm. As
easy as it would be to leave things there, this next part is the
most important. "I love you, Nicholas. I'm sorry I panicked
and ran away when you first mentioned the ring. It's not because I don't reciprocate your feelings or that I don't want to
marry you, because I do. I was just . . . scared. How silly is
that? I can face men like Bertram without swooning and stare
down the Gillian Pipers of the world without batting an eye,
but the thought of you willingly putting your life in my hands
is the most terrifying thing in the world."

"I know," he says.

"Aren't you scared?" I ask. "Even a little?"

He shakes his head. "No, Eleanor. I'm scared when you're
running around with criminals and voluntarily putting yourself

under hypnosis. I'm scared of how unflinching you are in the face of danger. I'm scared of how little value you place on your life and well-being." A strong arm snakes around my waist and holds me in place. "But I'm mostly scared that you'll wake up one of these days and realize that being stuck with a stodgy British entrepreneur is hardly the future of your dreams."

"You're not stodgy," I say, though my voice trembles and I'm suddenly grateful to have him holding me up. "You bleached your hair, Dr. Pierson. You wore a teal beach shirt. You went to a nightclub and danced with a man you loathe in order to pump him for information. And none too shabbily, if you ask me."

His face breaks into a smile that's so warm and inviting that I practically fall into it. "You liked my moves?"

"I *loved* your moves. In fact, I love everything about you. Which leads me to this next part." Clearing my throat, I add, "Nicholas Hartford the Third, will you do me the very great honor of becoming my husband?"

"Yes, Eleanor Wilde. I will. Can I kiss you now?"

I shake my head. Although I have every intention of sealing this deal with a kiss and anything else Nicholas has to offer, there's one thing I need to do first. Stepping back, I take a deep breath and shove the ring on the fourth finger of my left hand.

The snake wraps perfectly around my skin, his scales carved by time and exquisite workmanship. The gleaming rubies of his eyes are the only bit of color, shining up at me around the flat black of a diamond that absorbs all light in its vicinity. This ring and the man attached to it could hurt me with just one flick of the finger, but they won't. That much I know for sure.

They're strange and glorious and mine, and I love them.

Can't get enough of Ellie and friends?

Don't miss the other books in the series

Séances Are For Suckers

Potions Are For Pushovers

Curses Are For Cads

Available now from

Kensington Books

Wherever books are sold